DEEP SOUNDING CHAOS

LOVE, TAILS, AND BATTLE WAILS
BOOK 1

ADRIAN J. SMITH

NEEN COHEN

DEEP SOUNDING CHAOS

1

F*inally!*
Movement caught the corner of Zendalia's eye, drawing her attention away from the fluorescent red coral that she had never seen at home. Her heart raced wildly at the second sign of life, the one she had come there for. Another flick of the tail ahead of her prompted her to move.

She changed direction as quickly as the armor shielding her torso allowed. Zendalia stayed in the waves of movement created by her target. The dark water down here was difficult to pierce with her gaze, but she wasn't going to lose her prey again. Water sluiced along Zendalia's scales, guiding her speed and direction as she swam. Moving her tail back and forth, she kept her speed as she dove into the next sounding of the ocean, going deeper into the darker water and farther from home. The temperature cooled with each new plunge toward the ocean floor. She could taste victory already, knowing just how close she was to success after months of planning and searching. All the muscles in her body were taut with readiness—this was what she had trained for.

The armor pinched against the skin of her torso. It was a couple sizes too small for her, but she'd made do with what she managed to snag without causing waves. Her breath rasped in and out of the mask she wore to help with breathing. It was too small for her, but she would never be able to survive in these deep soundings without it. Pressure on her lungs beneath the armor made her pull harder on the device to the point that she wheezed. It had taken time for her to get used to breathing this way, but again, necessary. Movement again to her left brought her attention back to the goal at hand.

Revenge!

Another quick change of direction and Zendalia was back on top of her target. She wasn't going to let her get away again. That dark face hadn't left her memory in the intervening months, the way her cheeks had been hollowed out, her dark, almost black eyes that showed no emotion—no remorse. She'd been strong, her muscles tightening as Zendalia had gotten close to her, her tail long and powerful. But then she'd been gone before Zendalia could do anything. Everything had become about finding that treacherous mer again. Narrowing her focus, Zendalia followed the ripples in the water, the push against the current streams that would tell her exactly where her target had gone.

How did she move so quickly in these depths?

Light barely filtered through the layers of water, and the bright colors Zendalia had always known grew dimmer and further between sightings. Coral was a homogeneous gray while seaweed thinned and dust particles filled the empty space between rocks. Sound was harder to hear, though that could have been the straps on the mask pressed hard against her face so she could breathe. Zendalia slowed her descent and listened to what the water told her.

Her target dipped deeper.

Her vision blurred as the light faded, failing to pierce the lower soundings. Shapes turned into silhouettes, and she took her time, discerning rock from monster, tail from tentacle, anemones from coral. Zendalia held back her frustration, not wanting any bubbles or incongruous movement to alert the monster in front of her to her presence. Gritting her teeth, she waited for another sign, another disturbance in these unfamiliar parts of the ocean.

Zendalia reached for the stone around her neck, her thumb rubbing at the smooth, familiar surface. It warmed in her palm. Neyon's presence bloomed in her mind and their presence alighted before her, a mixture of purple and blue transparent lighting floating in front of her. She smiled until she noticed the hard edges of her familiar's presence, and how they weren't happy with her choices. She clenched her teeth, her jaw muscles bulging, sure Neyon wasn't going to be helpful in the way she needed.

Neyon splayed their tentacles in front of her face, giving her a perfect view of their ass before they spun in a swift circle and poked one tentacle at her. They were annoyed, and rightfully so because she'd known they wouldn't approve of her little revenge mission. But Zendalia had left Reine with one thing on her mind, finding that dark face and stripping her of life.

Zendalia wasn't getting into it again—not now. She hummed softly beneath the rasp of her mask. Their connection would allow Neyon to hear it even if the sound didn't make it beyond the mask itself. The edges of Neyon's spirit eased a little, and she smiled and breathed a little easier as the tingling sensation of Neyon's presence brushed past her cheek in comfort. What she wouldn't give to be able to truly feel them in the physical realm, but she wouldn't trade the connection she had with them, not even for touch.

"I have to avenge his death, Neyon." Her voice sounded so odd behind the mask, even to her own ears, but she knew Neyon would hear her no matter what.

Their soft pressure increased against her cheek and a small vibration tickled at her neck as a bright tentacle wrapped around her skin. She kept her hand in place on the stone at the center of her neck to keep the connection between them strong. They would forgive her, for now. She took as deep a breath as she dared and gave a small nod, ready to concentrate on the mission at hand.

She had a target to capture, a murder to avenge, and a life to honor.

Scanning the floor of the ocean once more, she narrowed her eyes, trying to focus on something other than darkness and shadows. But it was mostly a blur of shapes she couldn't distinguish. *How does anyone see down here?* A flare of panic rose in her chest, and she had to push it away. She couldn't fail this time like she had on so many other attempts. This time she at least had the tech to get where she needed to be.

There! To her left.

She took off, her fluke moving rapidly in the shocks of the water as her fins guided her. Water rushed over her and through her hair, the cold temperature turning her skin into bumps, but her scales protected her tail. She shot forward with force and determination.

She hadn't seen her, Zendalia was certain of it. She hadn't looked back, not once.

Zendalia would have her revenge—and soon. Her heart slammed against her ribs, her breath rattled harder in the mask, and she gained ground. Victory swelled in her chest as she got closer, radiating through her body and running in her veins. She would bring this murderer back to Reine, and she would face the consequences for killing an innocent life.

So close now.

Neyon's presence vanished from her, and she was left on her own to complete her mission, just like everything else in her life. Once she had this monster in her grasp, she could check on Neyon and see if she'd ruined that relationship too. Pistoning forward, Zendalia made everything in her about this one moment when she would succeed, when she would prove everything she had told the royals was right, everything her father had told them. She grunted as she dropped deep into another sounding.

A sharp turn to the right.

Another to the left.

Success tasted glorious.

A dip down.

Zendalia came up short, just saving herself from slamming her nose into a sheer rock face. Her chest rose and fell sharply as panic flooded her, her breasts pushing against the armor as she caught her bearings. *Where the hell did she go?* She pushed her hand against the rock, the frozen stone biting the skin on her palm and nicking her flesh. If she left it there too long, she feared she'd rip more skin when she moved away.

She spun around in a circle so fast brown wisps of her short hair blocked her vision for a fraction of a moment. The back of her skull collided with the rock, a pointy edge digging into the strap of the mask against her face. Her vision completely blackened for a moment too long and that panic set in firmly in her chest again. Gasping for breath, Zendalia flung her hands out to fight off her attacker.

Sharp coral bit into the skin at Zendalia's wrists as her arms were yanked behind her, straining her overworked muscles. That same feeling of panic, of failure, of dying with no one fucking caring filled her. Neyon had been right. She was doomed to fail from the start. She gasped in a sharp breath as her hands were tied together, pulling the armor tight across her chest, making it even harder to breathe. She just had to focus to get loose.

She whirled around, her back to the cliff face now. Pushing out with her tail, she used the force of movement to break free, but she was shoved against the rock again. Sharp edges of rock dug into her skin, ripping her open at each point of contact. Zendalia gritted her teeth in pain, an arm suddenly against her neck, pushing into her jugular and making it impossible to breathe. She clenched her eyes tight against the attack as shame opened up in her heart and consumed her. She had failed.

A merwoman floated into view, her long dark hair and skin hinting at a deep purple in the rare flecks of light that managed to pierce the water and Zendalia's vision. She was gorgeous in a state of dark brooding violence. Zendalia wouldn't be tricked into thinking this merwoman was anything but deadly. Her chest heaved as she floated an arm's length away from Zendalia, her jaw tight and features sharp.

Zendalia had never seen a mer like her before, which had been why it had been so easy to memorize exactly what she had looked like. Closer to the surface, her skin had stood out in the light, the shimmering purple undertones stark and glittery in the rays of the light that penetrated the water in the upper soundings where Zendalia lived.

Holding still, Zendalia waited to see what would happen next, what move she would make. *Will I be her next victim?* Zendalia's hands were tied so tightly behind her back that she couldn't break free, and she had missed when the coral had been wrapped around her fluke too, effectively pinning her in place. She had enough movement to keep her buoyancy and not sink to the ocean's floor, but that was it. She was completely at this monster's mercy.

"Let me go!" Zendalia screamed through the mask. Her voice was muffled through the technology, but she knew the words were clear as day to the monster floating in front of her. Where had this monster been hiding, and how had she snuck up on Zendalia so quickly?

"Why are you following me?" The mer's words were slow and hard. She rounded the words with her mouth in a way Zendalia hadn't heard before, her accent thick. How was it even possible for her to be down here without a mask? Without some way to help her breathe?

"Let me go!" Zendalia struggled against the coral cuffs. They tightened and bit deep into her wrists.

"Who are you?" The mer moved closer, heat radiating off her body in a way Zendalia hadn't expected in the cold depths of the ocean, but it warmed her and contrasted sharply with the cold of the water. The mer tilted her head to the side, gaze burrowing into Zendalia's as she squinted. "And why are you so bright? Are you trying to get yourself killed?"

"I'll kill you," Zendalia ground out, that same anger she had felt so clearly when she had left Reine coming back full force. She had hunted this mer for months, and finally when she was within her grasp, she couldn't break away to get her.

"You want to kill me?" She moved back, out of reach of Zendalia's head and tail. Her eyes widened, the dark purple such a stark contrast to the merfolk Zendalia was used to seeing.

Zendalia surged forward to try and intimidate this pathetic mer. She had the power in this situation because she knew what this mer had done. She would get revenge. "I WILL kill you."

"Well, that doesn't exactly make me want to let you go."

Why is her voice so calm? Every intonation without fear irked Zendalia even more. Zendalia growled and shook, trying to find some weakness in the damn cuffs, some way to break free and get what she had come after.

"Let me go."

"Are you going to try to kill me?" Now she sounded almost amused, as if this were a joke, as if Zendalia was pathetic. She couldn't believe that *this* mer was the last person her father had seen. He deserved so much better than *her.*

"I'm going to kill you." Zendalia clenched her jaw hard, more determined than ever to escape and exact her revenge.

"Then that's going to be a hard no." The mer slipped around Zendalia's writhing form and pulled at the cuffs that bound her hands. She made sure to avoid getting into any position where Zendalia would be able to harm her. "If you keep thrashing like that, I'll wrap your fluke tighter."

"You wouldn't dare." Fear surged, taking over her desire for vengeance. Without her fluke, she would sink to the ocean floor and die, unless this mer dragged her wherever she wanted to go.

Zendalia looked over her shoulder and stilled as it sank in how much danger she'd put herself into. The two met eye to eye. For a beat they lolled in the water, the sound of Zendalia's rasping breath through the mask all she could hear, her pounding heart in her chest all she could feel.

The mer jerked up on the coral tightly, and Zendalia winced, bucking her tail wildly. The strength this mer exuded was insane. She held tight to the coral while wrapping something else, something smoother and thicker, around her fluke, pulling it tight to the point it burned along her scales each time it moved.

"What the hell?" Zendalia raged, her voice ragged as she tried to force her entire body to move in a way that she could find freedom.

"I warned you." The mer held up a thin rope, made of something Zendalia remembered learning about when she was younger, but she couldn't place the name of it now.

Zendalia strained against the bonds, pushed with all her might to try and break loose, but it was so hard to move in the depths of soundings. She hadn't thought she would end up that deep, but the monster was well hidden and farther below the surface than she had anticipated.

"Let me go." This time Zendalia pleaded, a small whine to her tone as she begged to be released from whatever hellhole she had swum into.

"Are you going to kill me?" The mer spoke slowly, each word punctuated as if she had to work to get them out.

"Yes!" Zendalia screamed.

"Well, won't this be fun then." The mer pulled on the rope sharply, and Zendalia fell back, her head smacking hard against the rock face in the same place it had before, making her mind spin with pain and confusion.

Zendalia grunted in pain, a new hurt ricocheting through her veins. "Ouch."

"Uh-huh." The mer swam, dragging Zendalia behind her.

Anger and frustration added pressure to Zendalia's already tight chest. This had not gone according to plan. She had the cuffs in her pack. Not primitive coral ones but real ones that would freeze the wearer into place, rendering them unable to move or speak. The plan had been simple enough. Find this monster, restrain her, and then take her back to Reine and make her answer for her crimes. And now she had been captured by the same monster who had murdered her father.

Zendalia blinked, no longer fighting against the bindings, as the thought struck her.

Why had this mer captured her? She hadn't bothered to do the same for her father, or had she? Was this just all part of the monster's plan? Torture first, death later?

Despite the humiliation, Zendalia had no choice but to ignore the questions and the bindings and focus her attention on breathing. She shifted in small movements in the hope of relieving some of the pressure that squeezed her chest.

"If I take the threads from you, will you stop fidgeting?" Her voice sounded softer this time, as if that hard exterior was falling away.

Zendalia kept her mouth shut. She didn't want to talk to this mer as though she were something other than a monster. A murdering monster at that.

"Well, you haven't told me you'll kill me again, so I'll take that as a good sign." A slight tease this time. Zendalia couldn't keep up. One minute they were yelling at each other, and she was tied up the next. Now this mer had the audacity to think this all was a joke?

The mer pushed Zendalia to a small outcrop of rock. Zendalia sat awkwardly without the use of hands or fluke on the edge of the rock. She left the scowl on her face as best as she could when the mer came around to face her.

"If you fight me…" the mer stopped, curling her tail up so she floated lower than Zendalia and to make eye contact. She slid down to the waved sandy floor, and the mer began again, "I will put these back on, tighter, and then carry you over my shoulder if I have to."

Carry me where? A hot burn flushed in her cheeks while panic sweltered in her chest. She was not some helpless child and wouldn't be treated as such. And she wouldn't allow this mer to bring her back to her lair only to be tortured before she was murdered.

As though the mer could read her thoughts, a smile tugged at the corner of her lips as she unfurled back to her full height, carefully winding the thread back around her hand and arm before tucking it into a small pack Zendalia hadn't noticed earlier. It lay flat against her chest, unlike Zendalia's own pack that rested on her back.

"So what's your name?" The mer's tone was suddenly jovial, as though this conversation was a regular meeting in the reefs.

Zendalia narrowed her eyes and pressed her lips together, more confused than ever. She scanned the immediate water around them, narrowing her eyes to try and find a way to escape so she could come back and take out this monster.

"Well, I figured if you were going to kill me, the least I deserve is the name of the valiant soldier who is going to end my time in this desolate plane of existence." The mer rolled her eyes and pulled Zendalia up by the upper arm. "I'm Kaelin, since you were so kind to ask."

"Let me go." Zendalia meant for her words to be strong, but they came out as a whine.

"Not until you stop trying to kill me."

Zendalia pressed her lips together once more, unwilling to give up her quest for vengeance. She pulled in on herself, darting her gaze around to try and find an escape, a way to break free now that at least part of her bonds were gone.

"All right, how about we start with *why* you want to kill me?" That same amused tone as before was back.

Zendalia snorted, irked by the question. It should be obvious. Any mer who had killed would feel that burden and know they'd wronged. "You're a monster."

"Ah, well sure, that clears up everything," Kaelin muttered as she pushed off, half-dragging Zendalia by the upper arm as they swam at a pace that made Zendalia's head feel too light and glazed her eyes over.

"Where are we going?" *Do I sound out of breath?* It hurt to pull water into her lungs, to make her chest rise and fall. The armor she'd brought mustn't have been built for these depths. She should have fought harder for better material.

"We can't stay out in the open." A lash of fear echoed in Kaelin's voice, and it reverberated through Zendalia. If she was taken to someplace hidden away, no one would find her to help her—not that they were coming anyway. She'd snuck away from Reine and only Soulara knew where she'd gone. Neyon hadn't even wanted her to go, but she'd ignored their pleas.

Zendalia didn't ask why they couldn't be in the open. She couldn't imagine they would be easy to find in the darkness, but she had to stay focused. This mer was likely taking her some-place where she could be killed in the same ruthless manner her father had been brutally murdered. She would take her revenge —all she had to do was wait until this monster let down her guard.

2

Kaelin blew out a breath as she dragged this annoying mer into a cave. She pressed her deep into the back, the darkness a silk ribbon around the edges of the mer, even to Kaelin's well-adjusted sight. She knew there was no other exit except the way they had come in. She'd scouted it at one point, wondering if it was the solution to her banishment. It wasn't, but for this, it would do.

She pushed the mer a little farther until her back bumped against the wall of the cave and then floated away so she wouldn't get hit. Even if this mer did try to kill her, Kaelin was pretty certain she wouldn't succeed. She was clearly from a more surface tribe and didn't have the stamina to last in these depths.

Kaelin put her hands on her hips, raising an eyebrow as she stared at this mer, someone who had tried to kidnap her and completely floundered in even that attempt. Her scales were a rusty orange, not the same luminescence as the coral outside, but in these dark waters they would be a beacon of light for any enemy that came their way. And here there were enemies in abundance.

"You're too damn bright." Kaelin scrunched her nose.

The mer snorted.

"Right, so I'm Kaelin. Care to share your name yet?"

Her eye roll was what got Kaelin. She burst her tail in the water, shoving her entire form forward so she could press her arm against the mer's jugular and hold her against the cavern's wall.

"Look, I don't want to hurt you. I don't even know why you're here, but you've got to stop being ignorant when it comes to the depths of the soundings we're in. This isn't your world."

The mer clenched her jaw, her high cheekbones shimmering like they had a fine coating of glitter. Her eyes were a pure amber of hatred, and even though she couldn't move, Kaelin was sure she would try to kill again.

"What did I ever do to you anyway? You want to kill me, the least you can do is tell me for what."

Kaelin relaxed her grasp, knowing with the coral ties that this mer wasn't going anywhere. She could catch her in an instant if she needed to. Kaelin frowned. The violence she had shown since her banishment had come into full effect. It was astronomical and she needed to stop. It was so unlike her and not who she wanted to be.

Backing away even more, Kaelin blew out a bubble and gathered herself. "Why are you here?"

"To kill you."

"Just me? Or all of my people?"

The mer seemed confused by that, and Kaelin chastised herself for potentially giving away the fact that she wasn't alone. Except she *was* very alone. That all-too-familiar tinge of shame filled her, and with the stark reminder of her recent violent streak, she knew she deserved to be right where she was.

"You," the mer's voice wavered slightly.

Well, at least the mer was honest. Kaelin scrunched her nose and backed away farther, putting more distance between them. She moved her hand to her side, coming across the smooth skin of her companion and relaxed instantly as they wrapped around her side, the suckers from their tentacles clinging to her. At least the elders had let her bring her companion along with her when they kicked her out.

Kaelin clenched her hand, signaling her companion should go back into hiding. Their pull away from her was hard but necessary. Kaelin would do anything to protect them. As soon as she didn't feel them near her, she straightened her shoulders with a newfound burst of confidence and focus.

If she let this mer go, she would no doubt just come after her again. Kaelin could give chase easily, but there were dangers in the depths that this mer wasn't prepared for. She couldn't let her go out into the seas like the other one. She'd meet the exact same fate. And Kaelin wouldn't allow herself to be banished any longer than she already was. She had to go back as someone new.

The silence in the cave was deadly.

Raising her chin up, Kaelin moved again into the other mer's space. "Why do you want to kill me?"

The mer defiantly glared back, jaw clenched, lips pursed.

Right, this one wasn't a talker, she just repeated herself a dozen and three times without any explanations. Sticking her tongue out, Kaelin tried a different tactic, one that would have worked on her brothers and one that took the edge of violence out of herself.

She was greeted with a look of confusion in response. Not quite what she'd anticipated, but it was better than the glare. Kaelin canted her head to the side, something about this mer seemed so oddly familiar, in a way she couldn't put her finger on, but she wished she could. She wished her companion were closer by. Perhaps she could sense from them whether or not this mer was safe.

"Who are you?" Kaelin probed, this time with true curiosity, the answer on the edge of her mind. When she was given silence again, she sighed. "Well, do you like squid or fangtooth?"

The mer scrunched her nose up, eyes squinting, and her color shifted from that fiery orange to a gray color. She looked utterly disgusted.

Amusement flashed through Kaelin's chest. "No to the squid? It's one of my favorites."

What was she supposed to do with a silent prisoner? She didn't want to capture this mer to begin with. She wasn't even supposed to talk to anyone until her banishment was done, and this put that entire plan in jeopardy. With a deep breath, Kaelin stared this mer down hard.

"Please tell me what you're doing here. Why are you trying to kill me?" Kaelin's frustration was reaching an all-time high. This was the first mer she had spoken to in months and the conversation was infuriating. She was no closer to an answer.

Kaelin nodded to no one but herself. She grabbed the coral ties and wrapped them around a stalagmite tightly for her own safety. Then again, if this idiotic mer wanted to try and escape into the yonder without her protection, then so be it. Kaelin wasn't going to babysit her while she had other things she needed to get to.

Like food.

Kaelin wanted to be able to do that, but guilt stabbed at her with the reminder of her banishment and the consequences of her actions. She couldn't leave this mer on her own. If they were going to be stuck there because she had no idea what to do, they would need to eat. All of her supplies were back at her regular habitat, which meant Kaelin was going to have to scrounge. Not something she was looking forward to.

Swimming out of the cave, Kaelin moved above the rock cliff and looked for any kind of mollusks, grasses, or worms that she could find. She hadn't spent much time in this area yet, but she knew there had to be something around. She'd followed the monster that direction in hopes of figuring out where it was coming from and where it was going. If only to protect herself from it, along with her tribe if it were to attack them.

She huffed out a few bubbles of frustration and began

dancing her fingers along the tops of the rough dark coral, hoping for the skittering echo against her fingertips. Frustration built as no sensation returned her touch. Nothing living, nothing edible, lay within the coral. Of course not, that would have been too easy.

She flicked her tail and risked swimming a little farther away from the cave and her unwanted captive. How in Poseidon's Sea had she, the banished of her people, found herself with a captive? A captive who wanted to kill her no less.

She shook her head.

Digging into the small sand dunes, she burrowed and wiggled her fingers until she hit the hard shells of sea beans. She flicked, holding her breath in a halfhearted hope of finding something, anything. Kaelin's fingers stung, the edges of the beans seeming to grow harder and more jagged the more she flicked.

Finally, she flicked over a bean and smiled. Beneath the hard deep-brown shell were three water mushrooms. They wouldn't go far, between her and her captive, but it would stem the tide. Quickly she plucked the flat caps off the mushrooms, whispering a heartfelt thanks to the sea for providing. She re-covered the stems that remained carefully with the sea bean.

The tops were an average size, each a little smaller than her palm. She slid them into her bag debating if she should look for more or head on back.

Her companion made their presence known once more by landing lightly on the bean where the mushroom stalks would grow more caps.

"Hello, friend. Where have you been?" Joy filled Kaelin's chest along with comfort and safety. They always showed up right when she needed them, even if she didn't know her own self well enough to be aware of it.

She curved her fingers around their high back, moving into the caress and finding as much comfort in the touch as they did. She wished she could speak to them, understand what they were thinking, but her people had lost that ability over time. Settling into the companionship she craved, Kaelin looked around for other easy food grabs.

"I had to find food. It's been a long time since I foraged somewhere new." Her explanation was pointless, her companion would know everything, but she'd taken to talking out loud to them since her banishment, just to make sure her voice still worked.

The slick blue light of her companion danced and twirled in front of her as a memory of wrapping a half dozen sandbugs in seaweed came back to the forefront of her mind.

"Oh." She riffled deeper into her bag and smiled wider as she found the bundle. A little flatter than it had been, but there they were. How had she forgotten her emergency supplies? It had been a while since she packed them in there, not having needed them on her last trips out, but still. They were one of her companion's favorites, too.

Smiling, Kaelin swam back to the cave entrance, the weight on her shoulders sliding away as she found the solution to the most immediate of her problems. Food was good. And despite the mer's aggression and lack of conversation, Kaelin couldn't deny how nice it was to simply be around someone other than herself.

As she reached the mouth of the cave, the weight returned and settled deep into her chest. Nice or not, what the hell was she going to do with this mer who wanted to kill her and refused even the smallest of respects? No name and no reason for wanting her death. Kaelin prepared herself to meet the mer face-to-face again, and hopefully hold her own again.

But Kaelin wouldn't let the mer starve. She might have been banished, but she was still a daughter of her people and would be returned to the tribe as soon as she fulfilled her punishment. At least, she hoped she would, if she could manage to follow all the rules and seek repentance for her wrongs.

From just inside the entrance of the cave, Kaelin could see the mer pulling against her restraints. For a moment Kaelin bobbed, her long hair tickling around her face and down her arms. The mer hadn't seen her, even though she looked at the cave entrance several times as Kaelin watched. How she had ever found Kaelin with such poor vision was yet another question that itched at her.

"I found food," Kaelin called out and was rewarded with the mer's flinch and scowl.

She swam toward the captive and watched as she let the restraints tying her to the stalagmite go slack.

"No luck at running off then?" Kaelin would do her best to keep the conversation going, even if she was the only one talking. She'd been so used to it for seasons now it wouldn't make much of a difference anyway.

Even the growl she was rewarded with wasn't enough to dampen Kaelin's mood. She had food and company, not good company but beggars couldn't be choosers. Kaelin made quick work of getting food ready. She found two half shells in the debris inside the entrance of the cave, chipped and a little worse for wear but better than nothing. She placed a mushroom cap and a bug on each shell.

"Now, if I untie your wrists so you can eat, do I need to tether your tail instead or will you play nice long enough for food?" Kaelin couldn't believe her own audacity and chatter. She had spoken fewer words to many people of her tribe over the years.

"What is it?" The mer strained her neck to try and see what lay in the shells Kaelin carried.

"Just bugs and mushrooms."

"Mushrooms?"

Kaelin could almost see the drool leaking from the mer's mouth.

"Is that a yes?" Delight lit in Kaelin's stomach at the possibility of finally having found a connection between them. Maybe this would be the way to get information from her.

"Yes." It was a forced reply, slipping between her clenched teeth, but it was enough for Kaelin.

She turned her back, testing the mer's word and placed the shells on the ground in front of her. For a moment, she hesitated and then pulled the third mushroom cap from her bag and slipped it onto one of the shells. Mushrooms had always been a favorite treat of hers, but hopefully she would find some more later.

The mer didn't struggle. Kaelin swam closer, noticing the barely-there warmth from her skin. Kaelin frowned at it, concern lighting into her chest. Was it too cold down here for her? Kaelin clenched her jaw as she leaned in closer, her arm brushing against the mer's as she reached for the coral ties and slid the tight knot loose. Her heart raced as she backed away and held her breath.

Kaelin handed the mer the shell with the two mushroom caps before taking her own seat on the second rock. She watched as the mer tore off some of the cap, lifted the edge of her mask, and stuffed the piece in her mouth before replacing the mask. What she would give to see the fullness of her face. Perhaps Kaelin would recognize who this mer was then? Or perhaps she'd only dreamed about finding someone to talk to in her isolation.

The mer lifted her eyes after the third piece of mushroom cap and froze. Those amber eyes bored right through Kaelin's soul, her heart hammering at the thought that they had finally calmed the rage between them—at least for a moment. She was just about to ask tenderly if the mer wouldn't mind sharing her name again when her thoughts were interrupted.

"Poison?" Fear raced through the single word.

"What?" Kaelin's cheeks were warm after having been caught staring. And then the meaning sunk in. "No, of course I wouldn't poison you. All life is sacred."

The mer scoffed but slowly chewed again, not letting Kaelin's gaze drop. This was a test—it had to be. Kaelin wasn't going to survive on her own, so the ocean had sent a fiery mer who was going to ruin any chance of her returning to her people.

The mask the mer wore reminded her too much of another mask. She shook her head and unwrapped the bug on her plate. Her appetite, previously ravenous, now shriveled at the sight of the dead animal. She had caught it humanely when she asked the water to provide. But right now, none of that mattered. She truly believed what she had told the mer—all life was sacred, and that included the life she was about to consume.

She ate a few small pieces, knowing she would need her strength before she rewrapped the rest and tucked it and the mushroom cap back into her bag.

"So…" Damn, her usual shyness had returned with the near civility of sharing a meal. Her stomach fluttered as she grasped at straws to try and figure out what to say. "Are you willing to give me your name yet?"

"Zendalia." She murmured the name quietly as she shoved the last piece of mushroom into her mouth and reattached the mask.

"That's a beautiful name. Difficult to pronounce for me. May I call you Zen?" Kaelin raised her gaze, pleased that conversation was flowing and Zendalia had finally chosen to give in to communication.

"No, you may not call me anything." Zendalia pushed the shell plate so roughly from her lap as she rose that it shattered against small pebbles that littered the floor of the cave.

"I didn't mean to offend." Kaelin wanted to smack herself. Why was she always doing the wrong thing? So stupid. She should have just nodded and accepted the name.

"Why are you doing this?" Zendalia's voice was nearly a whisper, so hard to hear over her breath within the machine attached to her face.

Kaelin eyed her curiously, confused as to what Zendalia meant by the question. She picked at the pieces of broken shell on the cave floor, wanting to recognize the life it had once contained and the use it had given them. She would do that later, when Zendalia wasn't eyeing her so suspiciously. "Doing what?"

"Being nice. Feeding me and trying to talk to me." Zendalia's brow drew together, a line forming in the center of her forehead.

Kaelin paused, not sure where to go with the conversation. It hurt her soul to think Zendalia had never experienced this amount of kindness before. Just what were the surface tribes up to? "I'm trying to understand why you wish for my death so muc—"

The ground shuddered, and the cave walls trembled. The sound of moving rock echoed loudly in her ears. Panic swelled in her chest, clawing at her throat. It was next to impossible to breathe. Kaelin whipped around toward the cave entrance, every fiber of her being attuned for the moment the monster would attack.

"Oh no," Kaelin muttered, her eyes wide. She held her hand out, waiting for her companion to wrap around her in solidifying strength.

"What?" Zendalia remained undulating where she had risen, but her coloring dimmed when they locked gazes.

"We need to leave now."

"Why?"

"It found us."

3

Zendalia froze. Her heart thudded wildly as she looked into Kaelin's dark eyes. She could barely make her face out in the dark cave and couldn't even begin to fathom where the rest of Kaelin's body was. But she must only be inches away. The cave shook again, and the sound rattled her to her bones.

Crying out, Zendalia reached up to cover her ears and dragged in a deep breath. She pushed her fluke hard, forcing her body backward to try and get away from whatever it was. She crashed into the cave wall, her side slamming hard enough to knock the wind from her lungs. Pieces of rocks fell from the ceiling, the stalactites shattering and falling to the floor of the cave.

Kaelin pressed against her, full form, both of their flukes flapping sharply. Zendalia shuddered at the warmth of Kaelin's body, not realizing just how cold she really was. It was so hard to breathe, and she had to close her eyes to focus, but that only made the rest of her senses sharper.

An odd sound vibrated outside the cave. Swishing water, crunching rock, but something else that Zendalia couldn't identify. She'd never heard it before. Zendalia panicked. What the hell had she gotten herself into?

"Don't speak," Kaelin whispered harshly in her ear.

"What is it?"

Kaelin grabbed her wrist hard, twisting to the point of pain. Zendalia cried out, clenching her eyes shut tight against the onslaught. She tried to quiet herself but didn't manage, and Kaelin was at her ear again. "It'll hear us."

Fear ratcheted up another notch, and Zendalia's heart thudded. She relaxed her position slightly, staring into Kaelin's dark eyes. There was as much fear in them as she felt herself. Kaelin let go of her and swam to the entrance of the cave, staying back from it slightly. She waved Zendalia forward. It took everything in Zendalia to swim to the edge of the cave, just behind Kaelin, holding her position.

She had to trust Kaelin.

She had no other choice. Despite the fact that Kaelin had killed her father, Zendalia was stuck trusting that this mer would lead her out of whatever the fuck was happening or at least to where she could see this new enemy to fight. Zendalia pressed a hand to the small of Kaelin's back to get her attention and raised her eyebrows.

Kaelin nodded her head in the direction of the entrance to the cave, but Zendalia couldn't see much of anything beyond it other than blur and darkness. She hated that her eyes were too weak to see in the dark, and she should have grabbed something before she left Reine to rectify that, but she'd been in a rush when she'd stolen the mask and the armor. It made her instincts to fight harder because she couldn't see what she was fighting against.

"I can't see," she finally whispered, gasping in a breath when her head went light.

Kaelin took Zendalia's wrist again, moving in so her lips were right against her ear. "We're going to have to swim for it. Stay close to me."

Zendalia nodded firmly, still not knowing what was going to happen or where they were swimming to. Bright lights flashed in the distance, blinding Zendalia. She clenched her eyes against the onslaught as those lights turned on the cave they were in, shining against the rock and reflecting off it. Kaelin ducked down and dragged Zendalia with her, covering her body as Kaelin practically lay on top of her. For the first time in years, Zendalia felt completely safe—even with whatever was happening outside raging on, she knew she could trust Kaelin to protect her.

"Let's go," Kaelin said sharply, grabbing Zendalia's hand and pulling forward as she swam.

Zendalia had to work hard to keep up. Kaelin was so much faster than her. It was any wonder she'd gotten close enough to even think about killing her. She swallowed the lump in her throat, fluttering her fluke rapidly to keep up as best as she possibly could. They swam along the edge of the cave, dodging the lights that were shining all around it.

Kaelin stopped sharply and pushed her back to Zendalia's front, her side fins spreading out, covering her as they waited for a light to pass over the two of them when they couldn't avoid it any longer. Zendalia dragged in deep breaths as she stilled, sensing she had no other choice but to play along and listen. Kaelin at least knew what the hell was going on.

She was just about to shift to swim, her hand brushing against her necklace, when Neyon appeared next to her, their bright blue aura a beacon of light in the darkness. Zendalia's stomach dropped heavily until she realized no one could see them except her.

Kaelin's face flashed in her mind's eye as Neyon ran one of their smooth tentacles against her cheek. The sense of trust and safety increased, and Zendalia had no other choice but to listen to her familiar.

Zendalia didn't answer, wanting to keep as quiet as she had been told to. She stared at Neyon, comfort settling into the pit of her stomach again. This was it. This was the only way she was going to survive. She had to trust that Kaelin wasn't going to kill her as soon as they got wherever they were going, which she hoped was far away from this place.

Kaelin moved sharply when the light was off them. Zendalia pressed her hands against the cave wall and pushed off with everything she had. They dove deep, down to the ocean floor. The ripples in the sands were disturbed by the vibrations in the water and were no longer smooth and serene. She blinked, and they moved between two large outcroppings of rock.

They slid between them, Kaelin's hands on her hips as they stayed put. The sound got louder, that odd, almost-grinding sound. Zendalia whimpered and shifted in closer to Kaelin, their fronts pressing against each other as they had no other option of where to go.

"I can't see where they are," Kaelin whispered. "The lights are blinding."

Zendalia nodded her agreement. Down here in the pitch black of the deepest soundings in the ocean, it was blinding to see any light at all, and especially this kind of light. It moved swiftly and around, never staying in one place long enough to be able to focus on it and see anything. Her heart thundered, and she reached for Kaelin's hand, folding them together. Wherever Kaelin went, Zendalia was going to go too.

"We need to get out of here," Kaelin whispered again, her voice barely audible enough for Zendalia to hear it over the sound her mask made. Something was wrong with it, but she didn't have a second to even think about figuring that out. She pressed her forehead against Kaelin's shoulder and closed her eyes, centering herself.

Neyon's emotions filtered through her mind again, and she knew she had to trust and bring this mer with her. She still wanted to kill her, but she knew instinctively that she wouldn't. Neyon wouldn't let her.

Zendalia lifted her chin. "I can't see anything down here."

"I know," Kaelin responded, tightening her grasp on

Zendalia's fingers as if it would calm her to know that she wasn't alone just then.

Zendalia swallowed the lump in her throat. "Where are we going?"

"It's not too far, but it's safe. If we can manage to get there."

The vibrations in the water started again, but they changed tone and pace. It was high pitched, and Zendalia cringed, holding back her scream as pain moved into her ears and surrounded her skull. She refused to let go of Kaelin's hands, but she knew she had to be bleeding from the piercing tone.

"Now!" Kaelin said loudly, jerking Zendalia's hand.

They swam furiously, Zendalia half-dragged by Kaelin's powerful tail. They ducked behind another outcropping of rock, this time pushed to the sandy ocean floor. Zendalia once again found herself underneath Kaelin, her fins on the sides of her tail spreading out to cover her completely.

Kaelin dragged in a ragged breath, her heart pounding so hard that Zendalia felt it in her own chest. She choked on the water in her mouth. Clenching her jaw, she steeled herself for the fact that her mask might stop working in an instant. If it did, she was likely dead. She couldn't breathe this far down in the sea without it, and she doubted Kaelin would bring her closer to the surface. They couldn't swim there anyway, not with whatever was lurking after them.

Another loud noise kicked off, this time a sharp hum that vibrated the water in tiny waves around them. The sensation of small bugs crawling all over skin and scales, trying to burrow their way inside rippled across her. She couldn't make it stop no matter how much she squirmed against Kaelin.

"What is that?" Zendalia risked the question, hoping she'd get a response but also wanting Kaelin to be as in the dark about what was happening as she was.

"Suction. Shut up and stop moving. It'll see you," Kaelin ordered.

"How?"

"You're too damn bright."

Realization hit her that Kaelin wasn't only protecting her body from harm but hiding her from being seen by those bright lights that still roamed throughout the water.

"We're moving. Now."

Kaelin swam without warning, taking Zendalia by the hand again. They moved in a zigzag line, staying as covered as possible by whatever was on the ocean floor. Zendalia followed blindly, not seeing anything until it was right in front of her, and she suddenly had to dodge it.

The farther they moved the less the vibrations affected her. She had no idea how far away they were by that point, but they had to be a good distance if she could barely feel the disturbance in the water surrounding her. Kaelin slowed her pace, and Zendalia dragged in one gasping breath after another.

There was definitely a problem with her mask, but it could so easily be a seal or something simple. It didn't fit her right, and she'd found if she didn't keep it in place perfectly that it would do this. Once they had a moment of respite, she would try to adjust it so she could breathe easier. Kaelin relaxed slightly but kept their hands clasped together as they moved along the ocean floor, still staying hidden for a large part. If this was how Kaelin moved naturally, then it was a wonder Zendalia had found her. Kaelin could have so easily stayed hidden and Zendalia would never have been the wiser. Then again, Kaelin was a murderer, and no doubt she wouldn't want to miss out on another opportunity to take Zendalia out if she had it.

Zendalia's heart calmed slightly as they got farther away, but she was still left in the dark. Kaelin's hand was warm in hers, and she was reluctant to let go, needing guidance.

"Where are we?" Zendalia took in short breaths, her heart still racing too fast for the calm that they had found. Her head was dizzy from lack of oxygen, and she wished they would slow down so she wouldn't spin to her own demise.

"We're heading toward the shallows."

That meant absolutely nothing to Zendalia, but it seemed to be a specific place that Kaelin had in mind. Zendalia had to hope she'd be able to find her way out of it when she could. She stayed the course, listening to the emotions of her familiar and trusting that they had her best interest in mind. They should since Zendalia and Neyon had been together for some time now since Soulara had first given her the necklace as a gift. She smiled at the memory before flapping her fluke to catch up. Kaelin was so damn fast.

"Here." Kaelin dove down sharply.

They moved into a cave on the ocean floor. Zendalia frowned at it, not understanding why this place was called the shallows, but she didn't fight it as she followed Kaelin into another dark cave. It seemed to be where Kaelin lived most of the time, hiding in caves where no one could find her. Perhaps that was how all the tribes down here lived. Zendalia wasn't sure, and she didn't remember the lessons from her studies either.

Zendalia was consumed by darkness. It was impossible to see. Kaelin left her floating in the middle of the cave. Zendalia missed the sure touch of Kaelin's hand in hers as she stayed still, not sure where to go or what to do. In an instant, something glowed behind her, illuminating the cavern wall she was close to. Turning around, Zendalia gasped.

4

Kaelin jerked her head up sharply at Zendalia's gasp, her heart rapping in panic and her muscles ready for another fight. Blinking against the bright scales of the merwoman in the light of the cave, she let out her own slow breath as her eyes adjusted. Zendalia floated, staring not at her but at the mural Kaelin had made on the wall. Her companion had shown her, in their way, how to make the paints from the fluorescent coral, and since the start of her banishment, her style with the anemone frills had grown exponentially. She would never be a great artist, but she had found comfort in creating the shapes and patterns that now decorated her temporary home.

Warmth spread through Kaelin's chest, a strange mix of pride and nerves as Zendalia looked entirely mesmerized by the wall. Kaelin didn't want to get her hopes up that the half smile she could just make out beneath the edges of the mask had anything to do with her or her wall. But hope had a way of blossoming without permission.

As Zendalia continued to undulate gently in the current, Kaelin took the opportunity to look beyond the bright orange scales and the tech that covered half her face and chest. Zendalia wasn't as monstrous as she first came off. She was so slight, her fluke narrow and her fins barely a hand width wide on each side. Was it any wonder she had struggled to keep up with Kaelin? She wasn't built for the deep soundings.

Kaelin looked down at her own flared fluke and thanked the waters for giving her what she needed to not only get away but to cover Zendalia's brightness during their escape. She'd been able to protect them both in ways she hadn't managed to do before. Memories of pressing her body against Zendalia's made heat rush to Kaelin's cheeks. She had been so cold, shivering against Kaelin's warm flesh. She hadn't thought about the touch of another mer, but in her memory it flared, her isolation highlighted.

"Is this your home?" Zendalia asked, interrupting Kaelin's thoughts. Her voice was soft compared to any other time she'd spoken, and it threw Kaelin off.

"Oh, uh, yes." Kaelin hoped none of the tech Zendalia sported allowed her to read Kaelin's thoughts. Had they been working on such a thing? There had been rumors of it at one point, but Kaelin hadn't ever studied the surface tribes. It would be nice to be able to read her companion's mind, she supposed. But after all these years together, they had managed to understand each other most of the time through touch and feel.

"Do all lower tribes live such solitary existences? Or..." Zendalia let her words drift off as she threw a cursory look over her shoulder. This was the most relaxed Kaelin had ever seen her, and she couldn't quite figure out why. They had just escaped the kraken narrowly, and she knew that it would come and find them soon enough.

Zendalia's eyes widened, her face relaxed, her shoulders dropping as she released her tension. Their gazes locked in a tangible moment of connection. Kaelin had no idea what that look was about. Had Zendalia been checking if Kaelin knew the question was for her? But really, who else could she possibly be asking?

"We live the same way as our past elders." Kaelin would

have given anything to know how to change the topic, but she gave the vaguest answer she could think of at the moment.

"But how do you survive alone? Don't you ever get lonely?" Zendalia asked the questions as though they didn't rip a hole right through Kaelin's chest. Zendalia moved her attention back to Kaelin's mural. Her long slender fingers brushed the wall, a picture Kaelin had painted one evening of the tragedy that landed her in exile. She'd needed it to get her mind off it—escape it. But her painting took quite an artistic license and without knowing where it stemmed from, no one would guess the trauma behind it.

Kaelin pressed her teeth together hard. Her jaw muscles ached in mere moments, but she didn't ease up the pressure until she had taken three deep breaths and calmed enough to speak instead of scream.

"I wouldn't be able to stand this quiet dark all the time." Zendalia kept going, oblivious to Kaelin's bubbling rage.

"How do you live up there?" Kaelin snapped, surprising herself as much as Zendalia with the vehemence in her words. "Do you surround yourself with all your tech? Do you even have friends? Or family? Why would they let you come here all on your own? Is this a suicide mission or are you a spy for that monster?" Kaelin spat the questions, one after the other. She knew that she had been unfair, but this stranger had shown up, jeopardized the length of her exile, and had made her remember what touch with another mer felt like. The wounds of her punishment were too raw. With reality crashing around her, she grasped for the strings of normalcy.

"I'm not the monster here." Offended, Zendalia turned to face her, mural forgotten and voice rising over the hiss of the mask.

"Oh that's right. *I'm* the bad guy." Kaelin's fins whipped faster, moving toward Zendalia. Why did Zendalia have to trigger her rage? She had never had a temper before.

"*You're* the bad guy." Zendalia moved away from the wall

and met Kaelin in the middle of the open space, her eyes narrowing in anger, her fingers clenched tightly into fists.

"Well obviously." Kaelin let the sarcasm loose. "The evil mer who saved you from the kraken, kept you from being killed by more than just the one monster, fed you, and then brought you to her home. Tremble in my evil presence."

"Kraken?" Zendalia's shoulders slumped forward, but her eyes were still wide and locked on Kaelin's face.

"Yes," Kaelin answered, eyes narrowing, unable to read exactly what Zendalia's body language told her. How she wished she could rip off the woman's mask and see her face properly. The idea swirled like poisoned eel in her stomach. Nothing would make her risk the mer's life, not even a proper look at her face. The familiarity she had noticed more than once had shaken one memory from her mind.

She pushed it aside, too pained to think about it fully. The man with the other mask. The one that had haunted her days and nights since the banishment. The reason for the mural to begin with.

Anger and frustration at Zendalia deflated her like a wounded blowfish. Kaelin pulled her gaze away from the fiery amber eyes. Her heart clenched at the exact coloring match to the ones in her memory. She held the tension between them, her heart hammering while she pulled herself together again. She had to make this right—that was the entire point of her exile.

"There's a bed of moss around the bend to your right. Get rest while you can," Kaelin ordered, her voice wavering at the end as she was hit with emotion.

Zendalia jerked forward, her hand outstretched as if she was going to touch Kaelin's arm. Her eyes wide with confusion. Kaelin suspected it was with the intention of arguing the abrupt end to the discussion, but she glared at the mer who quickly pulled away and kept the space between them.

Busying herself with unpacking the items from her bag, Kaelin calculated how long she would have before needing to gather more food stores—a lot less now with a second mouth to feed. Surely having Zendalia stay wouldn't break the conditions of her exile. She hadn't searched her out. And what kind of mer would dive from the surface without her own food to sustain her?

What the hell would she do with Zendalia if she tried to kill her again? She wasn't safe in her own dwelling, which set her on edge. She waited every second for Zendalia to come after her, every nerve primed and ready to go. She wasn't going to sleep a wink that night.

"Thank you."

Kaelin tensed and turned around slowly. The words were unexpected, but the stony resistance on Zendalia's face made hearing them tolerable. Zendalia didn't look pleased to have said them. Her amber eyes were hard, staring straight in Kaelin's soul as if she could see and understand all of her fears.

"Does that mean you'll stop trying to kill me?" Kaelin asked, wondering if she had always been so forthcoming with her thoughts or if the time in exile had made her forget how to be around others. Then again, these circumstances weren't like any she had experienced before.

"Nothing has changed." Zendalia raised her eyebrows, tightening her shoulders.

Kaelin glanced down at Zendalia's hands, checking that they were still at her sides and not holding a weapon. She pursed her lips before eyeing her again. "Everything has changed. The kraken will find us sooner rather than later, and you'll need your rest if we have to move quickly."

"Why should I trust you?" Venom laced Zendalia's words, her anger returning. Her movements became jerky as she swam forward a little.

"You shouldn't." Kaelin raised an eyebrow, daring Zendalia to try something. She was ready for the next attack. Relief washed over her when Zendalia didn't move. She didn't deserve to be considered safe. She didn't deserve this time with another mer. She hadn't forgotten her punishment or her crime, and she should be isolated because of it.

She returned to her pack, shoving items around without intent or purpose but not wanting to turn back to a mask and half a face. If Zendalia was going to kill her, the least she could do was make it swift. She didn't deserve to see the face of any mer, let alone a gorgeous one like Zendalia, and she would take that punishment with pride.

"You could have at least remembered him—remembered me." The words were soft and teased her ears. She suspected Zendalia hadn't wanted her to hear them, to hear the cry of pain in them, but Kaelin was a daughter of the deep soundings, and very little would escape her hearing down here.

Counting her breaths, keeping the tightness in her chest pushed down as far as she could, Kaelin waited until the rustle and shift of Zendalia settling into her moss bedding reached her ears. She relaxed visibly once Zendalia was out of sight and no longer hovering around her. Without that immediate threat every second, she could get her work done for now. She swallowed hard, those same amber eyes rising in her memory. Pain tore through her again as she watched the light of life fade from them in an instant.

Swimming in her own guilt and shame, Kaelin left every second coral lit for her guest, captive… What the hell did she call a mer who tried to kill her only for her to save their life and bring them to her home?

The light in the cave dimmed, and Kaelin relaxed into her familiar surroundings. She could move around in the pitch black and not make a single noise if she wanted. The paintings brought a smile to her lips, and she found her own fingers, less delicate than Zendalia's, tracing the imperfect lines of her companion. If only Zendalia could truly see what she had painted. It would answer all the questions she hadn't asked or Kaelin hadn't dared to answer.

As if the movement called them into existence, the smooth

soft press of energy against her side told her exactly who was there.

"Hello, my friend." Kaelin smiled to herself, closing her eyes and reveling in the touch much like she had done with Zendalia's touch while they'd escaped.

They moved long strands of fibrous light around Kaelin's wide hips, hugging her and sending a low hum through her body. Kaelin sighed into the touch, relaxing instantly at the familiarity. She placed her hands over the light, feeling the soft vibrations tickling her skin. They floated, taking comfort from each other, though Kaelin suspected she always received more from her companion than they got from her. An unfamiliar rhythm filled her home, low and not entirely unpleasant. As it was, it still took her a while to realize it was the sound of Zendalia sleeping, her breathing mimicked by the technology on her face.

"How did everything get so flipped upside down again?" she whispered, though she suspected she would have been able to grind more dead coral for her paintings and Zendalia wouldn't awaken.

An image of her bed flashed in her mind. She smiled at the communication and question that lingered in the picture.

"It's okay. I don't need to sleep. I'll stay up, keeping vigil. But you can sleep, my little one." As she spoke, she lowered her body to the ground, tail resting heavy on the cave floor. Yes, it was her home but not the one she grew up in. Nothing like that.

Perhaps Zendalia did have a point. Nothing really had changed, her instincts to keep details of her people a secret had been a driving force in not wanting to answer her earlier questions. She could have answered them, spoken about the home she once had and explained that no, not all deep sounding mers lived as she did. She wouldn't have had to explain her exile. But she hadn't trusted Zendalia. A half answer that didn't explain the truth of her situation felt too much like a lie.

She leaned her shoulders heavily against the cave wall, and

the light of her companion shuffled to rest more comfortably on her chest. Humming under her breath, Kaelin ran her hands over the weight on her chest that pressed against her heart, reminding her she was not alone despite what her people had passed down as her punishment.

Images of Kaelin's mother singing the words of the song she now hummed played in her mind. Kaelin smiled and let her eyes close, just for a minute. Her companion and friend had never left her, had never condemned or blamed her. Because of them, Kaelin remembered what love felt like.

"Goodnight, Neyon," she whispered to her companion as she lulled off to some much-needed sleep.

5

The moss bedding wrapped around Zendalia in a way that reminded her of Soulara's bed. Her own sleeping area back home didn't have such a luxurious softness to it. Despite the exhaustion of the day, the fear that had consumed her during her escape from the kraken—an actual real kraken—her mind buzzed, and the idea of sleep was the furthest thought.

She groaned in pleasure as she sunk a little deeper into the moss, wriggling her tired fins and fluke to get more comfortable. It was so soft against her skin compared to the cave wall she'd been tied to earlier that day. She closed her eyes, thinking through everything that had happened.

How had everything become so fucked up?

Kaelin had definitely been the mer who had returned her father's body. Her voice had sounded different, and she had wondered briefly during the escape, but when the lights had come on in Kaelin's home, she could no longer hope she had been mistaken.

There had been no denying it. She had gasped and reminded the monster in front of her of her presence. But the sight of those wide strong fins and flared purple fluke had been the same. Her heart had raced, and it had taken everything in her not to let Kaelin know, to hide the truth of the moment.

Zendalia groaned into the dimming light. She hoped Kaelin didn't remove all the light from the cave. She would need it to be able to see and kill her eventually. She tensed at the thought—she'd never killed someone before. She hadn't ever wanted to, but with the pain from her father's death so present in her chest, she'd wanted to exact her revenge. She had fucked up, royally.

Why hadn't she just killed Kaelin already? She had been given the chance. Kaelin had kept her back to her, almost daring her to try. She'd been so close to swimming forward and wrapping her forearm around Kaelin's neck and slowly cutting off her ability to breathe. So where had the fire and anger gone?

The mask sucked louder, a small hissing coming from the bottom right corner. Holding her breath, she removed the mask and poked at the tech. Her eyes rested on the small crack, and she pressed her lips tighter together while scrunching her nose. That wasn't something she could fix any time soon, and it wouldn't do her any good to panic. Not yet.

A small crack shouldn't be too big an issue. As long as it didn't get any bigger it would suffice until she reached a high enough sounding for her to breathe on her own. She nodded, her eyelids feeling heavier by the moment.

Zendalia put the mask back over her mouth, locking it into place against her cheeks as tightly as she could. She sucked in a deep breath, her lungs expanding with the water that filled them. When she breathed out, she did it slowly to calm the panic that set in the pit of her belly.

Turning on her side, she curled tightly into a ball and stared at the far wall. This must be Kaelin's bed, the place she slept every night. She shivered at the thought, wondering why the monster would be so kind to her but so murderous to her father. There was no difference between them. They were from an opposing tribe. Her father hadn't even posed a threat. He'd just been exploring, trying to find answers to why the surface of the water was lowering. Her city was so close to breaking the crest of the waves that they were about to burst through them and be exposed to the air above.

He had been the one to try and find answers when no one else would, and it had cost him the very life he had treasured. Zendalia sniffled, holding back the tears that wanted to gush forward. She didn't have the energy for that today. She had cried too much since Kaelin had brought him to her, carrying his small body in her arms as she handed him over and swam away without another word.

If she closed her eyes and focused on the sounds in the water, she was greeted with nothing. A stillness and quiet that she envied. She hadn't felt that kind of calm since she'd cradled her dead father and performed the ritual ceremonies over his body.

She couldn't remember that now. Forcing her wandering mind to turn, Zendalia flipped onto her other side, her muscles protesting the move after the strain she'd caused them that day. She'd been through so much, but the proof she'd gotten about what her father had been searching for was almost enough for her to bring back to Reine.

A real-life kraken. She had survived a real-life kraken.

Her father hadn't been a crazy old man unable to believe his theory was incorrect. He had been right. There *were* monsters in the deep soundings. She'd seen it with her own eyes, barely able to make out what it looked like because of those damn blinding lights, but it had been there. She'd been close enough to touch it —not that she wanted to, and she was pretty sure Kaelin wouldn't allow her to do that.

Kaelin. Zendalia sighed heavily, sinking into the moss even more. It was getting harder to keep her eyes open and her body ready for action. Kaelin had saved her. She'd covered her, protected her, made sure that she survived throughout the attack, and for what? It made no sense that she would kill her father but save her.

She'd never been so covered by another mer before. In Reine, she was one of the larger mer, her lineage of warriors keeping their bodies strong and bulky, but she was nothing compared to Kaelin. The warmth of her scales had heated her skin, touched her in a way she wasn't ready to admit to yet.

Blinking back the thoughts, Zendalia focused on the kraken. She at least had a name for that particular monster now. Her father had been seeking proof of its existence. They had all told him he was crazy, that his ideas were outrageous. So when he left on his quest to find the answers to the questions only he was asking, no one had thought twice about it.

But fuck, he *had* been right.

Maybe she could find the proof, find out just how right he had been. Was this kraken the reason the water above was lowering?

Zendalia had seen the water levels fall and the light from the sun become brighter throughout the years. It hadn't happened rapidly at first, but in the last year the soundings above her city had vanished without anyone seeming to notice. Her father had. He'd tried to raise the alarm that something nefarious was happening. He'd used all his connections and influences, and no one had listened to him. He had worked relentlessly to save a tribe who didn't even know they were in danger.

Whimpering, Zendalia clenched her eyes shut and pressed her fist to her chest. She missed him. The pang of hurt took over and consumed her, and she allowed it in this moment, needing to work through that grief before she could move forward with her plans. When she pulled herself from her mourning, she blinked her eyes open and found the lights softened but still very much present. She would have to thank Kaelin for that when she woke. No...thanking Kaelin was the last thing she should do.

She just had to avenge her father.

The idea, once a warmth in her belly, now twisted with an unease that made her frustration mount to insane levels. She didn't understand what was happening. It all hurt too much for her to wade her way through it. She knew Kaelin had murdered her father. She'd brought him back to her, sliding his lifeless form into her arms.

Zendalia had been so consumed by shock and grief that she had wailed out. The vibrations had stung the water, and she'd clenched her eyes against the onslaught of losing the only family she had left. But that left her with Kaelin. This problem she wanted to end in order to avenge her father.

So what if Kaelin was beautiful and strong and everything she ever looked for in a partner? Zendalia frowned. Where had that thought come from? Yes, she couldn't deny that Kaelin was attractive, now that she had actually seen her face in the light, but that didn't mean she was exempt from being a monster.

It wasn't just attraction that made her hesitate, though. It was the warm hands against her hips as they pushed together between those rocks. The fact that Kaelin used her fins to completely cover the burnt orange of Zendalia's tail, hiding her first and foremost from the kraken. It was the simple moment of the heat of her flesh against Zendalia's, warming her from the cold waters.

Zendalia shuddered.

The mer was a murderer, an enemy. She had to keep reminding herself of that, because everything that had happened since Kaelin had wrapped her hands in that coral had twisted those thoughts into something else. Something akin to empathy.

Suppressing a shiver, Zendalia burrowed deeper into the moss and covered her tail with it. She hadn't realized how cold it was down there until she stopped moving. Zendalia clenched her jaw. The coldness she had anticipated from Kaelin hadn't ever been there, despite her desire to see it. She wanted to believe Kaelin was the monster so badly, but why would a monster save her from the kraken?

Zendalia growled as her whole body racked with shivers. Reaching up, she cupped the necklace she wore tightly in her fingers. "Ugh."

"Oh, so you've finally realized what a stupid plan this is?" Neyon slid from the dark corner near Zendalia's head, their form shimmering blue in the darkness. They were so small that they could fit in the palm of her hand if she wanted, but their skin never truly touched hers. Her familiar had been her only companion since her father had left, and she was grateful that Soulara had introduced them, even if that hadn't been the intention behind giving her the necklace.

"Where have you been?" Zendalia whispered, a smile gracing her lips despite the octopus's attitude. She sought so much comfort from them, every moment of upheaval in her life, and she'd gone right to them. They'd kept her safe and sane in the last seasons since her father's murder.

"I've been with you the whole time, you know that." Neyon slipped into the moss beside Zendalia, resting against it as if satisfied to have her attention. "You've just been occupied being an idiot."

Zendalia frowned and wrinkled her nose right before another giant shiver stole through her. She wasn't sure how much sleep she would manage to get that night, not with the cold seeping through her veins. She tried to cover herself with the moss, curling into a tighter ball as if that would stave off the inevitable.

"Well, at least you didn't kill her and then get yourself killed." Neyon stroked her hip with one tentacle, the touch a phantom but so clear in her mind. She craved the companionship, the friendship, the familiarity since she'd ended up in such a strange part of the ocean. Zendalia sighed into the peace she hadn't managed to find anywhere else.

"Yeah, heaven forbid you don't have a free ride around Reine anymore." She chuckled, sleep tugging at the recesses of her mind. It was getting harder by the second to keep her eyes open, even though she knew she needed to keep alert. The calm she had been searching for before wrapped around her. She needed Neyon in order to find that. Her world was so lonely without her family and friends. They'd all left her sooner rather than later—even Soulara had.

"Precisely." Neyon nudged Zendalia and was rewarded with an arm wrapped around them, pulling them deeper into Zendalia's side.

Her breathing deepened, and her eyelids fluttered shut. She'd needed Neyon in order to fall asleep, but Kaelin was right, as much as she didn't want to admit it. She needed to rest before they figured out what was happening next. She had to be on her tail when she attempted to wrangle more secrets and stories from Kaelin about the kraken.

Just what was it doing?

Where did it come from?

How could they stop it?

She would take up the mantle her father had left behind, and she would save her people from the monster they didn't see coming. Zendalia burrowed into the moss and relaxed her shoulders. She wouldn't let that monster be the end of her people. She could deal with the monster sleeping in the next room another day.

6

Kaelin's ears bled. She clenched her eyes against the screeching sound, as if that would stop it, but it didn't. Her heart raced as the vibrations in the water intensified, lifting her scales off her tail from the sheer force. She feared they would rip off if she moved too suddenly. Diving behind a rock, she flattened herself to the sandy ocean floor and tried to hide from the chaos of destruction happening.

Just moments before, she'd been running her fingers along the coral, the fluorescent colors brightening as she touched them, like a response to her hope and happiness. Pressing her hands over her ears, she tried to block out the sound, the deep thud happening so slowly. She couldn't predict when it would strike again, when the wave of water would rock through her.

Kaelin took steadying, deep breaths. She had to get back home. She had to tell them what was happening before they swam face first into this. No one was prepared for it. Swallowing the lump of fear in her throat, Kaelin bit down on her tongue to get her wits about her. She widened her eyes, moved her hands, and pushed up from behind the rock and swam as fast as she could.

It was impossible to see. Dust and debris floated through the water, making it impossible to distinguish what was in front of her. Kaelin kept her mouth shut, not wanting to breathe the grains of sand into her lungs. It would kill her slowly, and she couldn't let that happen, not without warning her people first.

Narrowing her gaze, she cringed. The sound clanged in her ears, more blood flowing from them freely as it hurt her. She pushed her fluke down hard, propelling herself forward in whatever direction she could. She had no idea where she was going, but she knew she had to get away. She swam hard, the vibrations getting stronger.

Gasping, Kaelin stopped short. A large claw-like arm shot out of the dark, right past her right side, scraping her arm in the process. She cried out in pain, blood seeping from her skin. She curled into a ball, waiting for the next attack to hit her. A second long claw-like arm shot toward her, hitting her full on and hurtling her back the way she had come. She spun in circles, no way to know where the ocean floor was from the way to the surface. Her head spun, her stomach swirled with bile from those shrooms she'd collected and eaten.

Kaelin cried out loudly. In an instant, warmth surrounded her, sweet familiar vibrations. She pried her eyes open, finding Neyon's fibrous light surrounding her and slowing her momentum, but she was going too fast for even them to stop her. Crashing into a jagged rock wall, Kaelin cried out as she collapsed to the ocean floor.

Her head pounded relentlessly as her world righted itself again, though she saw nothing of where she had been and barely any of where she was now. The vibrations hadn't stopped, they pushed against her skin, trying again to flip her over and push her away. The sand on the floor rose up toward the surface, mixing with the dark ocean water to form a thick cloud. Grains of sand scraped against her throat and her lungs every time she sucked in a breath. She would be coughing those out for weeks.

Orienting herself, Kaelin finally found where she had been. She'd been thrown so far she wouldn't easily be able to swim back, and surely not swiftly. Her mouth gaped open as she stared at the swirling murk and debris that had once been the coral she had brushed with her fingers moments ago.

The light was blinding, searing through the murky water and alighting on her position. Panic welled in her chest, ready to burst any second. *It found her.* She cried out as it blinded her eyes. Ducking on instinct and covering her head with her arms, Kaelin moved out of the range of the search light. She swam, slithering like an eel along the ocean floor, moving herself away from the monster she knew hid behind that piercing brightness and the murky death scene.

A sound, muffled and terrified, reached her ears. She stopped. Her heart clenched hard, and her stomach dropped again. Prying her eyes open wide, she looked around, desperately trying to see where the sound had come from. It was so different from the monster behind her—so like another mermaid.

Her blood roared, drowning out the sound of fear while her heart beat so hard she feared it might break through her chest. The dust and debris floated down around her, sucking into her mouth as she gulped the water too fast. Her mind whirled as shapes emerged from behind the thinning contamination to the water.

The golden tail whipped wildly against the ocean floor. It moved more debris into the water surrounding the mer. Kaelin blinked against the cloud and finally made him out. His fins were so small. Something odd covered his thin arms, his narrow chest, and his mouth, wrapping around his head behind his ears.

The light dimmed to the point it no longer hurt her eyes, and she swiveled her head back and forth to make out where it had gone and where the monster was coming from next. Kaelin's tail flapped back and forth too fast in the water, belying her otherwise outward calm. With no sign of the monster, she dropped back down to the ocean floor. The dark form moved away, the light polluting her world receded as the monster's shape shrank into the distance. It must not have seen her.

A strange sound shocked her attention back to the floundering mer. He leaned against a large rock, recently settled upon the sandy floor. The gurgling noise hurt her throat, as if she could feel the pain he was in. Then there was a whistle that pierced the thick water, making her squint her eyes from the pain. She stared at him bewildered, no idea what to do or say. She'd never spoken to anyone outside of her tribe before, but he looked so desperate.

"I'm Kaelin, daughter of the lower soundings." She approached carefully, hands lifted, palms out in a sign of serenity.

He breathed heavily. "Krak–en."

"What?" Kaelin furrowed her brow in confusion, and he pointed to where the monster had gone.

"Krak–en."

"The monster? It's gone."

He looked relieved until sounds joined the high whistle, but she couldn't make out any more words. She drew in a sharp breath and moved toward him. He should have left the ocean floor by now, but he hadn't budged since she'd found him. His tail flapped again, wildly, and this time, she could see the break near the base of his fluke.

"Are you all right?"

The mer's head shook back and forth in earnest. His eyes were wide, but it wasn't fear in his gaze. It was pain. Death.

"Come, I'll take you to my people. They can help."

He shook his head again, more ferociously this time, his shock of white hair whipping around his face and his large round amber eyes piercing into her own. She'd seen that death-look before, heard the rattle when one of her beloved companions passed from this world into the next.

"They can help," she whispered, pleading with him to allow her to take him. She clasped his forearm with her fingers, as though greeting an elder of her people and tried again. "It'll be all right. I'll take you there now."

He shook his head back and forth once more but with less enthusiasm, not resisting as Kaelin swam for home, half-dragging this stranger along beside her. The gurgling grew louder, the bubbles excessive as they floated in a trail behind them.

The sound, though stuttering on and off as it had done, finally grew quieter as she neared home. She thanked the near silence as the reality of what had happened struck her hard in her soul.

But the sound never returned.

Kaelin blinked her eyes open, tears filling the water near her face with warmth. Her breath came too fast, and her heart hurt her chest with the strength of its wild thuds. The sound—she could still hear it—pained from her memories as it had faded away. She closed her eyes, willed the last remnants of the nightmare away, begged and sobbed.

"Don't let me hear it when I'm awake as well." She reached her fingers out for Neyon, waiting for them to warm her hand with comforting vibrations, to wrap her in the peace she had sought for so long. She wanted nothing more than for the tears to stop, for the living nightmare to cease, to let her breathe just for a moment longer without the knowledge of what she had done.

She forced water in and out of her mouth, slowing as much as she was able to. She had to take her punishment, live through her exile so she could learn from her mistakes and go home stronger than before. But the mark of being banished would stay with her forever—it was her burden to bear. Sniffling, Kaelin wiped her hands along her cheeks. It would all be fine so long as the sound stopped echoing in her ears.

She opened her eyes wide, looking sharply from side to side.

It was real. *The sound was real.* But it wasn't the same, not exactly. The man had breathed a deep rolling sound. But this one, this hiss didn't carry the same timbre. It was that high-pitched hurt, but it wasn't as powerful.

Forcing herself upright, Kaelin looked for Neyon, her faithful companion who would show her what to do. But they were nowhere in sight. Fear knotted in her stomach and her fluke seemed sluggish as she slowly swam through her home, following the rattling pitch.

Dread pooled in her chest, ripping through her very being and making her skin prickle with fear. The sound came from her moss bedding. She turned the corner and found Zendalia tossing and turning, tangled up in the moss, her tail mostly covered, her breasts exposed. Relief almost settled on Kaelin, a smile about to touch her lips, until the sound came again in a great heaving rush as Zendalia's chest shuddered with her breath. As she released, she seemed to convulse on the bed.

"No," Kaelin murmured. For a fraction of a second, Kaelin froze, staring at her nightmare happening again. In a rush she came back to herself, swimming so fast that small ripples of bubbles pushed away from her fluke. "No, no, no, no, no, no, no."

She grabbed Zendalia's shoulders and dragged her into a sitting position. Her body flopped forward, and Kaelin's no mantra repeated as she shook the mer back and forth rather violently. A hissing gasp escaped Zendalia, and she pushed away from Kaelin.

"Get away from me." Zendalia gasped, taking gulps of water after each word. "Are you trying to kill me?"

"I'm trying to save you, you obnoxious..." Kaelin trailed off, the color draining from Zendalia's skin. Her arms were so cold against Kaelin's fingers, her skin and scales frozen.

The words floated around them, and they both stilled, floating in their natural buoyancy.

"Is your—" Kaelin groped for the right word, her hand

coming up to her face to make a circle indicating her meaning "—mask. Is your mask broken?"

"Were you trying to kill me?" Zendalia's eyes, amber and round, stared into Kaelin. The memory dislodged something deeper than the mer's own eyes looking at her. She shook it off. She had to focus on the mask, because she couldn't let it happen again.

"No." She took a deep gulp of water and forced her words to come out slower, gentler, despite the rushing fear that raced beneath her skin and tail. "I wasn't trying to kill you. I was trying to wake you. You weren't breathing properly."

"I…" Zendalia shook her head as though trying to shake off the remaining fogginess of sleep. That high-pitched noise hit them again. Zendalia shifted, the moss moving from her tail, and revealed Neyon wrapped around Zendalia's hips. "I'm fine. I don't sleep well. That's all."

Betrayal sat in the center of her chest, but Zendalia's words clanged inside of Kaelin's mind, and another painful memory rushed at her.

Retelling the story of her return journey home had been an agonizing and slow affair. Confusion had filled her mind as looks became dark and their eyes strayed to the dead mer who lay on the floor beside her own prostrate, bruised, and bleeding body.

The elders had found her guilty of ending a life when she could have saved it. She hadn't listened to the man's pleas for help, which she admitted he had tried to express to her through his eyes and his movements. She hadn't breathed life into him, given him what his body so desperately craved.

She had been guilty of the most heinous crime in their society. Taking a life the waters had not given her freely. The punishment had been her exile from the tribe. But before that began, she would need to return the body of the man's family.

The mer's sobs had rung in Kaelin's ears, and they had turned to screams once she had handed the body over. Those cries were Zendalia's. She looked at Zendalia with new eyes, recognizing the pain and hurt she had already caused her. Everything she had taken away because in her own denseness she hadn't done what was necessary, she hadn't seen there had been a solution.

"Kaelin?" Zendalia's words pulled her from the memory. "Are *you* all right?"

A sob nearly tore through her lips at the words she'd asked the mer all those seasons ago. The tears started again, and she pushed away from Zendalia, putting space between them. She stared down at Neyon, shaking her head at the betrayal she felt wrapping her heart tightly. She needed them—not Zendalia. They were her *only* companion.

"I remember you," Kaelin choked out. She stared at the amber eyes above the mask. She had known, some part of her had, but she'd avoided remembering that time of her life for so long that she hadn't been willing to dive into it again. Looking at Zendalia now, it was so obvious the familial relationship. "You are the mer's daughter."

Zendalia's face hardened, her eyes narrowing as she shook her head slowly. She stayed put in the moss bed, Neyon wrapped around her tightly. She spoke from behind clenched teeth, "His name was Zen."

7

Zendalia rushed forward, hands wrapping around Kaelin's throat, fingers gripping tightly. The muscles in her arms worked hard, as she exuded as much pressure as she possibly could. This was her one chance. This was the moment she had waited for, the chance to exact her revenge. She flapped her fluke, pushing even harder and shoving Kaelin against the wall of her home.

"Why?" Warm tears merged with the cold water between their faces. She had no idea if they were her tears or Kaelin's. She didn't care whose they were. She couldn't bring herself to think about it. Every moment she had was focused on taking this life in exchange for her father's.

"Why did you kill him?" she ground out. Zendalia tightened her grip, pushing her thumb into Kaelin's jugular and diminishing her life.

Kaelin didn't fight back. She didn't push Zendalia away. She didn't try to wriggle out of her grasp. She stayed there, pressed against the wall with Zendalia squeezing the life out of her second by second. She was going to succeed this time. She had to —it was all for him.

"Why did you drag his body back to me like some kind of prize?"

Kaelin lifted her hands then, wrapping her long fingers around Zendalia's wrists and squeezing. She didn't push them away or fight, but she lifted her gaze, those dark purple eyes with bright purple irises. Zendalia faltered in her hold. Kaelin used the moment to use soft strokes against her forearms.

Kaelin's face turned ashen, the gray consuming the deep beautiful purple of her skin. Kaelin's breathing slowed, each drag of water into her lungs stagnating to the next. Zendalia shook her head, the tears continuing to pool between them, and she knew in that instant that she was the one who was crying.

Something crossed Kaelin's gaze, something she had never seen before. Zendalia hesitated, her fingers releasing her tight grip as her stomach twisted with knots. She canted her head to the side, waiting for the explanation behind that look, behind Kaelin's lack of defense.

"Not a prize," Kaelin rasped, her voice raw from the pressure Zendalia had exerted on her throat. "Not a prize."

"What then?" Zendalia sobbed, dragging as much water into her lungs as possible, but it was so hard to do it. It took everything in her just to keep herself steady in that moment, answers ready to be revealed.

Kaelin's look sobered, and she slid forward slightly. She reached out her hands but dropped them to her sides, loose fists made and so much pain in her gaze. *Pain.* Zendalia shook her head against it, not believing what she saw. "Zendalia."

"Did you think I would be grateful?" Zendalia gasped. "That my father's murderer handed him…back…to me?"

It was so hard to breathe. A sharp sensation seared through her chest. Her eyes burned against the water. Her tail felt weak and slow to move, and her head light and dizzy, as if the spinning was just about to begin and never stop. She was floating, wasn't she?

"Zendalia. You have to calm down." Kaelin's voice sounded

so far away, but it was firm and demanding. Zendalia clung to it like a lifeline. Zendalia's vision blurred, going in and out from light to dark. It was so hard to make out Kaelin's face, the beautiful features that had greeted her as soon as they'd come into the light.

"Slow your breathing," Kaelin murmured, taking Zendalia's hand and pressing it to the center of her chest, right over her heart. "Feel my breaths."

Zendalia's ears picked up on a hissing, and it grew louder. Her head spun, and it was impossible to focus. The hissing took over her sensations, the loudness of it, the high-pitched whine that would mean her death.

"Zendalia!" Kaelin shouted, but Zendalia couldn't hold herself anymore. She drifted. Wherever Kaelin wanted her to go, she would have to because she couldn't fight it. She couldn't make herself move or focus. Relaxing all her muscles, she slipped away.

The mask was ripped from her face. Zendalia gasped for breath in the thick waters. Sharp pain entered her lungs, spearing through her chest. She spun around, her back colliding with the wall. She closed her eyes, ready to die. She had failed. She hadn't avenged her father. But at least she'd manage to find his murderer. Her lungs burned. Parting her lips, Zendalia let whatever happened happen.

Kaelin's mouth against hers was strong. Water pushed into her lungs, her chest expanding in a second. Zendalia closed her eyes against the onslaught, unsure of what was happening. A second breath. Her head still spun but not as much. She could feel her fingertips again. Her head felt less foggy. Kaelin left her lips for a brief second before coming back and forcing more water into her lungs.

Zendalia panicked. She shuddered and pushed Kaelin away, reaching for the mask that was still attached to her neck. She shoved it onto her face, holding it firm with Kaelin's hand over hers as they did up the straps along the sides of her head swiftly.

"Don't do that to me again," Kaelin muttered. They rested together, Kaelin's forehead on Zendalia's shoulder, Kaelin's breathing deep and slow. Her shoulders relaxed as she practically fell into Zendalia's waiting arms. They embraced through the aftermath.

Zendalia clenched her jaw, guilt and shame filling her. She closed her eyes tightly, the warmth of tears still very much present. Drawing on all the strength she had, she flipped them quickly. Zendalia pressed her forearm against Kaelin's neck, pushing hard while she rammed her fist into Kaelin's stomach. Kaelin doubled over, grunting in pain as Zendalia pounded against her again.

"You. Killed. Him."

Kaelin whimpered, clawing at Zendalia's arm as she tried to fight for control of the situation. Her tail flapped against Zendalia's. The force from her brute strength pushed Zendalia farther back. Zendalia had to work hard to keep herself where she was, to keep the pressure against Kaelin's neck.

The octopus who had joined her in the middle of her sleep wove their way in between them. Long fibrous tentacles wrapped around Zendalia's arms and Kaelin's shoulders. Then they wrapped around Zendalia's abdomen. Vibrations moved through them to her at a strong steady pace. A bolt of electricity shocked her.

Zendalia cried out, her voice ricocheting off the cave walls as she crumpled to the floor of the cave below. When the shocks stopped, Zendalia shoved upward and swam right at Kaelin again. Once more, the octopus got between them, electrifying the water with five sharp pulses. Zendalia collapsed to the cave floor in a tight ball, whimpering in pain.

When she pried her eyes open, Kaelin lay next to her. Her eyes were wide, her lips parted as if she had experienced the same shock. Her chest rose and fell rapidly. Zendalia wanted to try again, but she didn't have the energy. The leak in her mask had gotten worse, and she was at the point she couldn't keep up with it anymore. She dug her fingers against the rock floor of the cave and stayed put.

"What the hell was that thing?" she muttered.

"My companion," Kaelin answered, her voice breathy.

"Why…" Zendalia dragged in a raspy breath, deciding at the last minute to change her question. "…why did you help me?"

Kaelin groaned and rolled onto her side, away from Zendalia. "Doesn't matter."

Kaelin moved, swimming away more slowly than normal, and she wasn't entirely sure why. Zendalia stayed put, the sparks from that last shock still rolling through her body. She'd never experienced something like that before. She'd never thought that any creature in the ocean could do that. The long fibrous legs of the octopus moved near her, slowly hovering above her.

"That was nice, real nice." Zendalia narrowed her gaze at them.

They flicked a tentacle in her direction before swimming off in the direction Kaelin had gone. Zendalia hit the back of her head against the cave floor. She needed some damn sense knocked into her. That had been a stupid move. It might have been her only chance, but she should have planned it out better. And it would have gone as planned if her mask hadn't been cracked. *Fucking tech.*

Clenching her fists, she pounded them into the ground before dragging her sorry tail off the ground. What were they going to do now? Swim around each other? Zendalia followed the octopus's trail, sliding into the main room again. She shivered helplessly now that the cold seeped back into her muscles and veins. She had no idea how she swas going to survive much longer down there without finding a way to keep warm.

As she rounded the corner, Kaelin stuttered as she packed a sack. She tossed a glare over her shoulder and shook her head. "I didn't bring him to you as a prize."

"Then why would you do that?" Zendalia shouted, the burst

of energy coming from somewhere deep inside her, anger mixed with deep grief, blending seamlessly.

Kaelin spun around sharply, flinging her hand out at her side. Zendalia winced at the move, but she stayed her ground. She wasn't going to give this one up. She had to know.

Kaelin's cheeks flushed, the purple along her skin lightening to a light rose. She closed her eyes slowly, staring at the floor between them. "It was part of my punishment."

"Punishment? For murder you mean."

Kaelin's chin bobbed slightly, but she still didn't make eye contact. "Yes, for his life being extinguished."

"So you did kill him!" That same rage that had bubbled just under the surface for the last few seasons rose again, clawing at her throat to get out. She blinked hard, her fists clenched tightly at her sides. Her eyes blurred with emotion, and it took everything in her to stay put. She had no idea where that damn octopus had gone, but she had no doubt that they would attack again as soon as Zendalia took another chance. She would have to try when they weren't around.

Nodding, Kaelin seemed to close in on herself. She dragged in a few steadying breaths before raising her chin up to stare Zendalia directly in the eye. "I am Kaelin, banished daughter of the lower soundings."

"What does that mean?" Zendalia furrowed her brow, the formal language so foreign to her ear.

Kaelin shook her head reluctantly. "It means nothing anymore."

"What does it mean?" Zendalia's voice reverberated loudly as her impatience and anger took over her.

Swimming forward in an instant, Kaelin put her hand against Zendalia's chest again, holding firm. "Breathe slowly."

"Stop with that nonsense!" Zendalia shook her head wildly.

"You have to breathe slowly otherwise you won't be able to breathe."

The high-pitched sound of her mask finally reached her ears.

Zendalia listened, as much as she didn't want to, and slowed her breathing, calming her racing heart, and relaxing her muscles. It was much easier to draw the water into her lungs now.

"The elders banished me. One season for each year of his life. That's why I'm here." Kaelin put her hands out to her sides, indicating the cave. "That's why I'm not with my tribe."

Zendalia's lips parted. "He was sixty-three years."

"Then now I have an end date to my exile. Thank you." Kaelin nodded and turned back to the sack that she'd been packing when Zendalia interrupted her.

"You didn't even know?"

Kaelin shook her head.

"How would they know it ended?" Zendalia stared at her incredulously, her heart picking up speed again.

Kaelin shrugged. Zendalia floated higher, her mind spinning with curiosity, with pain, with wanting to know exactly how this had all happened and why she was still talking to this murderous monster.

"The elders do what they think is right. I took a life that wasn't freely given by the waters, so I will suffer the consequences of my actions."

"You took a life," Zendalia repeated, the words hitting her hard. Kaelin was freely admitting that she had murdered him. "He was my father."

Kaelin winced, whispering, "I know. I brought him to you so you could perform your rituals."

"My rituals?"

"Whatever it is you do with those who have passed from this life into the next."

Zendalia shook her head. "You mean interning his body?"

"Whatever it is you do. I'm sure we have different rituals." Kaelin frowned before ignoring her again.

Confused, Zendalia stayed frozen in place, her fluke keeping her exactly where she wanted to be. "What do you do when someone dies?"

"We strip their bodies, bathe them, prepare them with garments and place them in the lowest sounding. We sit with them for as long as possible until the last of us must leave. Then we leave them to go into their next life."

"That sounds almost beautiful," Zendalia murmured. It was so different than what she had done with her father's body. She almost pitied the lack of ritual in her own heritage. Lifting her gaze to meet Kaelin's dark purple eyes, Zendalia fought the guilt filling her soul. "What is the kraken?"

"He told me about it." Kaelin raised her gaze. "Your father did, before he died. He tried to warn me about it, I think. I've followed it since my exile. It comes and goes, devastating anything it touches."

"Where does it come from?" Zendalia raised an eyebrow, trying to make eye contact with Kaelin, but she wouldn't raise her gaze again.

Kaelin shook her head, her voice so quiet that Zendalia almost missed what she said. "I don't know."

The octopus swam around Kaelin's tail, wrapping around her and tightening their grasp against her scales much the same way Zendalia had woken in the night with them. Zendalia couldn't stop the smile that lit her lips. They had been protecting Kaelin—and she couldn't mistake the comfort she'd received from them as anything other than a mutual need for heat.

8

After a few slow and deliberate breaths, Kaelin relaxed her shoulders when Neyon squeezed a little tighter across her tail. It wasn't a natural easing of her chest, but a demand on her body, on her arms to pull her shoulders down and stop making her body ache more than it already did from the altercations with Zendalia, not to mention the escape from the kraken from the day before.

She took her time, her back turned to Zendalia as she prepared a simple breakfast of seaweed and bug salad. It wasn't bravery—she wasn't a brave mer. She didn't want to see those eyes staring at her over the cracked mask, hating her. She hated herself enough for the both of them. She needed just a few moments to gather herself, to remember what being around another mer felt like. And to wonder why she fought so hard against Zendalia's attempts to kill her when to move from this life to the next might be the better choice, but she couldn't let Zendalia meet the same fate she had.

She shook her head and pushed the thought away. Besides, she knew without a doubt that if Zendalia attempted to attack her yet again, Neyon would alert her and stop Zendalia as much as they could. Kaelin shuddered. She didn't need another shock to her system to wake her up this morning.

There were no noises from behind her except for that damned horrid hiss from the crack in Zendalia's mask. Had the crack gotten worse during their altercation or did the hiss sound louder only because she was on high alert for another attack? She turned, and Zendalia's gaze flew upward, a darkening in her cheeks as her eyes met Kaelin's.

Kaelin bit back a smile. Had Zendalia been checking her out? Checking out the curve of her hips and the swish of her tail? Surely not. Kaelin scoffed at herself. If anything, she was checking her out for any weak points, trying to work out her next move to try and kill her.

"It's not much, but it's better than nothing." She hesitantly held the plate out to Zendalia.

Zendalia's eyes narrowed, shifted to the shell, back to Kaelin's face, and down to the shell again. She drifted forward, and Kaelin flinched.

"This one looks better." Zendalia reached past the offered shell and took the smaller portion Kaelin had made for herself.

"Fine." Kaelin huffed, several bubbles floating out of her mouth.

Zendalia drifted over to a cluster of rocks that Kaelin rarely used. It seemed like a nice enough place to eat now that she watched Zendalia perch upon one of the smoother stones. She followed and settled down herself two stones over. They rested their tails between them almost close enough together to be considered hospitable, to even possibly be mistaken for acquaintances if not friends. *Almost.*

Nearby, Neyon rested on their own stone seating. It jutted out of the cave wall about chest high from the cave's floor. Their tendrils drifted in front of them as their eyes moved constantly between the two merwomen.

The cave's light stung Kaelin's eyes, and she squeezed them shut again, scrunching up her face against the onslaught. The lanterns she had kept lit for Zendalia's sake made everything far too bright and too sharp. She had never thought her home was filled with angles but now she saw little else but the jutting edges and rough walls. Warm water stroked her face as the tears became constant, but she could only imagine how much fear the darkness might create for Zendalia. Sight had always been one of her tribe's strengths. Not being able to see would have been a death sentence for Kaelin during her exile. Especially with the kraken. The thought worried Kaelin as she chewed on the sand bug, barely tasting the flavors of the flesh. How did Zen know about the kraken, but his daughter didn't? Is that why he had been down here?

"So what happens now?" Zendalia asked as she stabbed at the food on her half shell as though it might move if she didn't grab it with extreme force.

Kaelin blinked, more warm water leaking from the sides of her eyes and mixing with the cold around her before she answered as though it were the most obvious thing in the world. "We need to get you back to water you can breathe in."

"No, I'm not going anywhere." Zendalia shook her head, and the hiss of her breath hurt Kaelin's ears and her heart. Why wouldn't this stubborn mer listen to her? Didn't she understand the reality of the situation? There was the need for revenge, and then there were suicide missions.

Kaelin couldn't look Zendalia in the eyes. Instead she focused on Zendalia's bronzed fingers as they clenched tightly onto the jagged edges of the shell plate she held. Zendalia had eaten half of the bug and seaweed salad while Kaelin had nudged most of her own shell-full around, only able to stomach a few bites.

"You're going to die if we don't get you away from here." Kaelin couldn't hold in her annoyance, and the mouthfuls of food in her stomach roiled against the idea of another dead body for her to carry. Another long banishment that she knew she wouldn't survive. It had been hard enough to be alone for these seasons. Finding another mer who was willing to speak with her had been a blessing from the water.

"I'm fine. I can last a little longer." The hiss between her breaths belied Zendalia's words. "Besides, why do you care? You didn't care about my father."

Kaelin's heart sank, the words on the tip of her tongue, but she couldn't force them out. Her tongue became thick with emotion, and she held back. She stared down at the food in her hands, wondering how much she could force herself to eat and how much she could get away with not eating.

"You can't last, not without my breath." She ignored the rest of the words, though she couldn't avoid hearing them as they punched into her chest.

"You are not putting your lips on me again." Zendalia shuddered, and a twist of shame hit Kaelin's chest. Zendalia hated her—of course she did—to the point that she would truly prefer to die than to receive life-giving breath. That just wouldn't do, because the consequences were beyond Zendalia's life. They included her own sanity.

Kaelin's mind raced. What could she do if the crack got worse, or if Zendalia passed out again? She wasn't allowed within three leagues of her tribe. She had been told not to seek out other companionship until the term of her punishment was reached. At that time she would be contacted by a representative of her tribe and given the choice to return or to find another tribe.

There had only ever been three mers during Kaelin's life who had been sentenced to banishment. And the three combined had a sentence far less than her own. They had all returned and were now embraced by the tribe. But Kaelin had also seen the side looks and heard the whispers and the speeding up of tail fins when one of them approached. She'd been guilty of it herself, her own mother having warned her against them.

She'd be that person now, the pariah in her own community, and it would be a stigma she could never rid herself of. Then again, she did deserve it. She hadn't been strong enough to save him, or with-it enough to realize and understand what he needed. She ground her teeth together, her gaze resting on the full plate of food in front of her.

But still, she craved home. *Real home.* Not just this makeshift place that no matter how much she painted had never quite felt like her own. She missed the tiny mer swimming around the tails of the adults as they traveled from one place to the next, the sounds of their laughter as it echoed while they played, the gentle touch of her mother's hand against her arm when she was upset. Taking in a staggering breath, Kaelin brought herself back to the moment, although it wasn't easy. This was her reality now.

Silence settled over them. Kaelin forced another bite of food, but she continued to taste nothing. She wondered how much longer she could stand being here, in the cave on her own. For a moment the idea of giving in flitted through her mind. Would it really be so bad to let Zendalia win? To give her the revenge she so desperately wanted and deserved?

Fear bit into her stomach, churning it to the point that bile rose into her throat. All life was precious, even her own undeserving existence. And to make Zendalia live with the same fate seemed cruel. She looked up under half-closed lashes to where Neyon had stopped bobbing around alternating stares between the two and now glared down at Kaelin. She deserved that look, the harshness, for thinking thoughts that weren't allowed.

She couldn't give up. Whether she deserved it or not, the water had offered her life, and she would be no better than what they had branded her with if she threw it away so casually. Besides, what would happen if she gave up and let Zendalia win? Zendalia didn't stand a chance of making it back to the higher soundings. That clinched the decision more than angering her people or dying an outcast's death and never seeing her mother again. She couldn't let someone else perish because of her actions or inactions. She hoped she had the strength to honor Zendalia's wishes, but the very idea made her chest tighten.

"How old are you, Zendalia?" Kaelin asked, forcing her mouth around the entire name. The cave filled with a tense silence. Even Neyon stopped moving and glaring. She was certain she had spoken loud enough for Zendalia to hear her.

"What?" Zendalia's sharp word could have meant anything —confusion at the sudden change of topic, or perhaps her hearing was far worse than Kaelin gave her credit. Either way, it didn't change Kaelin's posture or tone. She had given up something in the moments of silence when her mind wandered to what possible future she might have or deserve. Whether that something was hope or a desire to keep believing she was strong enough to endure this exile, she wasn't entirely certain.

"How old are you?" Kaelin repeated.

"Why?"

"You'll die, and they'll add your life to my punishment. It would be nice to at least know when my exile will end or if I shall end my days in the caves."

Zendalia scrunched her nose, her finger positioned halfway between the plate and her mouth, a small bug pinched between her forefinger and thumb, no webbing on her hand like on Kaelin's. Those amber eyes locked on Kaelin's, boring directly into her soul. "Why would me dying from broken equipment add time to your punishment?"

Zendalia dropped the empty shell, and it floated down to the cave floor. Kaelin eyed it beside Zendalia's still tail. It was the first time Kaelin had seen her entirely still, and the effect was mesmerizing. The color of her scales was gorgeous in this light, the reflections from the bronzed oranges a balm on her eyes rather than an irritant. Kaelin squared her shoulders, tightening her grasp on her own plate.

Kaelin opened her mouth to speak, but whatever she had planned to say was abruptly cut off by the shudder of the cave's floor beneath their fins. The shell near Zendalia's fin jumped and cracked down the middle, the fin no longer still as it pushed off from the sandy ground, propelling Zendalia off her stone seat.

"What was that?" Zendalia's eyes were wide and filled with a swirl of emotions that met Kaelin's in the flickering lights.

"It found us." Kaelin's words were calm, though her heart hammered in her chest. Could Zendalia see her own emotions reflected back in Kaelin's violet eyes?

Kaelin looked around her cave, her home for the last few months, and grief sliced through her at having to leave her safe space. It wasn't truly her home, but until now it had been safe. Knowing it was doubtful she would ever return made her mourn for the hours she poured into the therapy of her art. The wall she had painted of her shame, the colors she had been forced to slow down in order to make correctly, were all part of her journey. She needed them to heal. Would having done it once be enough or was she now doomed to repeat her mistake in every aspect and moment of her world?

Another boom and the sting in her ears made her push past the sorrow as her survival instincts kicked in. She reached her arm out for Neyon. They swam down to her, wrapping around her hip and side, clinging to her for dear life.

She grabbed her pack and slung it across her front, grabbing Zendalia's hand and swimming for the cave's entrance. She didn't bother to look back as she flicked her tail hard up toward the surface of the cave. They shot out into the free moving water of the ocean just as the vibrations from the kraken hit, shoving them against the sandy floor. Zendalia screamed.

9

Kaelin twisted around sharply and pulled Zendalia against her chest, muffling the sound of her voice. Her chest rose and fell hard as the force of the vibrations knocked them backward. She clenched her eyes tightly as the rush of the water moved them. She couldn't fight against it, not with Zendalia in her arms.

Her back collided with a rock, knocking them hard to the ocean floor. Kaelin grunted and ground her teeth together when she landed on top of Zendalia. She continued to cover her, flaring her fins to hide that beautiful coppery orange color. Kaelin lifted her chin, still feeling Neyon pressed to her side. She narrowed her gaze, trying to make out where the kraken was this time.

With the force of that vibration, it was far closer than she'd anticipated. How had she not heard it coming before then? Guilt wracked through her, taking over her chest and her stomach, moving out into her fingers and her tail. She was never good enough to fight this thing. It was why she hadn't even tried. She'd avoided it as best as she could, but now it had taken her home, and she was left desolate in her banishment.

The hissing from the mask was loud. Kaelin ducked her chin

and stared down at the bubble escaping it. She cursed under her breath and reached up, pulling the mask back down into the proper position until Zendalia's hands could take over putting it back in place. Kaelin raised her chin up slightly, scanning the horizon. The murky cloud was rapidly coming near them. The kraken wasn't far off.

"We need to move," Kaelin murmured into Zendalia's ear. "But you need to stay quiet. As loud as it is, it detects sound."

Zendalia nodded, staying silent. Kaelin appreciated her willingness to listen this time around and not try to push her own agenda. It would make this easier in the long run. She tightened her shoulders and reached down to Neyon, patting their head. They dislocated from her body and swam off. They would help her find a way out if they got lost in the debris as it floated near them.

Kaelin had had far too many run-ins with the kraken lately, almost as if it was following her. Her heart thumped hard against her ribs. She gripped Zendalia's upper arms, holding still and waiting for the prime moment. They could go the opposite direction, but that was toward her tribe. If they got too close, then her banishment would be threatened again.

"Let's go." Kaelin made a split-second decision and shot up off the ocean floor. She kept Zendalia's arm in her grasp as she tried to skirt around the edge of the cloud, moving away from the tribe and toward the kraken but from a distance.

The loud humming she had learned to associate with it started instantly, the dust settling for a moment. This was her chance to get through the radius of attack without being caught. It wasn't usually so quick to stop its attack. She'd noticed it did that every time. It attacked, it stopped, it started again.

Her fingers tightened around Zendalia's cool flesh. She dragged Zendalia with her, not looking over her shoulder as she flapped her fluke in long, strong strokes. They had to go fast if they were going to manage to get through the waters before it started up again. It never took long.

Kaelin steadied her breathing, using her strength and endurance to keep their bodies moving. Zendalia tugged hard, her arm slipping from Kaelin's grasp. Crying out, Kaelin forced herself to stop. She spun around, trying to see through the sandy water and darkness to where Zendalia had gone. In an instant she caught a flash of her orange tail as she dove deep into the water and back toward the ocean floor, right toward where the kraken sat.

"Zendalia!" Kaelin shouted, knowing it wasn't going to make a lick of a difference. Zendalia had a mind of her own, stubborn through and through. In the short time they'd known each other, it had been clear she didn't give up on her ideas easily. Kaelin looked around, hoping to find Neyon's blue fibrous body somewhere in sight, but they were nowhere to be found.

Cursing under her breath, Kaelin folded herself in half, pivoted, and shot through the water to where she'd seen Zendalia's flash of scales. Zendalia was going to get her killed even if she didn't do it herself. She pushed her way through the water thick with sand and debris from broken rocks. It would eventually settle someplace new, completely changing the landscape of the ocean floor and leaving a giant circle where the kraken had sat to regain strength.

The humming grew louder. Kaelin held her breath to avoid breathing in the sandy water as she narrowed her gaze to see through the dust. She wanted to call out Zendalia's name, but she didn't want to wake the beast below them either. Finally she saw another flash of orange in the lights from the kraken.

"Fuck," she muttered the curse.

Zendalia was only a few tail flaps away from the monster itself. Kaelin sped up her descent, diving straight for where she'd seen Zendalia's form. She swam a straight line, pushing herself to move as swiftly as possible. She found Zendalia and moved her arms out, wrapping them around Zendalia's torso as they tumbled against the ocean floor, settling behind a rock.

"What are you thinking?" Kaelin hissed, but it was masked by the high-pitched whine of the cracked mask.

Zendalia's chest pressed against her sharply as she dragged water into her lungs. She shifted, moving upward and pressing her breasts into Kaelin's face as she looked over the top of the rock they were hidden behind. Kaelin tugged hard, pulling Zendalia back down to be completely hidden.

"What part of *you're too bright* don't you understand? It'll see you!"

"It's tech," Zendalia murmured right into Kaelin's ear as they pressed together. "It's all tech."

"What?" Kaelin let go and twisted around sharply. She'd never dared herself to get this close while it settled down. She peeked her head out from around the edge of the stone they hid behind. Lights blazed through the dark water, making it foggy. She struggled to clear her gaze and fight against the brightness. Zendalia mustn't have that issue since she was used to a brighter environment. Clenching her jaw, Kaelin waited to see the full-ness of the monster in front of her.

The humming continued, and finally she could see where the dust was being pulled toward the kraken. Drawing her brows together, Kaelin focused her gaze. The dust disappeared into the giant sphere on the underbelly of the kraken. The beast was held up by long legs that penetrated deep into the ocean floor.

"What's it doing, though?" Zendalia whispered.

Kaelin knew in an instant. The water rushed over her skin, the granules of sand scraping against her flesh and scales. Kaelin's long hair moved toward it, pulled by the movement of the water. She shook her head and pulled Zendalia behind the rock again, keeping her hands on Zendalia's shoulders since they had no time to waste.

"We need to get out of here before it wakes again."

"Wakes?" Zendalia frowned. "It's tech."

"It's a monster, and if we stay here, then we'll die like your father. You won't have the privilege of being the one to kill me."

Kaelin didn't hesitate as she grabbed Zendalia's wrist. "We're leaving now."

She pushed off the rock and swam. At first, Zendalia was a dead weight behind her, but instinct must have kicked in because within a few seconds, she sped up and it was easier for Kaelin to move through the waters. The pull of the current toward the kraken was strong, and it was a struggle to make any progress away. They moved sideways through it, inching their way forward as they tried to circumvent the drag of water.

They would have to talk about that later, or better yet, Kaelin could deposit Zendalia higher up toward her people and leave her there where she could survive on her own without the mask, and then she could dive down deep where Zendalia couldn't follow her. That was the better plan. She kept her grasp on Zendalia's wrist tight as they moved through the water until the current broke.

It stopped.

Fear ramped up in Kaelin's chest again. She stopped short and twisted around to stare at where they had come from. They hadn't made it far enough. She broke her grasp on Zendalia's wrist and put her hands up to shield her eyes as a bright light turned perfectly on them, putting them under the spotlight.

"Zendalia!" Kaelin cried out, clenching her eyes tightly.

The hand in hers was comforting. The gentle pull of Zendalia swimming away from the light was something she had to trust. When there was a darkness behind her eyelids, she dared to open them, finding the beaconed water in front of them. Kaelin shook her head and took hold of Zendalia again and turned upward.

Loud rumbles reverberated through the water behind them. Kaelin's stomach lurched as panic hit her. It was happening again. The exact same way it had all those seasons ago when she'd found Zen, when she'd first encountered the kraken. She swam erratically, dodging to different places and keeping Zendalia with her as close as possible.

No matter what she did, she couldn't lose Zendalia. She couldn't let her meet the same fate her father had. She wouldn't be able to take the extra seasons of banishment, assuming her people didn't exile her entirely.

Crack!

The large leg of the kraken shot down next to them, more lights turned on their forms. They looked like silhouettes in the darkness ahead of them, the light shining on them from behind. Kaelin swallowed a lump in her throat and turned down, but the lights followed. Then up. Again to the right, then left. She nearly cried out in anger when they couldn't lose them.

An outcrop of deep sounding coral shot up out of the waters. Kaelin glanced back at Zendalia and shot in the direction of the coral. It was their only chance. She pulled Zendalia along behind her, dragging her as fast as she could swim. When she reached the coral, she flipped onto her back and pulled Zendalia over her and spun around again.

She shoved Zendalia underneath her, fanning out her fins along her tail to cover Zendalia's orange scales completely. The lights flashed on them but roved away, searching. Kaelin breathed heavily, her chest rising and falling and pushing into Zendalia's. She wasn't going to let up, and Zendalia stayed still, although the hissing from her mask sounded loudly in her ear. If anything was going to give up their position, it was going to be the sound the mask made.

"What's happening?" Zendalia murmured.

"Shush," Kaelin whispered back. "It can hear us."

"My mask!" Zendalia's eyes widened. Within a second, she reached up after sucking in a breath and shoved the mask off her face.

Kaelin looked down on her beautiful face, the thin lines of her deep ruby red lips, a dimple forming in her cheek. Kaelin held herself just above Zendalia's form, her eyes wide as she stared down, not sure what to do or say. It was a stupid decision.

If she had just gone to the upper soundings, then they wouldn't be in this position.

Zendalia's fingers dug into Kaelin's forearms, her eyes widening, and she nodded silently at Kaelin as another loud crash sounded beyond them. Kaelin bent her neck. Her breathing slowed, her entire body heating in a way it hadn't for years. Her tail tingled, the ends of her fluke curling at just the thought of what was going to happen.

When Zendalia's nails dug deeper into her skin, she pressed their mouths together and breathed. She forced the water to leave her lungs and enter Zendalia's. The grasp on Kaelin's arms lightened, but the heat floating through her body didn't let up. She pulled away and looked into those amber eyes. Understanding floated through them.

The noises from the kraken moved farther away, and the lights stopped searching in their direction. Kaelin debated whether or not to grab the mask again, but instead she bent down and once more touched their lips together and breathed life into Zendalia.

10

Their lips met, and Zendalia slipped into Kaelin's softness, into her touch and tenderness. There was no longer the urgent need of the previous kiss. Had it even been a kiss? She knew without questioning that this one, this time, was a kiss. Or if it wasn't, at least it was more than simply giving her breath. It had to be, with that look in Kaelin's guarded gaze.

Something important nudged at the back of her mind, but she was so tired of the tension that had consumed her since her father died. She lifted her hands from where she had dug into Kaelin's arms and ran her nails lightly up, tracing the well-defined muscles. Zendalia had always been considered one of the strongest of her people, but these muscles left her own to shame.

"Shit." The spell broke the instant Kaelin moved back, eyes flicking over Zendalia's head, looking at something Zendalia couldn't see.

Her heart stuttered, preparing Zendalia for another blood pumping flight from the kraken, but there were no tremors along the seabed she lay against. Coldness swept over Zendalia's lips, and she slammed them closed as fast as she could. Whatever sound she made must have caught Kaelin's attention as she looked back down, her beautiful face scrunching up in what might have even been an apology.

The mask was back in Kaelin's hand, and she held it up, trying to place the tech back over Zendalia's face. Zendalia would have laughed if her lungs weren't screaming obscenities at her. As gently as she could, she relieved Kaelin of the mask and slipped it on. The crack had definitely grown larger, the relief only minimal as she sucked in water. The hiss an annoyance to her ears, but she noticed the pain that flitted across Kaelin's face.

Zendalia had paid closer attention to everything about Kaelin in the last few hours since Kaelin had woken her, so afraid that she was dying. She swallowed hard around that, the distaste that she cared to know what Kaelin thought and felt—not what she had wanted at all. She hadn't wanted that, and she shouldn't want that now.

Ignoring the temptation to argue with herself, Zendalia instead focused on following Kaelin's lead as she slid off and put space between them. The lack of warmth and closeness left a Kaelin-sized hole in her heart, and she hadn't noticed when Kaelin had snuck in there. Zendalia pushed aside what they had just done and looked around to figure out what had interrupted their moment.

Dust and debris still floated around them, settling from the churning effects of the kraken. Her exposed skin was covered in a fine layer of silt, and she was sure it was covering her hair and against her scalp. It stung her eyes and made her limited sight worse, but she saw the blue filaments of light in the distance.

"We've got to get somewhere safer than this," Kaelin interrupted Zendalia's scattered thoughts.

"Is there somewhere safer?" Zendalia stayed put, still looking up at Kaelin in all the strength and vitality that she had every time they ran from the kraken.

"Wherever the kraken isn't." Kaelin looked over her shoulder, her lip curled up on one side. Zendalia wished she could read that look, know what it meant. The soft looks Kaelin had given her only moments before were replaced with these, something she didn't fully understand, but there was a deadly touch to them. Kaelin was far more powerful in these depths of soundings than Zendalia, and she could have easily killed her a dozen times over by that point. Yet, she hadn't.

"Fair enough." Zendalia smiled wide, but she wasn't sure it reached her eyes. She also wasn't sure Kaelin could see it but allowed herself this moment not to care. She didn't fear for her life, not like she had anticipated when she'd first come to find her father's killer.

Kaelin took off, slow and careful, toward where Zendalia had seen the blue light. Dust particles floated up in the wake of her tail as she moved. Zendalia was pretty certain she knew who they were following. Finally forcing herself to turn onto her side, she tested the muscles in her arms and tail. Her back ached in a way it hadn't before, but overall, she didn't feel too awful—aside from her breathing. That was a problem she wasn't sure they could solve soon. Without the ability to take deep breaths, she was going to come up short when it came to moving. But she had a new reason for staying in the deep now, and it had nothing to do with avenging her father's death.

Zendalia pushed herself off the ocean floor, so she floated a few lengths of her hand above the sand. Kaelin vanished into the darkness, but the long fibrous legs of the creature Kaelin followed lit up brighter, like the beacon she had needed in order to figure out which direction to head. Flapping her fluke swiftly, Zendalia pushed to catch up.

They swam in silence, the sandy floor giving way to inclines of rock and recently settled debris. The hiss of Zendalia's mask continued to announce her every breath, but as they followed, the sharp pains in her chest decreased slightly. Not enough for her to remove the mask or feel even close to her normal self.

Zendalia stayed so close to Kaelin that every few pushes of Kaelin's fluke brushed her tail fins against Zendalia's arms. Neither spoke or moved away, and the anticipation of the touch sent a thrill through her. For the first time in seasons, she wasn't alone.

The octopus came into focus, the gap closing between them as they rounded a large coral wall. The beautiful intricacies of the coral were stunning, and Zendalia stopped short, mesmerized by it. The colors weren't bright, not like they were closer to the surface, but they held a muted power, a boldness that she envied. Zendalia's heart thudded as she dragged in another breath, her lungs coming up short. She could always blame the mask for her stop instead of being so taken with the beauty she had never imagined would be down here.

None of her people had come down here, no one but her father, in so long. All the lessons taught talked about the beauty that had been devastated by the war, the war her people won but not without destroying the beauty. But her teachers were wrong —it was still here. It looked as gorgeous as the coral in the upper soundings. It just looked different.

"Zendalia?" Kaelin's voice was clear as she spoke her name, no longer struggling to form the sounds as she had in the beginning. When had that happened? When had they gotten so familiar with each other that Kaelin could speak her name properly, although still with her deep sounding accent.

Zendalia ran her fingers over the coral, her eyes glued to one she found. The violet color twisted and reached up toward the upper soundings. It was the same color as Kaelin's eyes, the same flecks that were on the edges of her fins. Kaelin came back around, putting a hand on Zendalia's arm and startling her out of the reverie.

"Zendalia, is everything all right?" Concern etched its way through every word.

When she faced Kaelin full on, her head felt light, the movement so sudden that it seemed as though she was spinning in circles and couldn't stop, but Kaelin's hand was still on her arm, which meant she wasn't moving.

Clearing her throat, Zendalia took in some steadying breaths. "Yeah, I'm fine."

"Is it your mask?"

"I'm fine," Zendalia answered stubbornly. She moved her hand from the coral. "Where are we going?"

Kaelin shrugged her shoulders and pointed at the octopus. "They'll lead us somewhere safe where we can rest."

The octopus swam quickly around Kaelin's hips, a swirl of water following their movements. Zendalia burst with a sharp chuckle and snort, and her chest tightened at the sound, the contradiction of her mood to what her body was doing. How had it all gotten so complicated? She looked at Kaelin, this mer she had hated, the features burned into her memory of the heartless mer who had killed her father and taunted her by placing his dead body in her arms.

This wasn't the same mer. And yet, Kaelin had confessed to killing him.

The way Kaelin had said it, had admitted to being responsible for Zen's death... Zendalia shook her head, that same spinning motion coming back and causing her to lose her equilibrium. She had asked Kaelin directly, and Kaelin had confessed to being the one responsible for the murder. Who would do that? Wouldn't she hide away and push the shame from her?

And now Zendalia had saved her father's murderer from the kraken. The warmth of guilt and shame in her belly turned to roiling unease that barreled through to her chest. She couldn't rectify the complications Kaelin had thrown into her understanding of what had happened. There were moments where she had allowed Kaelin's lips on her own to breathe life into her. She didn't understand why Kaelin would save her but kill her father, but she'd allowed it for her own survival. But that last time. She had tasted Kaelin's lips. She had reacted, not just her body but her mind. She had *wanted* it.

"Tell me what happened." It wasn't a request. Zendalia needed it. She deserved to know the moment her father's body had been placed in her arms with no explanation. She ached at just the thought of hearing about it, but curiosity and desire for understanding outweighed the pain.

"What?" Kaelin's smile slid off her face, her octopus stopped their circling swim and clung to Kaelin's hips, wrapping several tentacles across her stomach in a protective move. Zendalia had seen them do that before, seen them protect Kaelin but also protect her. She narrowed her eyes at the octopus, just as confused as she was before.

Raising her chin up, she met Kaelin's eyes with the same fierce determination she'd had when she'd left the upper soundings. "Tell me what happened to my father."

Kaelin's head shook side to side, her eyes wide with fear. Her lips quivered, and her chest rose sharply. The octopus tightened their grasp on her, a gentle pulsing of electricity lighting in the water around them. Kaelin's purple hair floated around her head, strands breaking up the pain that creased her face.

"Please." Zendalia's voice broke just before the gasp from her mask took over. Her eyes stung with tears she didn't want. She was desperate.

"Don't make me do this," Kaelin whispered, letting go of Zendalia's arm and putting space between them. Kaelin met Zendalia's eyes, and that same pain she saw earlier shone through, bright enough for it to hurt even Zendalia's poor vision.

"Can I tell you about him then?" The words surprised Zendalia as much as they appeared to surprise Kaelin given her expression. "About why he came down here?"

Kaelin nodded and lowered herself to the rocky floor of the coral shelf.

Zendalia took as deep a breath as she dared, the hiss filling the silence. It took her longer than she wanted to admit to settle into the vulnerability she needed for this conversation. She dropped to the coral shelf next to Kaelin, keeping enough distance between them that they weren't touching but staying close enough that if she needed the support she could find it.

"My father, Zen, was an explorer. A scientist." Zendalia's eyes stung from the tears she held at bay. Cursing herself and her emotions, she lowered her chin to hide it and pushed on. "Up there, things aren't going so well."

"What do you mean?" Kaelin asked, head tilting to the side and hair floating away from her shoulders. The current of the water tugged at it, pulling it around Zendalia's body like barely-there touches of comfort, like the embrace she longed for from her dead father. He used to do that, run his finger along her arms and shoulders when she was upset.

"If you ask the royals, nothing is wrong. But they don't admit things until it's too late. But anyone bothering to look can see that the water is disappearing." Zendalia brought her hand up to wipe her face. This was easier than she had anticipated, but then again, she wasn't talking about what it was like to live without him, to swim into her home and have all of his things still there but not him.

"What?" Kaelin's back stiffened, and she sat up straighter. The octopus made their way up Kaelin's chest and wrapped themselves around her shoulders.

"It's too bright up there, even for some of my own people. The light has become too warm during the brightest times of the sun. The environment is changing. Coral and seaweed are dying, and we have to go deeper for fish. My father was the first to notice. He has—*had*—been taking readings since I was a child. For just histories really, but he had always included them as part of his reports."

"Readings of what exactly?" Kaelin reached out and curled

her fingers around Zendalia's, their fingers twining together in an exchange of strength.

"The water level above our homes is—*was*—the one he was most concerned about. He noticed that the measurements were changing exponentially. I mean, they always dropped a little, but then suddenly there were huge leaps in the numbers."

"The water is disappearing." Kaelin spoke the words though Zendalia got the impression they weren't really to her. Behind those violet eyes a whole other universe swirled. What she would kill just to have a small insight to what Kaelin was thinking at that moment. She almost asked, but she stopped herself. They didn't have that kind of friendship yet.

Taking another staggering breath that left her winded, Zendalia carried on with her explanation. "My father thought maybe the lower tribes were involved or had experienced some sort of war or change that we didn't know about."

"We would never take water away from your people. Water is what gives us life. Where would we take it?"

"I know that now." Zendalia smiled behind the mask, wishing she could have this conversation without her tech barrier. But then violet eyes met her own and it didn't matter as much as it might have, as much as it would have only hours earlier.

"Did your father know about the kraken before he came here?"

"How would he know?" Zendalia furrowed her brow, and Kaelin looked down at their joined hands. The silence thickened around them, but Zendalia's body and mind ached in sympathy. What she wouldn't have given to have another rest in Kaelin's moss bed. Images of doing just that with Kaelin wrapped around her flashed in her mind. Heat bloomed in her cheeks, and she hated herself all the more for it. She was supposed to despise Kaelin, and her damn hormones and body were telling her the complete opposite.

"What was your father hoping to find?" Kaelin's voice was soft in the waves of water, barely loud enough for Zendalia to hear her over the noise of the mask.

"An answer or proof he could take back to our people, so that they might finally listen to him."

"They didn't trust his readings?"

"I honestly don't think they ever truly looked at them." Zendalia shrugged. She wanted to defend her people, but she couldn't deny her anger, not down here in the darkness sitting side by side and chatting to her father's murderer. She had never been angry just with Kaelin. Her people were also to blame and maybe even her father.

"I'm sorry."

"For my people?" Zendalia blinked, her mind fritzing on what else Kaelin could possibly be apologizing for.

"For your father," Kaelin spoke so reverently Zendalia believed her words the instant she heard them. "You were close. He told you all of these things. I'm so sorry for your loss."

The breath caught in Zendalia's chest. The absence of the mask's hiss louder than the recent kraken attack. Their eyes met again, and she wondered how she had ever thought those violet eyes were anything other than beautiful.

"Thank you," Zendalia whispered the words. She hadn't been sure Kaelin had heard until she gave the slightest nod of her head. Zendalia frowned, her head spinning again even though this time she hadn't moved. She tightened her grasp on Kaelin's hand, closing her eyes to catch her bearings, but that only made the spinning worse. She gasped in a breath, but her lungs didn't fill. Sputtering, she faced Kaelin with wide eyes. "Kaelin."

"What?" Kaelin's voice was gentle as she faced her again. Shock hit her, eyes widening and lips parting.

Zendalia's vision went in and out, those bright violet eyes blurring and fading before coming back into view. Her heart thudded wildly, uncontrollably. Her hands were clammy and her skin hot. Zendalia swallowed again to try and find words, but it was so damn hard to think. Finally, she locked her gaze on Kaelin.

"Help."

11

Zendalia's lifeless body fell back. Everything happened in slow motion as the muscles in her body went lax. Her chin dipped down, her eyes rolled back into her head, and she slumped, her form crumbling toward the coral shelf. Kaelin grabbed her hard, moving her down gently. She ran her hands over Zendalia's shoulders and shook her, trying to wake her up as panic gripped her heart.

This couldn't be happening again. She had worked so hard to keep it from happening again. Neyon moved away from her, lying heavily against Zendalia's chest for the briefest of moments before their head popped up and turned on Kaelin.

Kaelin stared at them with fear in every inch of her body. She had no idea what to do. She couldn't think. One of Neyon's long tentacles came up and slapped against her face, a jolt of electricity zapping through her. Kaelin shook out the tendrils of pain before doubling down on her focus on Zendalia.

Right. She did know. Zen had told her.

Flashes of his hands to his mouth, his throat, his chest. He'd shook his head at her with those same amber eyes, wide and full of fear—but a calm fear, unlike what Kaelin experienced right now. She bent her head as she ripped the soundless mask from

Zendalia's face. She put her cheek against Zendalia's face, waiting to feel any signs that she was breathing even though Kaelin knew there was nothing.

Neyon slapped her again with another jolt of electricity. Kaelin shook as she reached up and put her hand around Zendalia's throat, her thumb on one side and her webbed fingers on the other. *Nothing.*

"Zendalia," Kaelin murmured before swiftly pressing their mouths together. This time she didn't do it slowly. She forced as much water into Zendalia as she possibly could and then pulled back to wait.

Zendalia didn't move. She did it again, watching out of the corner of her eyes as Zendalia's chest rose up sharply with the water now in her. Neyon crawled up her chest, electrifying the water around them. Kaelin blocked out the pain and breathed again for Zendalia. Ignoring the panic that clawed its way into the forefront of her mind, Kaelin turned her body and put some pressure against Zendalia's stomach.

She did it again and again, Neyon working their electricity into Zendalia's still form. She lost count of how many times she breathed into Zendalia before there was a tender pull of water from her mouth. Kaelin pulled back sharply, staring down at Zendalia's rounded cheeks and fluttering eyelids. This was it. She couldn't breathe down here.

Wrapping her arms around Zendalia's torso, Kaelin pulled her up. Zendalia rested in her lap, struggling to breathe again. Kaelin lifted her chin and pushed more water into her lungs. In a second, she turned Zendalia around as Neyon fell away, and Kaelin launched herself off the reef shelf. Using every ounce of her strength, Kaelin swam straight upward.

She kept her grasp on Zendalia's torso firm, using her arms to strengthen her hold. Kaelin moved swiftly, increasing the rhythm of her tail so they would move faster and faster. The temperature of the water changed around them, warming as it became lighter. Kaelin swam harder. The panic she had avoided earlier bit at her tail again, and she had to race to keep it at bay.

When she finally stopped, they were in the middle of the ocean, the lower soundings of it, but enough light streamed through the waters that she was able to see the beautiful fiery red of Zendalia's short-cropped hair. In the deep soundings, it had looked nearly black against her scalp.

Kaelin spun Zendalia around and pulled her close. Again, she put her hand against Zendalia's throat, feeling for every little change that she could find. The gentle beat of her heart rhythmically pulsed against her thumb. Kaelin breathed a sigh of relief, pressing her forehead to Zendalia's shoulder as she drew in ragged breaths. Emotions washed through her now that she no longer needed to hold them back. Fear. Rage. Understanding. Relief.

Kaelin held back a cry as she tightened her shoulders and lifted her head. When she looked around them, cradling Zendalia in her arms, she finally pinpointed where they were. She had never traveled that far before. They floated aimlessly, as Zendalia's breaths became deeper and with less struggle. They probably weren't far enough up, but Kaelin wasn't sure how she would feel any farther.

They were at a standstill, halfway between two worlds, and Kaelin wasn't going to let go of Zendalia until she knew without a doubt that she was all right, that she could float and swim on her own again. It took more time than she cared for, but small signs of life kept returning. Zendalia's ashen face had more color to it, the muscles in her arms and body tightened so she had more control.

Kaelin ran her fingers up and down Zendalia's arms, trying to use the small sensations to wake her from the state she was in. She kept her tail moving gingerly, taking them higher every once in a while, as she prepared herself for the lighter breaths, for her own head to get dizzy. She stayed in the center of the ocean, the light shining around them, rays of sunlight piercing the water and surrounding them.

There was nothing around them. No coral, no seaweed, no rock shelf, no place for Kaelin to set Zendalia down. Again she slid the tips of her fingers up and down Zendalia's arms, murmuring the prayers the elders had taught her when she was a child. They connected her to her people but also to the water, to the strength of the currents that would help to save them all.

Neyon swam, pushing their way through the water and up toward her. They always found her. No matter where she went, Neyon was never far. She'd watched them so carefully when they had been a small octopus in the fields of babies. They had chosen her, and she hadn't been able to survive without them since.

Their light wasn't as bright up here, but Kaelin could see them coming from quite some distance. She eyed Zendalia again, catching sight of an opaque stone that sat at the hollow of her throat. A weaving of metal wrapped from it all the way around her neck. Curious, Kaelin pressed her fingers to it and was stunned by how warm it was. Neyon flashed through her mind, the full force of their personality hitting her in an instant.

Jerking her hand away, Kaelin shook her hand like she'd been jolted with a strong shock of Neyon's electricity. Neyon, however, was still lengths away from them. Kaelin spotted them far off and held her breath as she waited. She wished she could speak to them, find out exactly what they thought and knew. Her people had been without that essence of communication between their companions for so long, and they had adapted, but it was difficult, and even though she'd never known it personally, she missed it.

Neyon reached her, the mask Kaelin had discarded captured in one of their tentacles. No wonder it had taken them so long to get there. The tentacle with the mask ended up next to Kaelin, and she took it while Neyon wrapped themself around Zendalia's torso. Kaelin shifted her form to cradle her more carefully, so that she could still hold her but also move freely since it seemed as though she was going to take her sweet time waking up.

"What do you think?" Kaelin asked Neyon, hoping they would somehow be able to share a message with her.

They tightened their grasp on Zendalia's chest.

"Yeah, me too." Kaelin sighed and closed her eyes. She focused on the warmth of Zendalia's body, the gentle rise and fall of her chest as she breathed freely, unencumbered by the mask for the first time.

Kaelin couldn't imagine what it would feel like not to be able to breathe. She'd had her breath stolen from her, like when the elders had handed down their sentence. They'd been so harsh and cruel, in ways she hadn't experienced before. Something else had happened between her bringing Zen to them and explaining what had happened and her sentencing. It had been swift, yes, but there had been a rippling tension in them she'd never felt before.

It had been the same when her other mother had died, but to be completely unable to breathe and not because she was overly emotional wasn't something Kaelin had ever experienced before. What would it feel like? She wished she could ask Zendalia, that there would be more signs of life from her, but there was nothing.

The mask hung lifelessly against her side as she continued to cradle Zendalia's weak form, much as she had with Zen, except his body had been lifeless. Zendalia's was anything but. Kaelin reached up and over Neyon, brushing the backs of her fingers against Zendalia's plump cheek.

"When will you wake?" Kaelin whispered.

They were completely exposed where they were, out in the open waters with nowhere to hide, and that set Kaelin's nerves on edge. She needed to be able to protect Zendalia, especially while she was in this weakened state. Pressing her lips together tightly, Kaelin looked around them before glancing down into Zendalia's open eyes.

Her stomach dropped, and she gasped. A smile lit her face, and she brushed her fingers against Zendalia's cheek again. Zendalia blinked, her body tightening as she tried to move.

"Stay calm," Kaelin ordered, hoping that would be enough of a chastisement for Zendalia to still herself.

"Where are we?" She sounded so weak.

"Your mask wasn't working properly. I brought you farther up in the soundings."

Zendalia turned her face away from Kaelin's chest, her gaze narrowing as she blinked slowly. "It's so bright here."

Kaelin chuckled. "This is nothing compared to where you live, I imagine."

"Reine? You're right. This is a nice color." Zendalia moved her hand from her body, swiping her fingers through the water as if she was trying to catch something. If she hadn't identified the name of her people, Kaelin would have worried there had been some damage done. "I must be heavy."

"Hardly." Kaelin's voice broke, and she cleared her throat to get it back, but she wasn't about to repeat herself. "You're light as a pearl."

Zendalia chuckled lightly. "How long has it been? Swimming up here must have taken some time."

"No time at all."

"Quit lying." Zendalia's face hardened.

Kaelin gritted her teeth, trying to figure out why she suddenly wanted to hide the truth. Her stomach twisted tightly, and she amended what she'd said before. "It's been half a day easily."

"Fuck," Zendalia murmured. "I don't remember much of what happened."

"Your mask stopped working properly," Kaelin repeated. "And you stopped breathing. My companion and I had to work together to get breaths into your lungs again."

Zendalia scrunched her nose and glanced down at her chest, as if just noticing for the first time that Neyon was wrapped around her. She lifted her hand and covered their bulbous head, stroking them. "Well, I guess you are good for more than simply leading the way."

"They are good for many things." Kaelin wasn't about to explain the number of ways Neyon had helped her in the past, especially these last few seasons, but they had. They had been her constant companion through all of it. "When you feel ready, you may swim on your own."

"Oh, not so light as a pearl now, am I?"

Heat rushed to Kaelin's cheeks. "Hardly, but I do want to make sure there isn't damage to your body."

"Sure, that's what you're doing." Zendalia shifted and took most of her weight, which was good because she wasn't paying attention to the rush of pink that tinged Kaelin's cheeks and chest. It wouldn't do them well for Zendalia to understand why she was so flustered.

As soon as Zendalia swam comfortably on her own, Kaelin pulled back and removed her hands from her hips. She pressed her palms against her sides to keep from the temptation of touching her again, but after hours of holding her tightly, an emptiness filled her without Zendalia against her.

"I think we need to talk," Kaelin started.

"Agreed." Zendalia looked around them, assessing the lay of the ocean where they were. "But where?"

Kaelin sucked in a breath and handed the mask over, realizing belatedly that it still hung from her shoulder where she'd put it after Neyon had brought it. Neyon detached themself from Zendalia's chest and spread their tentacles out before drawing them together.

Nodding toward her companion, Kaelin looked into Zendalia's eyes. "We'll follow them, and we'll go slowly until you're feeling more yourself."

"You're not struggling to breathe?" Zendalia's eyes widened.

Kaelin shook her head. "Not yet. We're not close enough to the upper soundings for that yet."

"But you can breathe up there without a mask." Zendalia said it so sure of herself.

Kaelin nodded sharply. "I can."

"Then why can't I breathe in the deep soundings?"

Blinking slowly as Neyon swam away from them, Kaelin moved her hand out. "We'll talk when we can find a place to rest."

12

They swam side by side following Neyon's light as it pulsed in the water, tentacles creating a hypnotic flow with every movement. As promised, the octopus set a slow pace, but Zendalia found movement became easier with each flick of her tail, her lungs able to inflate easily without the reliance on tech. Exhaustion washed over her, like the churned-up water of a young pod of pups learning to flip for the first time. While each breath no longer stabbed into her lungs her body struggled along, following the octopus as the pressure of Kaelin's words weighed upon her. And yet, a new relief and appreciation for her existence filled her with each unhindered breath.

The silence might have been a calming influence as signs of color and life came into view in the distance, but she knew when someone said they needed to talk, it was never good news. Her mind ticked over and over, thinking herself into a dark spiral, one she had found herself slipping into far too often since the season of her father's death. *Death, not murder.* She noticed the change in her own thoughts and guilt tightened her stomach.

"You okay?" Kaelin looked over her shoulder, tendrils of hair curling around her sharp features, a bunched vertical line appearing between her eyes.

"I'm okay." Zendalia smiled and nodded, but Kaelin's furrowed brow remained until she turned back and Zendalia no longer had to fake the expression.

She looked beyond Kaelin who swam half a body in front of her. Zendalia definitely didn't notice the powerful muscles as they moved beneath Kaelin's fluke or the delicious width of her hips or the span of her tail fins. Nope, not at all. She looked past Kaelin and focused on their guide.

She had no idea where the octopus was taking them, but Kaelin seemed to trust the creature without doubt or hesitation and so it seemed Zendalia did too. The realization shocked her almost as much as the electric zap they had given her when she had fought with Kaelin. But she couldn't deny her own faith in the creature. When she had brushed her shaking fingers over the octopus' bulbous head a calm familiarity had washed over her. She couldn't identify it, though it lingered in her mind, a mental scratch she couldn't quite reach.

Colors turned into shapes as they drew closer. A gasp from Kaelin made her smile—a real smile this time.

"I take it you haven't seen this place before?" Zendalia asked, pleasure floating through her chest at the mere thought of introducing Kaelin to something new, at seeing that same joy and pleasure run through her gaze.

"No." Kaelin rolled over, a smile beaming from her face as she continued to move, now backward, facing Zendalia, though a little lower in the water than Zendalia herself. "I've never been this far away from home except when..." she trailed off, and Zendalia didn't comment on it. They both knew what she was referring to.

"You mean this far up?" Warmth spread through Zendalia's chest.

"I haven't been anywhere near this far from the ocean floor."

Kaelin twisted back, and the gap between her and Zendalia grew.

Zendalia wanted to speed up, but her body objected before she could even suggest such an outrageous idea. Instead, she watched as Kaelin met her companion at the edge of the island. They danced around each other again, tentacles stroking Kaelin's fluke and fins.

Zendalia slowed, enjoying her buoyancy. Her fingers reached for the gentle weight around her neck, thumb rubbing over the smooth warm stone, and her mind became awash with thoughts of other familiar islands that scattered the ocean. Towers of rocks and coral, filled with hundreds of sea animals.

A flash of Kaelin's smiling face interrupted the vision, and Zendalia pulled her hand from the stone as though it burned her.

"What the fuck?" she muttered as she shook her head and made her way to join Kaelin. She supposed she was far more exhausted than she realized—that had to be what was affecting her mind.

"This is beautiful." Zendalia smiled as she approached, avoiding Kaelin's eyes and focusing on the octopus. She rubbed their head once more and again felt the overwhelming sensation of familiarity and rightness. It confused her, sending a shock through her heart that she didn't expect. She hesitated as she stroked them again, wanting that familiarity to form into some-thing tangible, something she could truly know.

"They're the best companion a mer could ever ask for," Kaelin said, her smile radiating.

Zendalia lifted her eyes, and for a moment she met Kaelin's. Heat swelled in the pit of her stomach and moved downward, right to her clit. Quickly she dropped her gaze once more as she made a noncommittal sound. Embarrassment filled her, and she wished she could make it go away. Instead, she was stuck with her cheeks burning and Kaelin's eyes glued on her.

A beat of silence echoed in her ears as the warmer water moved along Zendalia's skin, dancing with the unseen lives that lived in the ledge or the nearby crags and rocks. Zendalia was about to say something, give some excuse for her reaction, some flimsy explanation of what had just happened, but Kaelin interrupted her.

"I have some food. We can rest and talk." Kaelin's words were soft, a gentle pleading pulling at each word, as if this was going to be the end of whatever friendship they had formed, whatever balance they had found.

A sting of guilt hit Zendalia right in the center of her chest. The more she thought about it, there was something in Kaelin's tone that spoke of hurt. Had Zendalia done that? She frowned before she looked up again to meet Kaelin's gaze, and the embarrassment from before vanished. She needed some rest and some time to process. But what she wanted more than anything was to truly understand what had happened to her father.

Silently, Kaelin set out some food, taking her time and avoiding looking at Zendalia, at least from what Zendalia could see from the corner of her eye. She wanted to look around her, soak up the colors that danced in front of her, the waving beauty of life that housed creatures of all kinds. Simply being able to see so clearly was lightening her mood, and with that came the guilt.

"So you want to know why I can breathe up here and you can't breathe down in the deeper soundings?" Kaelin asked as she handed Zendalia a parcel of wrapped up seaweed and mussels. It looked intriguing, and even though Zendalia's stomach growled, she wasn't convinced her stomach could handle food right then.

"No." She took the parcel anyway. "Not really."

"Oh," Kaelin replied, and the tension in the silence returned.

The words sat heavily on Zendalia's tongue. She wanted to know, more than anything else, and yet she struggled to force the words out. She opened her mouth, and then closed it again. She opened it once more, but before she could force them out or at least attempt to, Kaelin spoke.

"I suppose you don't exactly need me here anymore." Kaelin's own parcel had only a small nibble out of the corner. "I'll leave you some supplies and head back soon."

"What? No!" Panic hit her first. Zendalia shook her head, every muscle in her body tensing. She sat up straight and stared at Kaelin's downturned face, her hands folded together in front of her, the way she looked so closed in on herself.

Kaelin raised her chin and looked up, meeting her eyes. Those violet eyes held so much, and Zendalia wished for one brief window inside, to know what Kaelin was thinking and feeling, to understand what was happening. That fear didn't go away. In all the seasons since her father died, she hadn't found anyone who looked at her like that, as if she wasn't an orphan but a mer, someone who could hold her own.

The heartbeat that lasted a million tail flips passed.

Again, Zendalia was about to speak, ask something, try to explain what was going through her mind after her outburst, but Kaelin interrupted her. Kaelin's firm and confident voice belied everything in the way she floated there, as though Zendalia had sucked the water away from her.

"Are you worried about not making it back home safely?" Kaelin asked, her words clear in her rounded way of speaking.

"No." Zendalia shook her head, her voice so gentle now compared to before. Frustration wrapped around her. She couldn't do this. Soulara had told her time and again that this wasn't her strength. She was awful at sharing what she was feeling and thinking and too often flew off the handle. "Please, please don't go."

"You want me to stay?" Kaelin's voice filled with hope, her eyes widening as if there was something else between them. Zendalia supposed there was—something had happened in the deep soundings that she couldn't explain, something that turned this murderer into someone she could trust.

"I want to know what happened…with my father." Zendalia swallowed, a lump forming in her throat as the words left her.

She tried to hold back all the raging emotion before it exploded out of her in a way she couldn't control.

"Oh, of course." All hope drained from Kaelin's voice, and she closed off again. She became so small.

Zendalia wanted to stop the defeat that overtook Kaelin's words and made her shoulders slump forward. She wanted to, but she couldn't. She couldn't be thinking any of the thoughts she'd been having about Kaelin. She couldn't let her own fear and run-ins with the kraken overshadow why she had risked her life and punishment from her people by stealing the equipment for the deep soundings.

"Your father told me about the kraken." Kaelin wouldn't look at her, and Zendalia longed to see those violet eyes locked on her again.

"Why?"

"I don't know. It was attacking, and I was hurt from it."

Zendalia's stomach dropped. She couldn't imagine Kaelin hurt, bleeding, the fact that she wasn't strong enough to swim away from it, hide from it, fight it was impossible.

"I didn't know what was happening." Kaelin's words washed away on the current.

"And you killed him for it?" The words fell from Zendalia's mouth before she could stop them. She bit her lip to keep herself from saying anything else as flippant as that. She wouldn't get any answers if she forced Kaelin to completely shut down.

"I suppose so," Kaelin murmured, staring out into the vast ocean in front of them. The food was completely forgotten, settled on the sand next to them.

Zendalia resisted the urge to pick it up and fling it out to where she couldn't see it. She shuddered and clenched her eyes against the onslaught of turmoil that wrapped its way around her heart. She had to stay in the moment to get the answers she wanted. She'd gone down there for revenge, but if she could have that and answers, she would take it.

"Why?" Zendalia's voice cracked, and she met Kaelin's eyes.

Kaelin's eyes glistened with pain and unshed emotion.

"Please," Zendalia begged again. Not entirely sure exactly what to ask and positive she would be unable to say anything else as a lump filled her throat entirely.

"During the kraken attack…" Kaelin folded herself up and lay on her side, discarding the barely touched parcel onto the floor of rock beside her and wrapping her arms around her bent tail, pulling it to her chest. "…his—his mask was broken. I didn't know what the sound was, I didn't know what it meant. I'd never seen a mask like that before."

Zendalia slid to the floor across from Kaelin, so they faced each other. Zendalia's tail stretched out, the back of her hands turning a paler shade of orange as she pressed her palms down on the floor as though needing the contact to stop herself from doing something. From what exactly she had no idea, but the feel of rock beneath her fingers remained a necessity.

"What happened?" Zendalia pressed, needing to know everything in those last minutes her father had.

"He tried to tell me. He tried to explain what the mask did, that he needed more oxygen than the water in the deep soundings gave. But I didn't understand. I didn't realize what he was trying to explain. He couldn't talk." The words were coming out faster and faster, Kaelin's voice deeper and huskier as the emotions consumed her. "But he used his hands, he was talking to me, and I didn't listen. I thought he just needed a rest. A healer from my tribe could fix any issues from the attack."

"What did you do?" Zendalia's voice filled with a roughness reminiscent of the jagged rocks that surrounded them. What could Kaelin have done to kill a mer who was already dying? What would possess her to do that?

"I took him to the tribe. I carried him the last league." A muffled sob escaped Kaelin's mouth, and she gulped several mouthfuls of water before she continued. "By the time I arrived, he was gone."

Zendalia's heart hammered. She clenched her fingers against

the rock, the hard surface scraping against her skin a sharp reminder that the truth wasn't always what it seemed. Kaelin hadn't described a murder but an unfortunate and untimely death. In fact, it seemed as though she had tried to save him— much like she had saved Zendalia so many times since they'd met.

Raising her gaze to meet Kaelin's sorrowful eyes, she asked the only question she could think of. "How did you find out how the mask worked?"

"Um," Kaelin blinked. "A member of the tribe studied it, and your father, and learned how different our bodies are from those living near the surface."

Silence settled over them, though Zendalia kept her hands pressed down, unwilling to raise them. She feared what she might do as the emotions swam around inside of her, threatening to crash into each other. She held the silence, waiting for Kaelin to say something else, to explain how this could possibly be a murder, but Kaelin remained stoically silent, curled up on the rock.

Zendalia flipped onto her back and clenched her eyes against the tears that slipped away from her. She had done far too much of that since she'd left Reine. She was tired of it. She needed to get a damn hold of herself and fight for something that was truly worthy of her anger.

"You didn't kill him." A cold relief washed over her as she uttered the words. It was the only truth that she needed, the only way this story could play out. Not once had Kaelin lied to her since they had met or tried to prevent her from doing anything other than hurting herself.

"I did, Zendalia. I didn't listen to what he tried to tell me. I could have helped him, but I didn't take the time to stop and work out what he meant. His life was given to me to save, and I owed him the debt of my own life on top of that. I did kill your father."

Zendalia opened her mouth to argue, but Kaelin's companion

swam up in front of her, blocking her view as their sudden presence shocked Zendalia. She reached up to the stone against her neck out of habit and ran her thumb across it. Flashes of her father's face, bruised and bleeding, of Kaelin's fear, her own blood floating around her head as she stared wide-eyed at Zen.

The sob tore through her hard. She clenched her jaw and held tight to the necklace, using it to center herself as she watched Kaelin grab Zen's hand and drag him, her words as she told him she was going to get help, a healer, the panic in her voice that hadn't been present one time since they'd been together.

Releasing her grasp on the stone, Zendalia stared at the blue octopus in front of her. She held her hand out to them, and they wrapped around her forearm. She had no idea what to say with everything blowing through her in such a sharp, painful way. She glanced at Kaelin, those eyes locked on her as if waiting for a response.

"I need to rest," Zendalia whispered, her voice cracking from the depth of emotion she'd been tossed into. "I'm not fully recovered yet."

"I understand," Kaelin said, eyes still glued in her direction.

Zendalia knew she wasn't giving her any kind of resolution to the turmoil Kaelin was going through. But it hurt so damn much, and it was next to impossible to say the words. Taking her hand off the stone, she reached over and put her hand on Kaelin's shoulder. "You didn't murder my father, Kaelin. I don't believe that."

Kaelin didn't nod. She barely shifted the features in her face, staying completely unreadable. Zendalia suspected they were both still tossed in the uncertainty and pain of memories revisited. Time passed between them, neither moving, the tension slowly ebbing away like the water on the beach. Zendalia frowned when Kaelin shifted, straightening out and swimming slowly away.

Zendalia's insides twisted, unsure if she would ever see Kaelin again or if she really had just gone somewhere to rest.

This entire time Zendalia had hated the one who had tried to help her father, who had not been able to because of tech she had no way of knowing about. And for that, her people had punished her beyond any reasonable measure.

Zendalia's heart broke as she thought of everything Kaelin had been through, how much she had suffered for nothing. She piled the pain on top of her own, and the water warmed in front of her cheeks as she cried.

No wonder Kaelin didn't want to be around her.

Anger bubbled up inside of Zendalia. But for the first time she felt as though the anger was finally being directed to the right place—the kraken.

13

R*ejected.*

Kaelin swam away from Zendalia, the isolation that she had lived with for the last few seasons overtaking her. She could barely hold back the tears. She'd told Zendalia just about everything, but not how the elders had decided she truly had killed Zen, which she agreed with, or how her punishment had been doled out, or how they'd even found Zendalia so she could return Zen to his people, but she'd shed enough hurt for one day.

Kaelin took a shuddering breath, swimming far enough away from Zendalia that they couldn't see each other. For the first time since Zendalia had tried to kill her, Kaelin wanted to be hidden away from all mermaids, and even Neyon. She wanted nothing to do with anyone. Her chest ached, as if someone had slammed their fist hard into her and expected her just to go on normally.

That had taken every ounce of effort she had. Zendalia had her answers. What she did with it was her choice, but it wasn't like she was going back down into the deep soundings. At least that was a comfort for Kaelin. She wouldn't have to worry about the kraken killing her too. That blood wouldn't be on her hands.

When Kaelin finally looked up, she was surprised to see how

far she had gone. She glanced over her shoulder, unable to find Zendalia in the craggy rocks of the island. It was exactly what she wanted. She swam even farther, ignoring the pain that forced her to look over her shoulder again.

Zendalia wasn't ready for what the rest of the ocean had to offer. Her father hadn't been either. It had been what killed him, but then again, without him being there, Kaelin never would have found the kraken or watched it over the last few seasons, trying to protect other mer from falling into its trap.

Her heart wrenched. She slid toward a sandy spot and collapsed against it. The small granules scratched at the skin on her arms and side, but she didn't know what else to do. Curling into a ball again, she held her tail tightly and clenched her eyes shut. Every emotion she had held back while retelling the story of murdering Zen washed through her.

Shame. Guilt. Devastation.

It hurt so much. She would never recover from that. The elders had been right to send her away because she wasn't worthy of staying with the rest of the tribe. She had nothing to offer them except for someone to ridicule. And they had done it. They had watched her leave their home with nothing on her back, and they had thrown her things onto the ocean floor as she passed through the path of mer.

Even Neyon seemed to like Zendalia better than her. They were always curled up around her, comforting her. Kaelin drew in a shuddering breath and ground her molars together. She was pathetic and weak. Nothing was going to change that, and nothing was going to shift the fact that she had murdered Zen. That would be a burden she would have to carry with her through the rest of her life, a mark against her. She would never be fully accepted back into her tribe and would forever remain on the edge of it—not that she hadn't been there before, but now there was a reason they could all point to.

Kaelin wrapped her arms tighter. She wished she could just die most days, but she'd never managed to follow through with anything like that. She would be banished from the afterlife if she took her own life, no hope of redemption then. She would never see her mother's again, and she would never find the peace that was promised to her. Though she doubted it existed.

She rolled onto her back and stared up at the ocean above her. She'd never been to the surface of the water before, perhaps she should try that someday soon. She wasn't locked into staying near her tribe like she had chosen to do, but now that she was halfway there, what difference would it make? What would the sun feel like on her face?

The jolt of electricity startled her. Turning her cheek to the side, she was greeted by Neyon, their tentacles sliding to wrap around her, electricity humming. They were agitated. Kaelin could tell even without being able to speak directly to them. She raised her hand up, cradling their head against her palm and sliding her thumb back and forth in an attempt to calm them.

"What is it, friend?" Kaelin murmured, hating herself for giving in so quickly to anyone's need for affection.

An image of Zendalia flashed through her mind, those orange colors so vibrant now that they were out of the dark water and into a place where the sun managed to break through a bit. Her eyes were such a beautiful amber, dark sparks throughout, and they were so damn expressive. Zendalia didn't hold back from her emotions, not like Kaelin did.

One of Neyon's long tentacles reached up and slapped her cheek. Kaelin scrunched her nose and covered the side of her face with her palm. "Ouch!"

Their head moved side to side, as if she should have expected the wake-up call. Kaelin frowned and rubbed her cheek to try and get the sting out of it.

"What was that for?" Kaelin turned on Neyon, anger lashing through her voice. She was tired of being someone that everyone just walked over, someone they abused.

Neyon straightened up, their tentacles firm against her now. Kaelin growled out a sigh before settling back into the sand.

"Fine, I get it," she muttered. "Don't be so hard on myself and stand up for myself. Blah blah blah."

Another tentacle came out and slapped her this time. Kaelin jerked up, moving swiftly enough to dislodge Neyon from her chest. "Enough of that!"

Neyon put up one tentacle in front of her, as if to tell her to shut her mouth. Kaelin was about to yell at them when she saw a sudden flash of Zendalia diving deep into the waters, her chest heaving, her breaths short, the damnable broken mask on her head.

"What the hell is she doing?"

Kaelin jerked with a start, pushing off the island shelf and shoving her body back the way they had come. She didn't even wait for Neyon, knowing they would catch up or find her soon enough. Zendalia's mask was done for, and there was no way she would survive in the deep soundings without it.

Moving as swiftly as she could through the water, Kaelin speared her way through the waves, needing to reach Zendalia before she tried to kill herself again. *What happened to resting?* Didn't the mer need some kind of rest after the drama they'd had earlier that day? And what was Kaelin's obsession with saving her? At this point, if Zendalia was so set on meeting her father in the afterlife, should Kaelin just let her do that? At what point did saving her life become a hindrance to her desires?

Putting her hands against her sides and using only her tail, Kaelin swam as fast as she could. The temperature changed as soon as the shadows reached her. The sun struggled to reach this far into the depths. Kaelin was short on time to try to find Zendalia, though she had a really good feeling she knew where she was going. She'd been so dead set on avenging her father when she thought Kaelin had murdered her, so now with the blame shifted to the kraken, it would make perfect sense that she would go after it.

Kaelin should have realized that sooner. She should have seen the tactic to separate them, to go out on her own without

Kaelin to fight with or drag her back up toward the surface. Kaelin flapped her tail harder in anger. She had been blind to Zendalia's motivations, just as she had been blind to Zen's attempt to explain how to help him.

As soon as she reached the mid-level depths, Kaelin stopped. She had no idea where to go, and her companion had been left in the dust. Her chest rose and fell heavily as she tried to narrow her eyes to see through the waters to where Zendalia may have gone. She panicked. If she lost another soul, she would be exiled forever, never allowed back into her tribe. As much as they pained her, they were the only family and home she had ever known.

Taking deep calming breaths, Kaelin closed her eyes and used her ears and other senses. She knew Zendalia would be heading to where they had last seen the kraken, assuming she could even find it since she'd been unconscious when they had left it last. Kaelin was just about to dive again when that familiar hum of electricity reached her.

Zendalia, swimming, the mask on her face but certainly not working. A sharp edge of a rock dug into her shoulder as she shimmied her way farther down into the rocks below. In an instant, Kaelin knew exactly where she was. She had cut her own shoulder on that rock more times than she cared to admit. With Neyon wrapped around her torso and climbing toward the back of her head where they loved to sit on long swims, Kaelin dove straight down.

She didn't have long if the image was anything to go by. Zendalia was ridiculous for even thinking she could manage this, and it was obnoxious that Kaelin once again had to rescue her from herself. She really did have a death wish, didn't she? Kaelin moved as swiftly as she could manage, her tail fins already protesting the ache from all the exertion that day. They really would need a long rest before anything else could happen.

Kaelin swallowed hard, pistoning herself through the water. She finally caught sight of that orange tail, a beacon in the dark.

She shook her head and twisted hard to follow Zendalia's path. She was still too far off to do anything useful at the moment, but it wouldn't take her long to catch up. Kaelin put her hands out to the sides, using her webbed fingers to help her maneuver through the rocks that jutted out. They were decently close to where the kraken had been last, but still quite a few soundings up from where it had burrowed down to do whatever it was that it did.

Twisting sharply around the rock that Zendalia had hurt herself on, Kaelin managed to squeeze through without a problem. She finally caught sight of Zendalia's full tail. Shooting toward her, she wrapped her arms around Zendalia's torso and held on tightly as Zendalia fought against her. The screech of the mask as she drew in each wild breath hurt Kaelin's ears. She resisted the urge to cover them and pulled Zendalia to her chest, holding on tight as she fought against it.

"You're an idiot!" Kaelin shouted. "Why would you come down here again?"

Zendalia stilled, as if realizing who exactly had captured her. Her chest heaved, the whistling noise and bubbles around her face obscuring Kaelin's view of her perfect lips and little dimple. She hated it.

"I needed to find it."

"The kraken? It'll kill you. It'll kill all of us."

"Probably more than you know." Zendalia relaxed, her breathing still ragged. "How did you...how did you find me so quickly?"

"Doesn't matter. Here." Kaelin ripped the mask off Zendalia's face and pressed their lips together, pushing water into her lungs. Anger filled her chest, swirling in a vortex of contempt. She shouldn't be the one doing this, yet again. Zendalia should just go back to her people and leave Kaelin alone to deal with her banishment.

She shoved the mask back on Zendalia's face, her breathing much more even and regular now. Kaelin raised an eyebrow at her as if to prove her point that Zendalia couldn't survive down here without her. Zendalia touched Kaelin's arm gently, holding still right against Kaelin's body.

Kaelin shivered as they held the moment of tension between them. She didn't know what to say because all she wanted to do was yell and scream and chastise her again. But those wide amber eyes, they said something Kaelin wasn't sure she wanted to read, something that couldn't happen. She wasn't worthy of it.

Zendalia opened her mouth and then shut it again sharply. She held up her hand. In it was a small black box. Kaelin reached for it, the metal cold against her fingertips. There was a silty layer of dust against it. She wiped it off, brushing her hand against her hip as she studied it. She had no idea what it was. Shaking her head, she handed it back to Zendalia.

"What's that?"

"It can tell us what they're here for."

Kaelin scrunched her nose and rolled her eyes. "I know what they're here for."

Zendalia's lips parted, but instead of words, a choking gasp resounded between them. Kaelin's heart thudded hard, an echo of the fear she had felt when Zen couldn't breathe, when Zendalia hadn't been able to before. Kaelin gripped Zendalia's wrist hard, making sure that she wasn't going to lose contact.

"We have to rise."

Zendalia nodded sharply as if understanding. This time, Kaelin ripped the mask from Zendalia's face and breathed water into her with confidence. She dropped the mask below them, letting it sink to the ocean floor while she pulled Zendalia higher into the soundings. She would breathe for her as long as she could.

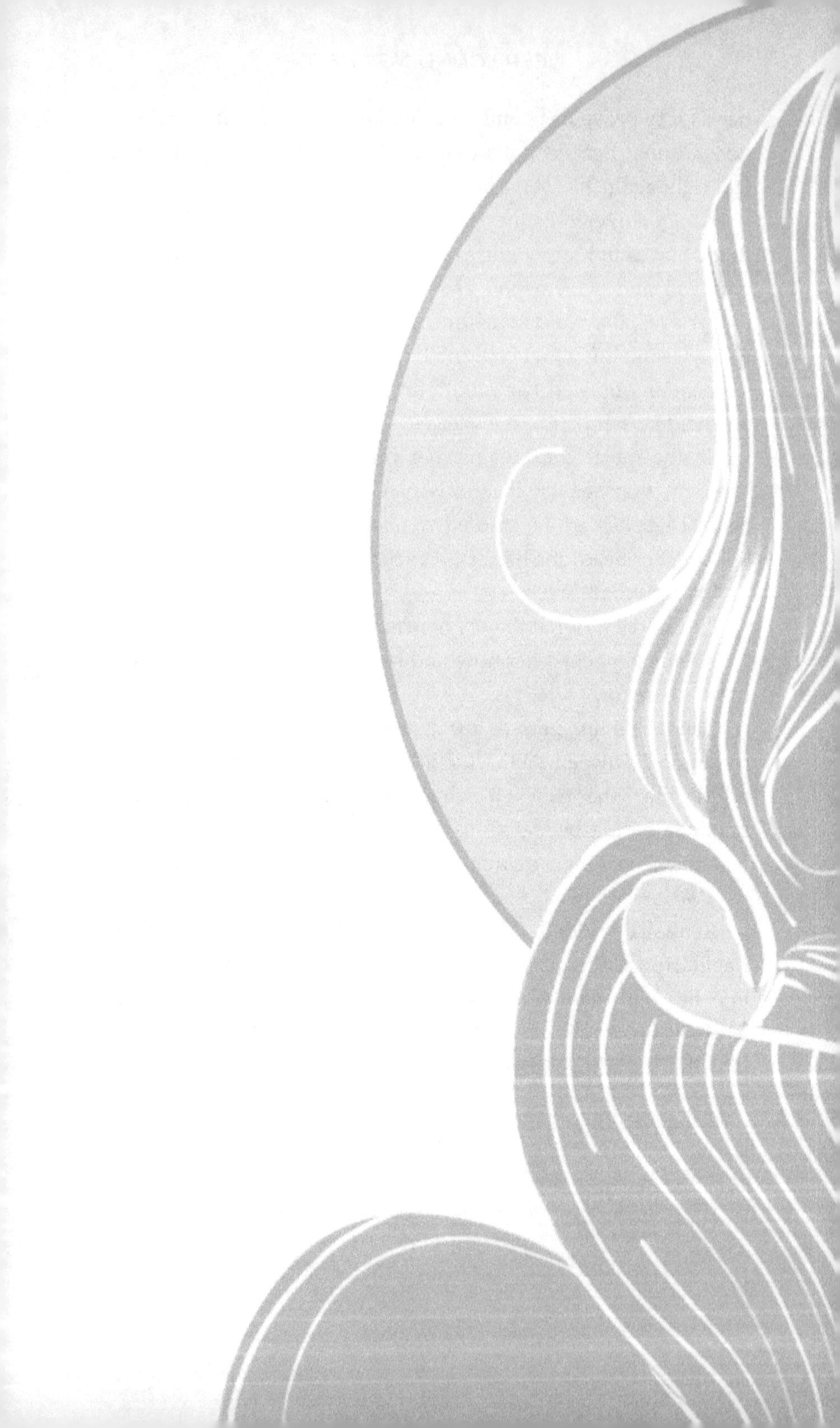

14

Three more—that's how many times Kaelin's lips pressed against Zendalia's before they reached the rocky outcrop where they had last spoken. Where Zendalia had learned the truth of her father's death. If it were to be classified a murder, the culprit was the kraken. And that fact had been enough to send Zendalia off in search of the beast. Anger had tinged her vision a red that saw nothing but the need for revenge. She hadn't thought much about her own life, or what she would do when she found it. But then the small box had shimmered at her, half-buried beneath disrupted coral. The plan had formed as the mask finally failed completely. She could use the box to find the kraken. The kraken and whoever programmed the tech had killed her father, not Kaelin.

Relief washed over her at the thought. And each time Kaelin's lips pressed against Zendalia's mouth pushing life-giving water into her lungs, that small spark that had twisted her up inside ignited and caught alight. But could she really admit to liking Kaelin?

No, she shook her head and floated down to the rocky outcrop, eyes following Kaelin as she joined her, two flukes' distance away. Kaelin looked tired, so very tired. Guilt knotted in

Zendalia's chest once more, as though it was so familiar with the sensation now that it missed the pain. So much for feeling better. But this time, the guilt was of her own making, and she had every right to feel it.

Kaelin had believed herself obligated to come and rescue her. And Zendalia couldn't blame her. Her tribe had punished Kaelin for trying to help a dying man. What would they do if she hadn't followed Zendalia's half-cocked plan?

Kaelin's eyes fluttered open, and Zendalia smiled, her fingers aching to reach out and brush away the white strand amidst the deep velvety purple of Kaelin's hair. She hadn't noticed it before, but it suited her, a light streak in the darkness.

"I'm sorry," Zendalia coughed out.

"I'm tired." Kaelin smiled, a small chuckle escaping her lips before she closed her eyes once more.

Zendalia shuffled forward, closing the gap between them, ignoring the scratch of rock and pebble against her arm, until she could finally reach Kaelin's hair. She tucked the white strands behind Kaelin's ear as they faced each other, lying on the cold ground.

Kaelin was beautiful. Zendalia had always known that, but now there was a freedom to allow herself to admit it and admire Kaelin's strength. Zendalia ran her gaze over the broad shoulders and voluptuous curve of Kaelin's hip. She had never seen such a broad fluke on any mer, and the width of her tail fins was beyond impressive. The warrior in Zendalia admired not just the size and shape of Kaelin, but the way she had been able to move in the water, even up here, with such ease, speed, and grace.

Heaviness pressed down on Zendalia's eyelids and though she fought it, being so close to Kaelin made her feel safe and warm. The blackness of exhaustion stole over her, and she welcomed it.

Zendalia woke with her heart pounding and warmth in the water in front of her cheeks. She gasped for breath as her eyes forced themselves open against her body's desire to sleep longer. But images, horrible and painful, danced in the darkness on the back of her eyelids.

Purple and white came into view and then Kaelin's face.

Zendalia took another deep breath, not as wonderful or as helpful as the kisses she had shared with Kaelin. *No, not kisses.*

The corner of her lips tugged upward.

Who was she kidding?

The pounding boom of her racing heart dulled in her ears, and she smiled as Kaelin continued to sleep. She had shifted a little from her side, rolling almost entirely onto her back now. Her hand lay open on the ground between the two of them. Zendalia held up her own hand and examined the differences between the two of them. While her own fingers were long and tapered, separate from each other, Kaelin's were joined by a thin webbing. She had vaguely noted the difference earlier, but now she stared at them, wondering at such a change between the two tribes. Or perhaps Kaelin's webbing was unique as well? Zendalia suddenly decided the history of their two people was incredibly interesting, and she couldn't wait to find out more about them, about one specific member to be exact.

Kaelin's hand twitched, and the small metal box tumbled out of her palm and turned twice in the water before landing on the ground.

Zendalia pushed all thoughts of sleeping beside her away and scooped up the black box. It had been a miracle that she had seen it in the debris and for the kraken to have ever lost it in the first place. But Zendalia could thank the waters another time. She wasn't yet ready to forgive them for making her an orphan.

Manipulating the small box in her hand, Zendalia focused on the small bumps that rose on two sides, opposite each other. After several frustrating minutes of manipulation, a satisfying click resounded. In the near silence around her, she shushed the inanimate object, hoping the noise and her own grumbling didn't wake Kaelin. She needed all the sleep she could get. Despite the minimal rest Zendalia herself had had, she felt alive with the thrill of discovery.

One more click, and the box opened, revealing the hinge on one edge opposite the now open side. An image, faint and wavering in the light and movement of the water, floated up, mostly blocking Kaelin's sleeping form.

Zendalia narrowed her eyes to clear her still sleep-blurry vision. A small red dot pulled her gaze as it shifted over lines and shapes. She stared so hard at the image that her eyes burned, and she had to remind herself to blink and refocus. The red dot moved, slowly but steadily. After three blinks, it stopped and disappeared.

Zendalia sat back, unaware until then that she had been hunching herself forward. Aches pulled at her shoulders and up both sides of her neck. She rolled her head one way and then the other.

"Ouch," she said automatically as a crack echoed through her skull, one knot released.

"That's what you get for having such terrible posture." Kaelin's voice sailed through the projected image, and Zendalia snapped the box shut again, certain she would be able to open it faster and easier now she knew the trick of the tech.

"Sorry if I woke you."

"I don't think you did." Kaelin shuffled up until her arms no longer needed to hold up her head, her stomach growling as if on cue. "I'm pretty sure that's what woke me."

"Oh." Zendalia didn't know what to say. This mer whom she had been determined to hate now looked at her with eyes that made her want to find every violet-colored coral and grass in the water just to have reminders of them.

"Are you hungry?" Kaelin asked, pushing herself up to full height with her tail. Her buoyancy had definitely returned, while Zendalia wondered if she would ever have the strength to even be a warrior when she returned home.

"Zendalia?" Kaelin asked, head leaning forward and eyebrows raising. Not to mention the creases around her almost-smiling lips. Nope, Zendalia was definitely not mentioning or staring at them.

"Yeah?"

"Are you hungry?" Kaelin asked again with a laugh in her words.

"Oh famished, but I really—"

"Nope." Kaelin cut Zendalia off and an enjoyable warmth spread through Zendalia's chest. She really did have a thing for the bossy ones. "Food first, and then you can tell me what that thing is."

"Okay." Really, what else could Zendalia do? Kaelin had saved her life, yet again. The least she could let her do was feed her.

"Good, now I need you to search over there and see if you can find any grub or mussel. I'll start collecting some grasses and things over here."

Zendalia looked at Kaelin, her own forehead creasing as she raised her eyebrows.

"Go on, off you go. And then you can show me what you risked our lives for."

Ouch. The words, though spoken with a playful lilt, hit Zendalia right in the chest. She really had risked both of their lives. She had never truly believed Soulara when they had fought about Zendalia's tendency to hyper-focus and not think about the consequences to herself and those around her.

With a nod, she wandered over to where Kaelin pointed and was happily impressed at the plethora of sea grubs she found.

She doubted Kaelin had simply lucked onto the exact place Zendalia needed to find food, and her appraisal of Kaelin gained another tick in the amazing column.

It was a simple platter, but there was plenty still there after both leaned back, satiated and happy.

"So, what's the black box, and what were the weird floating lights?"

"Okay." Zendalia's pulse raced beneath her wrists. The excitement helped her remain buoyant without much effort on her behalf. "It's a projection using tech. That much I know, but I actually have no idea what it's for."

"How do you know anything about it?" Kaelin's brow furrowed as she reached forward to touch the box.

"There are buttons on the side. I had already seen them when I first collected it. It's inscribed with a symbol that my people have come to know as meaning information." Zendalia pointed to the symbol.

"Come to know how?"

"I honestly don't know." Zendalia shrugged.

"May I?" Kaelin reached out her open hand, and again Zendalia was caught by the magnificence of the webbing.

"Sure. Want me to open it?"

"Yes, please."

Zendalia placed the metal box into Kaelin's open hand, the tips of their fingers brushing as she found the right position on the box once more and the hinge opened, the projection appearing just as faint and wavering as earlier.

"Wow. I never would have been able to do that," Kaelin said in awe.

Zendalia had thought Kaelin would have been looking at the image, just as she had been, but when she flicked her eyes to Kaelin's face her gaze was stuck on Zendalia's hands.

A heat washed up the sides of Zendalia's neck and burned in her cheeks.

"I guess that's why we don't have the webbing. We've

learned to manipulate the tech for so long because we need to get to places that we wouldn't be able to otherwise." Zendalia's throat felt dry as she forced down some more water. It didn't seem to have as good an effect as before.

"That makes sense."

Their eyes met, and they smiled at each other. After everything they had been through the last few days, Zendalia felt ridiculous for the nervous uncertainty she had now while looking at Kaelin.

Kaelin blinked, smiled, and then turned her face to the projection.

"I'm not sure what all the symbols mean, but there was a red moving light earlier." Zendalia didn't want to hold back any information. If Kaelin knew something that could be helpful, then she would need it, and she had no doubt that Kaelin knew more about the kraken than any other mer in the ocean.

"I know what this is." Kaelin smiled, pride beaming from her face as she met Zendalia's eyes again. "It's a map of the floor of the ocean."

"What? Are you sure?" Zendalia stared at the lines and shapes that remained meaningless to her.

"I'm positive. See here." Kaelin moved in closer, and oh dear water gods, her skin brushed Zendalia's and sent her pulse beating a quick tempo once again.

"Mm-hmm." It was all she could manage at that moment.

"That's the ravine where my home used to be." Kaelin forced the words out.

"Oh." All thoughts of Kaelin's incredible qualities slipped away—all right, most of the thoughts—and were overtaken by the empathy and anger for all Kaelin had been through.

"And that's where you found the box." Kaelin's voice was stronger now as she danced the tips of her fingers over to a swirled shape.

"The red dot?"

"I have no idea." Kaelin shrugged. "You?"

"Yeah." Zendalia the warrior would never have admitted suspecting something without having found proof and confirmation first. But she wanted to discuss it with Kaelin. "I think it's the kraken."

"So why isn't it here now?"

"I suspect the kraken has shut down to recharge, or it had to go someplace to do that."

"Huh?" Kaelin even looked adorable when she was confused —the furrowed brow, wide eyes, and slightly parted lips.

"Tech sends out a beacon when it's on. But when it's not on, it goes to sleep, and the beacon shuts off. But we can track it with this, we can find it and figure out exactly what's going on."

"No, we can't." Kaelin placed a hand gently on Zendalia's forearm. "You're already starting to struggle to breathe here. Don't think I haven't noticed."

Zendalia had no words. How had Kaelin even realized she had begun to struggle with the water? Though it wasn't entirely because of how far down they were and had more to do with the fact that Kaelin was still pressed very close to her side.

Zendalia swallowed hard, trying to refocus on what needed to happen next. "We need to take this to my people."

"What?"

"They will have to believe me about the kraken being real if I show them this, and…" Zendalia pushed down any idea of ulterior motives and made herself finish her thought aloud. "…if you're there to back me up and tell them the truth of what happened down there."

"Me?" Kaelin squeaked.

"Yes."

A sharp shock of electricity jolted them both. The box closed back together in Kaelin's hands, and Zendalia followed Kaelin's eyes, both looking down to see Kaelin's companion making their way up Kaelin's fluke.

"I guess they're coming, too?" Zendalia asked with a laugh, a real laugh. She hadn't thought she'd ever hear that sound from her own mouth again.

"They go where I go." Kaelin smiled and rubbed her cheek against the octopus as they made their way up to Kaelin's shoulder, seeming to shrink as they settled in for the ride, hiding behind Kaelin's hair.

15

"I'm not so sure about this," Kaelin mumbled as they swam away from the oasis they had found. Her stomach had been twisted in knots since she'd agreed to travel back to Reine. It wasn't technically against her banishment. She remembered those words every moment of the day, as though they had just doled out her punishment for murdering Zen.

Now she had his name, and his daughter was someone she may even stretch to call a friend. Kaelin shuddered as the warmer waters brushed across her scales. She'd only been this close to the surface once, and never with any intention of staying longer than a few moments. Everyone in Reine would feel the same way about her as Zendalia. She had killed Zen, and as much as Zendalia didn't believe that anymore, Kaelin did.

"Sure about what?" Zendalia swam beneath her, flipping up to stare at Kaelin, those wide amber eyes curious and beautiful.

Kaelin could fall into them in an instant if she allowed herself to, but she couldn't. "Going with you."

Zendalia stopped swimming. Kaelin had to bend down and double back, this time ending up below Zendalia. From this angle, she was given a full view of her, the light at her back giving her a glow that she hadn't had before when she was in Kaelin's shadow. Her skin looked like it glowed a fiery red-orange in this light. It was stunning. Kaelin's stomach flipped, and she swallowed down the attraction.

"Why wouldn't you want to? You can't go home. This is better than being out on your own, isn't it?"

The stark reminder that she couldn't return to her people was more than Kaelin had expected. It was true, she couldn't go back to her tribe—not yet—but at least she had been able to stay close to them. She must have frowned or shown her disappointment because Zendalia swam closer, touching her arm lightly.

"That was insensitive. I'm sorry. I'm really struggling with the idea that you were banished for something you didn't do and couldn't prevent. On top of that, the punishment seems extraordinary."

Kaelin swallowed hard, raising her gaze to meet Zendalia's. "We hold all life sacred."

"We do too," Zendalia burst in.

Shaking her head, Kaelin tried again. "No, I don't think you do quite like we do."

"What do you mean?"

Kaelin blew out a breath and started swimming again. If they didn't keep moving, they would never get there, and as soon as they arrived, she could at least deposit Zendalia in a place she wouldn't likely get hurt or killed, and maybe someone there had some influence over her to keep her in place and not go after the kraken.

"Before we eat anything, we give thanks to the waters for providing for us."

Zendalia scrunched her nose up. "Only the traditionalists do that."

Kaelin shook her head. "Every time we eat something or use something that the water has provided, we give thanks for it."

"You sound like you're from the olden times." Zendalia

swam down under Kaelin and then back up next to her on the other side. "Not that you're old."

"I'm one of the younger ones in my tribe. Well, younger grown. I'm no longer a child." Kaelin wasn't sure how to even begin explaining her tribe to someone who came from a completely different world. They may have come from the same source if they went back far enough in history, but they were no longer similar in how they lived.

Zendalia blew out a breath. "I didn't mean to call you old. In fact, I think you're quite young and spry."

"Why does that still sound like an insult?" Kaelin raised an eyebrow at Zendalia, enjoying the way the flush of colors in her cheeks lit up her face. She must have hit some kind of nerve in her, embarrassed her perhaps. She should feel guilty about that, but instead a playfulness sparked through her. It was such an odd sensation, one she hadn't really experienced before—or at least not in a very long time.

"It's not," Zendalia squeaked. "I mean…yeah…it came off that way. I'm sorry." Zendalia dove again before bobbing back up, swimming around Kaelin again in a giant circle before landing on the opposite side than she had been before.

"Do you ever stay still?" Kaelin questioned, frowning.

Zendalia chuckled lightly. "Depends on who you ask, but ultimately, I struggle not to be doing something or moving around."

Kaelin grunted, the frenetic energy surrounding Zendalia hitting her full force. As much as she wanted to tame it, she wanted to let it wash over her and consume her as well. Her lower lip quivered at the thought, her tail heating at the fantasy of grabbing Zendalia to still her and ending up entangled with her. Shaking her head free of the image, Kaelin focused on Zendalia. "I'm not banned from joining with other tribes during my banishment, but it is frowned upon. It's not seen as a true punishment."

Zendalia stopped her with a hand on her shoulder. "But this punishment you've been given is unjust."

Kaelin shrugged off the touch. She didn't deserve it, and she certainly didn't deserve the pity or understanding—she wasn't sure which it was—in Zendalia's gaze. "I will go with you to help bring awareness of the kraken, but I'll not be staying with your people."

"But you could learn so much about us."

Kaelin wrinkled her nose, unable to stop the initial reaction. Eventually it blossomed into a smile. "Learning about your people would be pleasant."

Zendalia shook her head. "You say things in the oddest of ways sometimes."

"So do you." Kaelin spun in a tight spiral, enjoying the feel of the water around her, the feel of being with another mer, talking with someone who wasn't afraid to speak with her. Kaelin would relish that for as long as she could.

She wasn't sure what they were going to talk about for the rest of their journey, but she at least knew she would enjoy the time. The closer they got to the upper soundings, the brighter the light got. It started to hurt Kaelin's eyes, but she didn't make any mention of it. She didn't want to show any kind of weakness if she could avoid it, not after what they had been through in the last few days.

Zendalia spun around her again, catching the tips of Kaelin's hair and tugging on them. "What are your family pods like?"

"I would think similar to yours." Kaelin frowned. "We have parents and children."

"Two parents?"

"Sometimes." Kaelin shrugged. "I had three parents, two mothers and one father."

Zendalia canted her head to the side. "We only have two parents typically, sometimes mothers, sometimes fathers, sometimes both."

"Interesting."

"Yeah, but Father always used to say that it didn't always make sense and that historically we used to live more like the pods you were talking about." Zendalia spun again, her tail fins brushing against Kaelin's. It sent a shiver through Kaelin, one that was filled with pleasure but also a sense of familiarity. Aside from her family and tribe, Kaelin hadn't met anyone from another tribe, but Zendalia brought with her such a sense of confidence that it was impossible not to like her.

"We've always had pods like that as far as I know, but it wasn't a question I ever asked of the elders either."

"So you have elders? What do they do?"

"They guide us through decisions, like when to move, where to go, how to stay safe and where to find food."

Zendalia frowned. "You move around?"

"Every few seasons or so, when the tides change and the waters shift." Kaelin floated on her back, staring up at Zendalia. "Don't you move?"

Zendalia shook her head. "No. I've grown up in the same reef my entire life. And we don't have elders, we have a king."

"King?" Kaelin's brow furrowed. "As in passed down through bloodline instead of age?"

"Yeah, that's it." Zendalia circled her again, this time it wasn't just her fins that touched Kaelin's tail, but the very tips of her fingers. Or maybe it wasn't, but she swore it was. Pleasure surged through her. She hadn't been touched like that in so long, and even then, she'd done it mostly in secret so as not to alert the tribe to the fact she was thinking about bonding.

"Do you have bonding ceremonies?" Kaelin cringed at her question. She hadn't intended to ask that, or steer the conversation in that direction, but it was already out there, and there was no taking it back.

"Yeah, we do. But they're pretty simple."

Kaelin frowned. "Ours take a whole season."

"Season?" Zendalia stopped her movement, floating still in the waters.

Kaelin moved on ahead of her, stopping when she realized that Zendalia wasn't keeping up with her. "What?"

"A whole season?"

"Yes." Kaelin wasn't sure what was so surprising about that, but she kept moving. They had to get to the city, otherwise she would never be able to return home. Making sure that Zendalia arrived safe was her new priority, and she would give up everything to be able to do that.

Neyon floated between them, wrapping one tentacle around Kaelin's wrist and the other around Zendalia's. Kaelin frowned at them, not sure what they were doing. Zendalia gasped, her eyes fluttering shut and her cheeks turning a rosy color. Kaelin cocked her head to the side, reaching out and grasping Zendalia's fingers. Neyon did everything with a plan, that much she knew about her companion. They weren't an octopus who did things without a purpose.

Zendalia's eyes flashed open, the amber pouring between them and into her soul. Kaelin's lips parted in surprise, in hope, and then in shame. She wasn't someone who was worthy of any of this, and she had to put a stop to it. She tried to pull away, but Neyon held them together, a vibration stealing through her.

"We should keep going," Kaelin said, her voice wavering.

"I agree," Zendalia nodded, but she didn't break her gaze. "Kaelin…"

Kaelin shook her head. "No."

Breaking Neyon's hold on her was harder than she thought it would be. She pistoned herself forward, clenching her eyes shut as she moved toward the surface, closer to Zendalia's people. She couldn't stay there and be subject to that look because everything in her would break if she let it. Her heart was already against her, and she couldn't let it be known to anyone but herself and Neyon because they knew everything about her.

"Kaelin! Wait up!"

Her heart sank. She wished she could forget the last few days, crawl back into her cave which was now destroyed and live in the silence of her banishment. But Zendalia had changed everything, and she had to accept that.

"I didn't mean to offend." Zendalia breathed hard, having worked to catch up.

Kaelin could tell the water was thinner up here, but it hadn't started affecting her yet. Not like the light had. "You didn't offend."

"Then why did you swim off?"

Kaelin heaved a sigh, stopping short. "Yes, bonding takes a full season in my tribe."

"Why did that question bother you?"

"It didn't," she answered with a clipped tone.

"It did."

"Leave it alone." Kaelin tried to move forward, but Zendalia snagged her wrist and tugged hard.

"Tell me what's wrong? We went from having a good conversation to this, and I want to know what I said."

Kaelin looked up, their eyes locking again. She found the confusion, the worry, and even a touch of fear in those amber eyes. "You didn't say anything."

"I did. What was it?"

"I'll never have a bonding," Kaelin blurted out. Zendalia's brow furrowed. "Because of my banishment, no one will want me. I've seen it happen before."

"Kaelin," Zendalia's voice broke. "You didn't deserve this punishment."

"I did, whether you believe that or not isn't up to me. The elders decided and that is the law. I didn't uphold the values of our tribe, and I didn't save your father."

Zendalia moved in swiftly, taking both of Kaelin's hands in hers, lacing their fingers together. Kaelin stared down at their hands and then just over Zendalia's shoulders, unable to meet her gaze.

"Look at me when I say this, please." Zendalia's voice was sweet, sensitive, and pleading.

Kaelin took a deep breath, telling herself that she wouldn't do it, that she wouldn't raise her gaze, but she also couldn't deny Zendalia anything that she asked. She swallowed hard, bolstered herself, and then looked up, finding Neyon wrapped around their joined hands.

"It wasn't your responsibility to save him."

"It was."

"Shut up." Zendalia rolled her eyes. "I don't agree with the elders, and my father took a risk going down there. He knew the risks, just like I did, and he was impulsive, just like me, and it wasn't your responsibility to correct his mistakes."

Kaelin drew in a shuddering breath. "But—"

"No buts." Zendalia nodded sharply. "It was his decision to make and his life to risk."

Kaelin had no idea what to say. She parted her lips, her heart racing. It wasn't pity she saw in Zendalia's gaze. It was compassion. Leaning in, they floated closer. The water between them warmed from their bodies. Kaelin stared into those amber eyes, listing herself forward. The edges of their fins touched in the water. Her chest heaved, and if she didn't know better, she would think that Zendalia was going to kiss her. But that was improbable. They had way too much history between them, even though they'd only known each other truly for a few days. Zen's death tainted that.

Everything stilled, the tension between them increasing. Kaelin's heart thudded hard. She wanted to, but she would never be the one to make that move. She couldn't do that to Zendalia. She had to be a constant reminder of her father's death, and she wouldn't wish that on anyone. A jolt of electricity shocked them both, their hands shifting apart sharply. Kaelin brushed hers against her tail, removing the sweat from her palms. She cleared her throat.

"We should get going if we want to be there before nightfall."

"Uh, yeah, I guess," Zendalia answered.

They shifted as one, moving back into a position where they

could swim next to each other. Kaelin tried to brush off the feeling of being together, the way their tails moved in sync with each other, the sensation of Zendalia so close. She couldn't believe they had almost done that, that she had almost given in and kissed her. That would be the worst mistake of her life, and she couldn't afford another one.

16

At some point during the swim, the tension fell away from Zendalia's shoulders. Light filtered through the water more clearly, and she breathed deeply, her lungs celebrating the ease. She was nearly home with the truth about her father's death and evidence that his research, what he had lived and died for, was right. A bubble formed in Zendalia's chest, a pressure that filled with emotion and dangerous thoughts, but she quickly gulped down more water and forced it away. She had to focus on the mission, on the reason for risking her life, for dragging Kaelin up to the surface. But the excitement of that last part filled her and chased the last of that suffocating bubble away. How could anyone want to live in the dark when such beauty was mere leagues away. Hope swelled in her chest. Could Kaelin find a home here with her?

Zendalia chased the thought away. *How ridiculous.* Yes, of course she was attracted to Kaelin, anyone with half a brain would be, but Kaelin wasn't like anyone Zendalia had ever met, was nothing like anyone from home. She gnawed on her lip. Would that be a problem?

Beside her, Kaelin had seemed to relax as they swam closer to Zendalia's home. Her movements became more fluid, and her speed relaxed—no longer slicing through the water as though trying to race Zendalia to the surface.

Around them, more colors came to life. Blues and oranges popped as life flowed more freely than she had experienced in the deep soundings. Her heart sang, and she hummed, her muscles relaxing more.

"Home," the word fell reverently from her lips.

"Huh?" Kaelin's word came out almost slurred.

Zendalia looked over as Kaelin turned her head and met her eyes with half-lidded ones. Red lines zigzagged around the almost black surrounding the violet irises.

"Kaelin, what's wrong?"

"It's just…" Kaelin squeezed her eyes shut and then forced them open a crack. "It's very bright."

"Oh." Zendalia felt like the biggest fool in the whole entire ocean. How had she not thought about that? "Of course. You're used to the darkness. How dense of me."

"It's okay." Kaelin's smile was less than convincing. "I'll get used to it."

Not likely! Zendalia kept the thought to herself, knowing it wouldn't help and surprising herself at her own ability to bite her tongue.

"Come on, I'll take you to my place." Zendalia touched Kaelin's shoulder lightly, hoping the connection would guide both of them together.

"This is your home?" Kaelin looked around, still squinting.

Zendalia had the urge to kiss the small pucker between Kaelin's brows but resisted, satisfying herself enough with pulling Kaelin into her side and swimming directly toward home. She would take the most direct route possible.

"Not quite yet." Zendalia chuckled as she adjusted her swim to half carry Kaelin. It was incredible how easy it actually was. She had expected Kaelin to be heavier, but her weight had a strange buoyancy that only heightened Zendalia's interest.

"Where were you going then, if not home?"

"I was going to head directly to the castle."

"The king's castle?"

"Yeah." Zendalia smiled at the incredulity that seemed to radiate from Kaelin at the idea. She still couldn't quite get her head around the idea of a nomadic existence. Home meant something solid and permanent, not something to be changed every few seasons. Zendalia closed her eyes and wished she could rewind some of her earlier words, when she was still the mer who spewed words before she thought. "Oh."

"What's wrong?" Kaelin stiffened in her arms, pulling away slightly as if preparing herself.

"It's okay." Their eyes met, and though the redness around Kaelin's eyes had increased, she opened them wide, ready to go into battle with whatever was troubling Zendalia.

"Zendalia, please. What's wrong?"

"I feel like an idiot." The words were slow, Zendalia's tongue feeling as though it had swollen inside her mouth over the last few seconds.

"Why?"

"Can I ask you a question?" Zendalia's heart raced with the honesty that was about to show up.

"Umm, okay." Kaelin's weight leaned heavier against Zendalia once more as she slapped her tail and started them moving once again.

It should have worried her how easily they fit together despite the size difference. They swam side by side, tails curving toward each other, Kaelin's fins cupped around Zendalia's in a touch so intimate she never felt anything like it before. Sure, she'd been intimate with enough mers but there was an electricity that thrilled her through scale and skin alike.

"What does home mean to you?" Zendalia's throat constricted on the question, as if she would offend Kaelin by even asking the question, but she needed to know. Maybe Kaelin had the answers to the questions she didn't dare ask.

"Home?" Kaelin asked, and Zendalia nodded. "Home is my tribe."

The confirmation slammed into the pit of Zendalia's stomach as though someone had just thrust their balled fist into her.

"I'm so sorry." Zendalia's voice cracked, her jaw clenched tightly against the raw emotion pushing through her.

Kaelin slumped further against her. "My head is so sore. The light."

"I know. I'm sorry." Zendalia flapped her fins a little faster. "Close your eyes. I've got you."

Zendalia's mouth suddenly dried as her words registered. She looked over, nerves on edge to see what Kaelin's reaction had been, but Kaelin had closed her eyes, her mouth softer than Zendalia had ever seen it.

Zendalia did her best to hasten the journey but refrained as best she could from too much speed as fear of jostling Kaelin overrode her thoughts. She barely noted, from the corner of her eye, the landmarks of home that usually brought smiles to her face no matter her mood. The corners of her lips twitched as she passed under the rainbow-colored coral archway leading down to the reef of her home, but the majority of her focus alternated between the path ahead and Kaelin's slouching form.

Gritting her teeth, Zendalia wondered if this was her punishment from the water gods for the pain and worry she had given Kaelin over the last few days. *Had it really only been days?* Her life had changed so much she hardly recognized it. Even as the thought surfaced, she found herself surrounded by all the familiarity of the home she'd grown up in. Perhaps what she didn't recognize was the turmoil that rolled around in her head and heart, not to mention her stomach and lower.

She let out a self-annoyed breath. Her friend was in pain, and all she could think about was the way they touched, the slight brush of fins against fins, fingers pressing into the small of her back as Kaelin held on, the rise and fall of her chest as she breathed shallowly. She longed to slide her fingers farther around Kaelin's waist, holding her closer and more tenderly.

Zendalia swallowed hard, turning her chin and catching a whiff of Kaelin's scent. It sent shivers throughout her body, her mind distracted by Kaelin's very presence. She glided in closer, their sides brushing more intimately than before, but she pulled back. She shouldn't.

A newly familiar tingle ran over her fingers, and she looked over at the hand that pulled Kaelin into her side. Her companion had slunk out of their resting place and now sat, half on Zendalia's fingers and half on Kaelin's arm.

"Nice of you to show up," Zendalia murmured with a half-smile on her lips.

The tingle turned into a low-grade zap.

"Hey." Zendalia flicked her fingers, hoping to dislodge the octopus but not yet willing to let go of Kaelin's body. She could have sworn the damn thing tilted its head in the cockiest of fashions. She narrowed her eyes and kept swimming.

"Be careful, buddy, you're in my territory now."

Kaelin's companion laughed at her—she was certain of that as small bubbles escaped their mouth and floated in a swirl above their head.

Muttering a curse under her breath, she continued on, feeling buoyed by the smoothed-down path of sand beneath her tail. She allowed her fins to brush the sloping floor to her home and sighed into the sensation. Plants lining both sides down to the eastern reef seemed to wave, as they always did, through the movement of her passing, and this time, with home in sight, she allowed herself the smile she had been holding back.

The smell of the algae on the rocks and the brush of life blooming around her lit her up from within. Her favorite anemone was right where she left it, and three new pups quickly followed their parents back into their home, hiding from the big bad mer. Life goes on. It was what Soulara had told her, and while Zendalia had known it had never been meant to hurt, she had held that dark bitter anger in her chest ever since.

But now a calm washed over her. Oh sure, there was still plenty of anger and pain, amidst heartache and loneliness, but the calmness was new. Perhaps it was merely a form of numbness. She hadn't grieved like this in her memories of her mother's passing, but then she had had her father's strong arms and solid heartbeat to cling to.

A hiss from Kaelin brought her back to the present. She now carried her more than guided.

"We are nearly there. I promise." Zendalia tightened her grasp, unwilling to let herself drop Kaelin and fail in taking care of her.

"So bright…my head…"

"Shhh I know. It's okay, baby."

Baby? What the hell? Thankfully there was no response from Kaelin, and the mortification that had swept over Zendalia slipped away slowly, like a blowfish after a scare.

Her home rose up in front of her. The coral cave glowed a cool blue, and Zendalia could almost feel the soft moss beneath her fluke. Her muscles ached and gained weight with the mere anticipation of being home.

"Almost there," Zendalia muttered, to herself, to Kaelin, to her body. It didn't matter. The truth of the statement brought a warm wetness to her eyes.

The cave wasn't just her home. It was the central place for all the residents within. Four families lived there—well, three and her now. She swallowed down the lump in her throat and ground her teeth together because she wasn't a family any longer. Her family had lived in the blue coral cave for four generations now, and Zendalia wasn't entirely sure how to live anywhere else. How could she? She would lose all the memories of her life. Again, she shuddered and then stiffened her back as the uncomfortable idea of how Kaelin lived in the deep soundings turned into anger at her people. Home was her tribe, and they had stolen it from her for insane archaic reasons. She growled, trying to contain the emotions.

Her neighbors floated from their homes to find the source of the noise.

"Zendalia." Reices' soft tones met Zendalia like an embrace. "You're finally home. We were worried."

"I am so sorry. I left unexpectedly and didn't get the chance to explain." Zendalia tightened her grip on Kaelin, wondering just what this mer would think of her dragging in a half-dead woman who clearly wasn't from Reine. Her colors were all wrong for their people. She held her breath and waited for an answer.

"It is all right, child," Reices gently moved forward and took Zendalia's free hand. "Princess Soulara came and explained she needed you to run an urgent errand, and she wasn't sure when you might return. Still, so many days away from home."

"Yes, I've missed it, and you all, very much." Zendalia wasn't fooled by the silence. She could still feel the presence of all those behind her staring. They did try, she gave them that, but she was a warrior of their people and an orphan at such a young age. No one understood how to speak to her anymore. If she couldn't notice the tiny ripples that barely brushed against her fins, then there was no chance any of them would survive long with the kraken lurking in the deep soundings. And who knew if there was only one of them? The idea made her shudder.

"Oh dear." Reices patted the back of Zendalia's hand three times before releasing her. "I have kept you too long, you and your companion."

For a moment, Zendalia's heart beat a little too quickly as she looked down at her hand still gripping Kaelin to keep her in place. She had expected to see the octopus sitting there smirking, but instead it was just her bronze fingers against Kaelin's slick dark skin. Her skin and scales reflected hidden colors in the brighter light, and for a beat, Zendalia stood mesmerized by the beauty, by the shameless contrast of differences that blended together into a masterpiece.

"Please pass on our regards to the princess," Reices said as a way of leaving, extricating himself from the conversation and Zendalia's sudden lack of attention.

"Yes, thank you. I will." The words parroted out, and Zendalia shook her head. The shuffling came from behind, and finally she heard the soft swing of seaweed falling over entrances.

Soulara. *Shit.* She had hoped to get some rest and freshen up before going to the castle but needs pulled at her. News would reach her before Zendalia did, no matter how fast she swam, but the sooner she arrived after the word of her return, the better.

What in the waters had possessed Soulara to protect Zendalia like that? She had said she wouldn't, and she had never known the princess to lie before. At least, not to her knowledge. The idea twisted uncomfortably in her stomach as she pushed through her own seaweed barrier and found her home exactly as she had left it. She wasn't entirely sure what she had expected but perhaps something unusual, something different that would mimic the changes she felt within herself.

"Oh, still bright, but better," Kaelin muttered next to her.

"Good. Now keep your eyes closed, and you can sleep on my bed." Zendalia liked the idea of repaying Kaelin's kindness, though the situations were worlds apart right now. "I need to leave just for a moment."

"What? Why?" Panic filled her home, and Zendalia squeezed Kaelin closer in response as she helped guide her through to her resting moss.

"It's okay. I need to make sure things are all right with my friend, and there is also something she might be able to help you with." The idea popped into Zendalia's mind as she spoke it, unsure if Kaelin heard it as she crumpled up in the moss with a soft whimper.

Soulara was the most tech-savvy mer Zendalia had ever

known, and while she couldn't imagine why such a thing would exist, she cradled a small light of hope that the princess could fashion something to help. As Kaelin settled into the moss, her breathing no doubt deepening as she succumbed to the pain of being so close to the surface, Zendalia waited. She brushed her fingers over Kaelin's forehead, moving the long strands of hair that now had a shimmer to them.

Zendalia pulled her lip between her teeth and did it again, staying still as Kaelin fell into a deeper slumber. She didn't want to find Soulara. She wanted to curl up with Kaelin's arms wrapped around her and sleep until they woke naturally, some-place they would both be safe. Closing her eyes, Zendalia fluttered her fingers across Kaelin's cheek to her hand just under her and along the small hairs on her arm.

"I promise to take care of you," Zendalia whispered. "And I promise I won't be gone long. I wish I didn't have to go."

Kaelin didn't answer with anything more than deep, steady breathing. Zendalia clenched her jaw tightly and closed her eyes. She forced herself to back away and swim silently toward the entry. When she glanced back, she found Kaelin's companion taking a silent guard. They flicked a tentacle in her direction. Zendalia gave them a half-hearted smile and a wave before she disappeared through the seaweed and coral.

17

"Well, well, well, look what the shark dragged in," Soulara drawled as she looked up from her workbench and saw Zendalia standing in the archway to her workshop.

"May I enter?" Zendalia's heart rapped hard. She hadn't ever wanted to come begging for more help, especially after not listening to Soulara the last time.

"Oh please, don't try that repentant game with me, Z." The smirk on Soulara's lips helped Zendalia release her held breath as she floated through and buoyed herself up on the other side of the bench.

"Thank you, Soulara."

"What for?" Soulara tucked her chin and looked at Zendalia from beneath her top eyelids. "And do please be specific, I have done many amazing favors for you."

"Yes, yes, you have. Why?" Zendalia furrowed her brow, staying by the entryway and hoping Soulara would make her tease out an answer but knowing luck wasn't in the cards for her that day.

"Specifics." Soulara singsonged, and Zendalia wondered, not for the first time, if the royal lineage descended from sirens.

"Thank you for not telling anyone about the stolen mask or the armor."

"I see you're not wearing either, but..." she made a show of looking Zendalia up and down "...where is my mask?"

"Broken," Zendalia squeaked out, her heart pounding so loudly she knew Soulara could hear it from across the room.

"Impossible creature that you are, Z, I hope the lost tech was worth whatever made you run off like an eel on mushrooms."

"And thank you for covering for my absence." Zendalia would get to Kaelin and the kraken soon enough, but right now she found she needed to smooth things over with Soulara, and maybe she would even go see her estranged cousin later. What an odd thing to consider. Perhaps paying Soulara's parents a visit instead would be easier—it was certainly more palatable.

"Oh dear." Soulara stopped fiddling with metal shards and other pieces of tech Zendalia couldn't identify even under threat of torture or death. "Something is very wrong. You gave extra gratitude without my demanding it."

"No, I didn't." Zendalia's shoulders tightened, and her tail straightened without intention.

"Why so defensive, my dear?" Soulara's half-cocked smile was obnoxious.

"Ugh." Zendalia ran her hands through her hair as frustration and confusion whirled around her. A handful of days away in the deep sounding didn't change the core essence of a person, so why was Soulara acting as though Zendalia had never thanked her in her life?

"Okay." Soulara lifted her hands, palms out in surrender. "No more fooling around." She joined Zendalia on her side of the bench. "Tell me what happened."

"I think we need to speak with the family. It's about Father and his studies, and Kaelin." Zendalia squared her shoulders. She hadn't wanted to bring in the entire royal family on this one, but she had to at some point. Soulara, while a wonderful contact to have when it came to needing tech, wasn't a politician in her own right. She wouldn't have the power to make decisions like King Pregtox did.

Soulara canted her head to the side, those pale shimmering eyes scanning through her as if searching for some kind of answer. The tone of the conversation had gone from oddly flirtatious to serious at the snap of Zendalia's fingers, but she had to take it that direction. She thought of Kaelin's webbed fingers and whether or not she'd even be able to snap them but shook the thought. When she focused back on Soulara's rounded face, she shook her head.

"This is serious."

"I can see that. Come." Soulara grabbed Zendalia's hand, and they swam together through the castle halls, weaving around mer as they went about their duties and ignored them. It was reminiscent of when they had been together all those seasons ago, when they would sneak around the castle to find different places to fuck, places just outside the reach of other mer, where the threat of being caught loomed. That had always been more Soulara's thing than Zendalia's, but she'd gone along with it because she was such a good fuck.

"Stop thinking," Soulara murmured in her ear. "You think too damn loudly sometimes."

Flushing with embarrassment, Zendalia did as she was told and cleared her mind of those memories.

"Much better," Soulara drawled again. "Mother is gone, but Father is here still, along with Makryn."

Perfect. Soulara's brother and spare to her heir, and someone who really wanted it, unlike Soulara. He and Zendalia had never gotten along well, and she imagined this part of the conversation was not going to go well.

They bypassed the throne room, and Soulara took Zendalia to the wide-open space behind it. Zendalia knew from past experiences that this was where most of the work was done. She straightened her shoulders as they swam in, Pregtox and Makryn leaning over a table as they were deep in discussion.

They both looked up and straightened themselves when they saw Zendalia following Soulara.

She bent herself in a bow, first to Pregtox and then to Makryn, keeping her chin down as a sign of respect. She'd been in front of the royal line before, but never in this capacity. She'd witnessed others do it, but the responsibility had never been solely on her shoulders. The weight of that was heavy, and she suddenly understood why all those mermen had quaked at the thought.

"What have we here?" Pregtox said, and his drawl was similar to Soulara's when she wanted information.

Zendalia bowed her head again, Soulara's hand leaving hers. She was just about to speak when Soulara interrupted her thoughts. "Daddy, Zendalia has some information she needs to share with us, something about what her father was studying?"

Pregtox said nothing, but his lips pursed tightly as he stared down his nose at Zendalia. She hated this, feeling so small and insignificant and up against the entire ocean. But she wasn't. Kaelin had her back. She'd never once faltered from that, and in this instance, Soulara was there too.

"I recently went to discover more details about what happened with my father's death." Zendalia swallowed the rapidly growing lump in her throat. Pregtox didn't have a long attention span, so she knew she needed to make this quick. "While there, I discovered this."

She pulled the small black box out of the bag against her side and set it on top of the table that the mermen had been leaned over. She took a deep breath and backed away slightly.

"It's a metal I've never seen before, but it belongs to a kraken."

Makryn jerked his head up, his short auburn hair flinging wildly about his face as he stared with wide eyes at his father. "So it *is* true?"

Pregtox didn't even look at him.

"It's attacking the lower soundings. They are bearing the

brunt of the physical attack, but we're feeling the effects of what they're doing." Zendalia's hands shook as she reached forward and pressed the side buttons on the small box. It opened just as it had before, but unlike then, nothing happened. Fear swept through her. Everything was going to fall apart because the tech suddenly failed her. She couldn't keep herself together as she reached forward, her hands shaking. "It's not working."

Panicked, Zendalia grabbed the box and tried it again, closing it up and re-opening it. Nothing happened. Her stomach swirled with bile, and her mind raced. It was the only proof she had, and now it was gone. Her heart hammered.

"Enough of this," Pregtox didn't sound angry, but he was certainly annoyed. "If the lower sounding tribes are being attacked, it's their responsibility to deal with it. We separated from them eons ago."

"I know," Zendalia murmured, still trying to mess with the box. She was very near tears. Her entire plan of telling them what was happening, of calling in the guard and helping Kaelin's people, had gone out the ocean in a flash. She was defeated before she could even get to battle.

Soulara stilled her hands, covering them and taking the box from her fingers. The move forced Zendalia to lift her chin up and look into Pregtox's shimmering blue eyes. They were the exact same eyes Soulara had, and she'd never been able to resist them.

"Leave it be, child." His voice was calm, pitying but with a tenderness Zendalia hadn't expected.

"But it's killing the entire ocean!" She blurted it out, desperate to get some attention on what was happening.

Pregtox shook his head slowly. "Not if it's only attacking other tribes."

"That's great until it attacks us!"

"Zendalia," Soulara warned. "I know you're upset about your father—"

"This isn't about him." Zendalia was nearly in tears again,

her head pounding from everything that had happened and the fact that no one seemed to listen to her, even Soulara, the one mer who should listen. "This is about an enemy that's destroying the ocean."

"Enemy?" Makryn swam forward, his face right in Zendalia's. "You don't understand the word."

"I'm a more decorated officer than you." Zendalia straightened her back, willing to argue. "I've seen more battles than you have, and I have certainly taken more life than you. *You* don't understand that this kraken is more enemy than we have ever dealt with. My father did the research, he went on the hunt to find out what was happening, but I'm the one here telling you that if we don't deal with the kraken, it'll destroy every single one of us."

Makryn jerked forward, but Pregtox snagged his hand sharply and put him back into place. Soulara swam in front of Zendalia, putting her entire body between them. "Touch her, brother, and you'll regret it."

Zendalia's heart pounded. She'd never liked him. Pregtox waited until his son stood down, backing away slowly before he turned on Zendalia. "Come to me again with proof and we'll talk."

"I have proof!" She snagged the box, her fingers tight around it as she lifted it in front of her. "This is proof."

"It's a box," Makryn shouted at her, his agitation going higher every moment.

Zendalia sighed. "It's a metal we don't have, and it's a map to where they're going next."

"The kraken?" Soulara asked, taking the box back and studying it. She easily opened it again, but once more, nothing appeared.

Zendalia was devastated. It must have broken on their journey home. She hadn't realized it had been jostled that much while she and Kaelin had returned. She had to find some way to deal with this, to get her point across, to make them understand.

Soulara reached down sharply and gripped Zendalia's fingers, tightening her grasp around them. "Father, let me look at it, please. If I find something, we'll bring it back to you."

"Please listen," Zendalia pleaded. "I wouldn't come in here with nothing."

"Zendalia, your father was a good mer." Pregtox's voice was gentle, patronizing. Zendalia shivered at it. He was only trying to be kind, but she heard the dismissal that was in his words. "He was very smart, and I relied on him for many seasons. I rely on you now, not as a scientist like your father, but as one of my warriors. Zen will never be forgotten."

Pregtox straightened his spine and made a fist, covering his right hand over his heart in a symbol of dedication and honor for those who have died. Zendalia was taken aback. He'd done that before, at the ending ceremony, but she hadn't thought Pregtox had admired her father that much. Her lips parted, stunned into silence. She bowed again, her face to the floor as she tried to gather her thoughts and feelings so she could try again.

"Thank you, your excellency. But—"

Soulara jerked her arm, catching her attention. She gave her a sharp look. "Come along, Z."

She hesitated once more before listening to Soulara. They left the room, Makryn sneering the entire time. Soulara would make such a better ruler than he would. She still couldn't figure out why Makryn was kept around.

They swam in silence back to Soulara's lab. She was overcome with failure, and she really wished Kaelin had been there with her. Then they would have to believe what she had seen, what was lurking in the deep soundings.

"I should have brought Kaelin with me."

"Kaelin?" Soulara raised an eyebrow, but she didn't move her gaze from the black box she set on the table.

"A mer I met in the deep soundings." She was so much more than that, though Zendalia wasn't able to put words to what she was feeling just then. She didn't want to.

"Why didn't you?"

Zendalia gnawed on her lip. "She's not well. The light is too bright for her, so I left her to rest and perhaps get used to it."

"Too bright?" Soulara spun around, an eyebrow raised as she looked Zendalia over. "I might have something for that."

"Really?" Zendalia's stomach flopped, hope resurfacing, though she still felt damned for failing to get her point across to Pregtox.

Soulara hummed as she set the black box onto the table where she'd been seated when Zendalia had come in. Zendalia was going to ask her another question, but she looked so busy, so perfectly perched as she dug through a bag of things that she couldn't bring herself to interrupt her again, not after what she'd just gone through. Her stomach twisted at the thought. She didn't understand why Pregtox had never believed her father, but she'd known going in that it was going to be hard to convince him. She hadn't thought it would be impossible.

"Kaelin's lived near the kraken for several seasons. She could explain everything about what it's doing," Zendalia said, not quite sure why she was explaining when she didn't have to. She should be protecting Kaelin from anything that might come their way, including her own people.

"What is it doing?" Soulara asked, distracted by her search.

"I...I don't know, but it's affecting the water up here."

"Your father was never able to prove that." Soulara jerked her head up at Zendalia. "It might do you well to stay away from his research and truly take some time to grieve."

Zendalia frowned, shaking her head. Nothing was the same as when she'd left. She may not have fully grieved Zen's loss, but that couldn't be done in one season or two or even ten. She would always grieve losing him, and since Soulara hadn't lost a parent, she wouldn't understand that. She shifted her stance, prepared to leave. "Are we done here? I need to check on Kaelin."

Soulara licked her lips, putting the bag down next to her and piercing a look into Zendalia's heart. "You've mentioned her several times, worried about her, concerned for her well-being."

"Of course I would be." Zendalia's defenses rose sharply. That look in Soulara's eyes was never good.

"Well, I never thought I'd see the day." Soulara's smile was big, *too big*. Zendalia didn't like it. Her muscles tightened as she prepared to fight, although this wasn't a physical battle, and she knew she would lose. Soulara was too smart for her own good.

"See what day?" Zendalia nearly choked out the words, but she knew what Soulara was going to say, exactly what she was thinking without even having to hear it.

Soulara winked but relaxed, which helped Zendalia to realize that this wasn't an attack, at least not the kind in which she'd be the victim. "When you would start having real emotions for another mer."

"Excuse me?" Zendalia panicked. "I have real emotions for you. I had very real ones once upon a time."

"Yes, Z, but they were never like this." Soulara waved a single finger, drawing figures to indicate all of Zendalia.

"What are they like?" Oh how Zendalia wanted to smack herself for the squeak that escaped her mouth. Her chest constricted tightly, her heart hammering for an entirely different reason. She hadn't anticipated the conversation taking this drastic turn.

"Oh Z, you really have it bad." Soulara winked and went back to digging around in the bag she'd pulled up.

"Two Zs in one conversation." Zendalia smirked, though her pulse pounded almost painfully in her temples. Her stomach was doing funky things, and if Soulara could sense it, surely everyone else could. She'd have to work better at hiding it. Taking on a bit of Soulara's distraction tactic with her attitude, Zendalia flung her hands out to the sides. "Now I'm really scared."

"You should be." Soulara pulled out pieces of scrap from a woven basket of reeds on the edge of the table, having given up on the bag. She didn't raise her gaze as she put the pieces together in a pattern in front of her. "Love is terrifying."

Zendalia stared at her, but Soulara didn't look up, and if she noticed Zendalia's silence she ignored it. They stayed in silence for another few minutes, Zendalia slowly calming down from the confrontation with the royals, but now she was in complete turmoil over this obvious crush she'd developed and everyone finding out. She couldn't be in love with Kaelin—they barely knew each other.

"Now, I can make a crude pair of goggles, but I had an idea for a better one that I can develop once I know this hottie's dimensions, and the exact needs she has."

"Hottie?" Zendalia scrunched her eyebrows together so hard that an ache caught her off guard.

"I love you, Z, but for someone to get you this riled up, I'm betting she's a true stunner. Now shut up and let me work."

Zendalia hesitated for one brief moment, but just as she went to move, Soulara's voice reached her again. "Come find me again in the morning, and I'll give you these. Once I meet her, I'll make another—better—pair."

"Right." Awkwardly, Zendalia swam out of the lab and left the castle.

18

Kaelin woke and for three heartbeats she thought she must still be in the deep soundings, alone in her cave far away from her tribe, sad but safe. Her breathing was the only sound she heard, and the water lay still against her skin and scales. At least the ones that weren't snuggled up nice and warm against moss.

Moss?

Fractured memories of light and pain, of Zendalia's touch and Neyon's reassurance as they curled up at the base of her neck.

She fluttered her eyes open, sleep hanging on to her for just a little longer, and her head pounding at multiple spots, the base of her neck now empty of her companion's presence. She felt a sharp twinge at her temples.

"Fuck." She whimpered, unable to force the word out as loudly as she wanted, hindered by the excruciating pain that seared through her head. Slamming her eyes closed again, she fought against her racing heart. In and out, she took deep breaths, counting each and holding them until the pain receded back into an almost bearable throb.

"Zendalia?" She forced her voice as loud as she dared, an involuntary whimper escaping.

Silence greeted her.

Where in the serpent's teeth was Zendalia?

A familiar touch of tentacles on her scales made Kaelin smile, which quickly gave way to another moan. It seemed even the slightest movement of her head hurt, but she carefully shuffled her hand inch by inch, searching for more of that familiar touch.

As her fingers wrapped around the bulbous head of the small octopus, Neyon vibrated, and images of soothing colors filled Kaelin's mind. She relaxed, her body sighing into the comfort and familiarity that she had longed for and that only Neyon could provide.

"Thank you," she whispered, lips carefully moving the bare minimum, but the pain didn't spike. The touch seemed to take the sharper edges away, blunting them enough for Kaelin to think almost coherent thoughts. As she cracked her eyes open the tiniest of fractions, light poured in and almost suffocated her with the colors she had never truly experienced before. Opening her mouth she breathed slowly and deliberately, demanding her body adjust to the conditions around her. Except for the dulling of the corners, her body plainly ignored the command.

Tentacles wrapped around Kaelin's wrist, head resting against her webbed fingers as they nuzzled into her palm.

"Hey, little friend, is that you making this possible?"

The vibrations increased, and this time Kaelin's smile wasn't accompanied by sounds of pain.

"It's still too bright," she spoke softly, "but much better."

Images of a smaller darker area flooded her mind. She reached for it, needing it. Her muscles tensed as she prepared to move wherever Neyon took her. It took everything in her focus to think through the pain and make herself functional.

"Where is it?" Her voice cracked, her head spinning slightly at the thought of having to move long distances. She hoped wherever her companion was bringing her was going to be nearby.

A tentacle uncurled from her wrist, lengthening and pointing across the room to a smoothed doorway. The electricity flowing through her increased, and she knew she was going to have to move sooner rather than later, that Neyon was going to see her through this step by step. They always did. That had been part of what she loved about them. No matter what happened, they were there for her.

It took time, too much time, but Kaelin forced herself out of her moss bed, buoying herself up just enough to get moving, using her tail fins against the floor of the cave. She passed the smoothed doorway and stopped. She nearly filled the doorway, and the sudden realization of how much bigger she was compared to Zendalia hit her. She wouldn't easily fit into this world.

She couldn't quite reconcile the items around her—the colors and the beauty—to a home. Homes were transient. Even the cave in the deep soundings she had taken Zendalia to had been a silliness on her behalf and only temporary. But without the tribe, she had to keep her things somewhere safe, unable to carry everything all on her own. But she came and went from it, never staying more than a season at a time.

Zendalia's home was cluttered with items that pulled her attention though she didn't know why or what they could possibly be. Stacks of shiny silver shapes littered a shelf that stuck out from a wall. A ring of stones all moss-covered took up one corner. There were splashes of colors everywhere, coral and seaweed scattered among pieces of shaped metal, twisted and worked to be items that reminded her of the camps back home, but with inlaid colorful stones.

"Hey, I'm so glad you are finally ba—" The words died in the throat of a young mer who bobbed with wide eyes just inside what Kaelin thought might have been the front of Zendalia's home. "You aren't Zendalia."

"No." Kaelin clenched her teeth, not sure what to say or what to share, and she just wished she could open her eyes wide enough to see the features of this mer, memorize them in case she needed to know who they were later. Every nerve in her body was on fire, ready for fight or flight, and she would prefer the latter if necessary.

"Know where I can find her?" The mer cocked her head to the side, and Kaelin would know that defiant look anywhere. She'd worn it many times in her adolescence.

"No." Kaelin swallowed hard, staying as still as she could and using the gentle vibrations from Neyon to keep her in one place. She was defensive and protective, that much she knew and couldn't avoid, but this mer had just come into Zendalia's home without warning and Zendalia had left her without so much as telling her where she was going.

The young mer rolled her eyes and shook her head. "Got anything else to say except no?"

For a moment Kaelin felt the word once again dance on the tip of her tongue. But before she could say it, two other mers, female and older, followed the younger mer into Zendalia's home.

"Oh. And who are you?" The more striking of the two asked and swam a little closer than her fellow intruders.

"I'm Kaelin," Kaelin whispered, hoping the mer would get the hint. She did not.

"I'm San, and this is my wife, Ther, and our child Santher. We're fellow cavers of Zendalia. And how do you know our Zendalia?"

"I," Kaelin stammered. She was being stared at by three mers now—three. Would they even let her back into the tribe after this?

"Oh that's enough. The girl is obviously hurt," Ther spoke. She was a little wider in fluke and fin though not as wide and powerful as Zendalia's let alone Kaelin's own, and so bright Kaelin couldn't look directly at her.

This one moved with a slow surety as she approached Kaelin.

"It's okay. We won't hurt you."

"Speak for yourself," San muttered under her breath.

Ther glared at her wife. "We didn't know Zendalia had brought someone home."

"I don't know where she is." Kaelin squeezed her eyes shut. They were all so bright. Did they not realize how much they lit up the room and filled Kaelin's head with a pulsating throb? Of course they didn't, but surely Zendalia would have been aware, and instead of keeping her safe and away from all these mers, she had run away to—

Pain lanced through her chest to add to the pain that flooded the rest of her body. A memory surfaced in her mind. Something about a fellow mer. Zendalia had abandoned Kaelin to go find a merwoman Zendalia had mentioned before. She had left her, not even bothering to tell her fellow cavers about her, and here they were forcing their light and disregard for her banishment onto her.

Kaelin's stomach roiled, and everything felt heavy. She couldn't keep her eyes open any longer. They closed as the world spun, and she began to sink to the floor of the room.

"Oh no." The voice was one of the older mers, Kaelin knew that, but she had no idea which one. It didn't matter, not until she felt the fingers, strong and unwebbed, gripping both of her arms.

"Let me go." Pain screamed in her head as the words came out in a growl.

The fingers left her, and she opened her eyes to stare at these strangers who had dared to touch her, had dared to speak to her. She would never be allowed back to her tribe, to her own home. Anger burned inside of her, she knew it wasn't their fault, these three strangers who looked at her, with wide eyes filled with concern.

"She's with Soulara," Kaelin muttered and slunk farther

back, wishing she had never moved from the moss. "I had forgotten. She has gone to be with Soulara."

She hoped they would leave on their own with this information.

"Are you certain you're okay?" Ther asked, or was that one San? It didn't matter.

Kaelin gritted her teeth and gave a slow nod, up and down. It didn't matter to her if she wasn't going to survive. She didn't want them there with her. They only made everything worse, the pain in her head and behind her eyes, they made it all ten times worse.

"We should leave." Ther gave a smile that reminded Kaelin far too much of the last ones she had seen from her tribe as she was swam out of the protection of their camp. It was filled with pity, concern, but mostly filled with fear because of who she was and what she had done. She'd murdered someone. She'd killed Zen. The pain from that memory ricocheted through her.

"T." *Okay, this one was San.*

Kaelin closed her eyes, she didn't know what else was said, she heard the rush of whispers and the brush of ripples over her body. Images of that smaller dark space filled her mind again and a rub of familiar energy brushed against her cheek.

"Okay." She forced herself up enough to swim and followed the directions of her companion.

The small room held nothing that sparked Kaelin's pain or interest. A darkened corner in a world too bright. She curled up, pulling her tail into her chest as she lay down in the cool darkness of this space.

Abandoned in a place she couldn't even open her eyes, by a mer who only days ago had wanted to kill her, and rightfully so. She should have known better than to trust Zendalia not to leave her. She deserved to be abandoned, but that didn't make the pain seeping into her chest—not a physical pain but one that reminded her all too much of that moment her sentencing was handed down to her—any easier to bear. Zendalia had been warm when they'd traveled there. She'd been concerned, she had blocked the kraken's light so Kaelin had been able to see once again.

Zendalia had protected her, but it had all been a falsehood, hadn't it? She had been tricked into believing Zendalia cared more than she had, but Kaelin was there for a purpose. She was there to prove that the kraken existed and that there was a threat to the ocean. That was the only reason Zendalia had been so kind to her, had helped her, had changed in the last few days. Kaelin was being used, and she had allowed it to happen.

The water in front of her face warmed, her head pounded, and she was no longer able to hold back the tears. Her body racked with sobs. Every decision she made came back to haunt her, and this one was the worst. This one left her far from her people, unable to ever reach them again even after her banishment was over. This one would be the end of her.

She wished she had never seen Zen, had never learned what attacked her people or threatened their way of life. But more than anything, she wished vehemently that she had never fallen for a mer who cared only about her own skin. The moment they were here, she had swum off to this *Soulara*, swam off to pass on the information that had turned Kaelin's entire world upside down.

The skin on her arms tingled from the stranger's touch. She sobbed harder. Despite the fear, something inside of her had cracked open with joy at the feeling. A feeling that she was not allowed and would undoubtedly never be allowed again. Noises echoed outside of her safe dark corner of this inhospitable place, and she hoped it were someone, something, come to finally end this forsaken punishment of hers.

19

"Did you bring me here to kill me?" Kaelin's voice boomed through the small home as soon as Zendalia swam inside.

Zendalia stuttered to a stop, her heart racing from the unexpected attack. Her eyes were wide as she searched the room for Kaelin, finding her huddled in the darkest corner of her home. Her heart shattered at the image. "No. I would never—"

She stopped, because she had wanted to kill Kaelin, several times, before she'd known the fullest extent of what had happened. She couldn't say that and be truthful, and she never wanted to be anything but that. Swallowing hard, Zendalia swam closer, settling onto the floor next to Kaelin. She brushed gentle fingers against Kaelin's arm, which Kaelin jerked back.

"How are you feeling?"

"Sunny," Kaelin fired back.

Confusion filled Zendalia, unsure of exactly what had transpired between the time she had left and now that would cause such a shift in Kaelin. When she'd left, she'd been hurting and needed rest, and while she could tell Kaelin was still in pain, she didn't seem as bad.

"I asked Soulara to find something to help your eyes."

Zendalia kept her tone soft, cooing the words as she tried to calm Kaelin down. She reached forward again, wrapping her fingers around Kaelin's. When she was little and struggling, her father's soft and comforting touch like this always made her feel better. "She's working something up for you."

Kaelin snorted loudly. "So I can see you better when you swim away next time?"

Zendalia tensed, guilt pulling into the center of her stomach. So that's what this was all about. She sighed heavily and brushed the tips of her thumb against the back of Kaelin's hand. She wasn't quite sure what to say. She'd told Kaelin she was leaving, that she had to speak with Soulara and get some things taken care of, but then again, she had left her here thinking Kaelin would sleep the entire time she was gone.

"I'm sorry I left," Zendalia murmured, keeping her voice gentle. "I needed to talk to Soulara about the kraken and try to warn them all about what's happening in the deep soundings."

Kaelin said nothing, but the muscles in her jaw moved as she clenched and tightened all over. Zendalia scooted in closer, using the weight of her body to give Kaelin something to rest on.

"When did you wake up?"

Again, Kaelin remained silent. Zendalia's heart stuttered as she waited for some kind of answer, needing to know what was going through Kaelin's mind so she could soothe the worry or fear or whatever was wrong. She didn't want Kaelin to think the worst of her.

"Kaelin—" Zendalia started but stopped. "Kaelin, tell me what happened."

"You tried to kill me by bringing me here. Again. I should have known better than to trust you."

"Then why didn't you leave?" Zendalia pushed, wondering briefly if logic was the way out of this one. "You could have left at any time, and if you're feeling better, then why not just go?"

"I don't know the way."

"Like you couldn't find your way out? You're resourceful,

Kaelin." Zendalia took a risk and moved her hand from Kaelin's, reaching up and touching the side of Kaelin's face. Her skin was warm to the touch, and the connection sent a shiver through Zendalia's body. "Why didn't you leave?"

"I can't see."

"Try opening your eyes," Zendalia whispered, a hint of amusement in her tone. "That might help."

Kaelin kept her eyes clenched, and Zendalia waited patiently to see that beautiful violet gaze. She longed for it, to see Kaelin's muscles relax, and her lips curl up into a smile again, to feel the touch of her webbed fingers against her hand, her body. Zendalia gasped. She raised her gaze, her lips slightly parted.

"Kaelin," she cooed. "Please look at me."

It took more time than she wanted, but eventually, Kaelin pried her eyes open. Relief flooded her at the sight of that pure purple. Zendalia smiled, brushing her thumb against the edge of Kaelin's chin. Her breathing deepened.

"I didn't abandon you."

Kaelin's eyes watered.

"I'm not like your people, and I know that sounds harsh, but I won't abandon you. I don't want to kill you, not now that I have my head on straight and I know what really happened." Zendalia leaned in, their faces moving in closer. "I promise you that I don't want to hurt you ever."

Kaelin nodded. "I was scared."

"I know," Zendalia murmured. "I didn't think it through, and I should have stayed until you were well enough for me to leave or for you to come with me."

"Did she listen?" Kaelin didn't move away, the tension between them sharpening.

Zendalia's stomach swirled, but this time it wasn't fear or guilt. It was entirely pleasurable. She'd felt this way before, with Soulara, with others, but as much as it was similar, this time was so different. Her tongue swelled as the thought entered her mind. It wasn't the first time, but there would be no mistaking it. Zendalia hitched her breath. "Soulara did. The family didn't."

Kaelin tilted her head into the gentle touch against her skin. She closed her eyes, but they weren't clenched, and it didn't look as though she was in pain. "Will you try again?"

"Yes. Soulara has the black box. I'm hopeful she'll find some way to make it work better." Zendalia leaned in, concern flitting through her in an instant. She'd never gotten an answer to one of the first questions she'd asked since coming home. "How are you feeling? Truly."

Kaelin opened her eyes again. "Well enough. The light is still bright, but my head doesn't hurt as much."

"Good." Zendalia's lips curled up. Her heart hammered away, the edge of Kaelin's fin brushing against the scales on her tail sending arousal licking like electricity through her. "Kaelin, I'm so sorry I left before you were ready."

"Forget it," Kaelin muttered, her gaze downcast again.

Zendalia would recognize that look of shame anywhere, and she despised it. Kaelin was strong and resilient, and she deserved the oceans.

"No." Zendalia shook her head, sliding closer and shifting her hand from cupping Kaelin's cheek to just under her jaw, but she didn't force Kaelin to look up. "No, I won't forget it."

"You should. I'm not worthy—"

"Just stop," Zendalia whispered, her voice so gentle that if they weren't that close no one would have heard her. "Stop thinking like that."

Kaelin's lips parted in surprise. She raised her gaze finally, locking her eyes on Zendalia's.

Zendalia grinned broadly. "You deserve the world, Kaelin. I wish you would believe that."

"You didn't believe it before."

"That was before I got to know you." Zendalia didn't move, scared that if she budged even an inch Kaelin would swim away. She didn't want that. The more she stayed there, the more she realized she didn't want Kaelin to leave, not when they were just figuring each other out. "Kaelin?"

"Hmmm?" Kaelin didn't look away, that steadiness exactly what Zendalia needed in order to make this step.

She hadn't been sure until then that this was what she wanted, that it could even be possible, but surely, she could find a little bit of hope in the storm that had found her, couldn't she? "I can't stop thinking about this."

Confusion swam in Kaelin's eyes. "About what?"

Zendalia paused, trying to decide if Kaelin was dense or if she just needed to be more specific with what she was talking about. To her it was so obvious, the attraction that pulled between them, and since they had traveled back to Reine, it had only gotten worse. Had she made it all up in her head? Taking a leap of faith, Zendalia held her ground instead of pulling away.

"Kissing you," Zendalia whispered. "Ever since we found that box, well, probably before then." Zendalia let out a light chuckle, a tinge of embarrassment sliding through her. "I've wanted it. I've wanted your lips against mine for an entirely different reason than breath."

Kaelin didn't tense. She lifted her chin, her lips parted, her pink tongue peeking out against them. Zendalia wanted to lean in and taste, to know what it would feel like with this intent. It would be so different, she knew that, but what would it be like? What would Kaelin taste like? Her body heated, her clit tingled, and her nipples hardened. Gods, she wanted this, and she'd gone from hesitating about it to full acceptance.

Finding Kaelin so small, so wounded, had been her tipping point. Zendalia never wanted to be the cause of that again. But she also wanted more. She sounted to see what connection held them so firmly, tied them together in a way that she couldn't let go.

Kaelin reached up, her webbed fingers trailing over Zendalia's collar bone. Zendalia's eyes fluttered shut, her breathing coming in quick rasps as she let Kaelin explore her.

She had never been touched so reverently before. It had all been quick fucks, pleasure, and getting off as swiftly as possible so they could do it again, but Kaelin took her time. The pads of her fingers brushed against the tops of Zendalia's breasts before raising back up to the side of her neck.

Zendalia was at a loss for words, wanting and needing more from this moment than simple touch, but she would take anything that Kaelin gave her. She held still, keeping her hopes firmly in place and her dreams right between them. Kaelin would either give in to the temptation or she would pull away—so long as she followed her heart, Zendalia would be happy with her decision.

"Kaelin," Zendalia murmured, her lips curling upward again. "If you keep touching me like that, I'm going to want far more than a simple kiss."

Kaelin's fingers hesitated for one brief moment before she continued her exploration. "A kiss isn't simple, especially between us."

"I'll give you that one." Opening her eyes, Zendalia met Kaelin's gaze. Somehow in the last few moments she had gone from meek to fierce. Zendalia wasn't sure what had prompted the change, what had pushed her to that confidence, but she loved seeing it. It melted her, gave her hope that she hadn't been wrong when she assumed, that they both wanted this.

"I fear they won't let me go home," Kaelin said, her voice wavering toward the end. "I'm banished, which means I'm not to find a new tribe to live with."

"Did they tell you that?"

Kaelin's mouth opened, but then she slowly shook her head. "No, they didn't specifically say that."

"I don't want you to be unable to return home. I won't jeopardize that."

The touches against her neck, the top of her chest, her collar bones became firmer and more confident. Zendalia was so tempted to lean in the last few breaths between them and take a kiss, but she resisted easily enough. This had to be Kaelin's decision.

"Zendalia." Her name was pure as it rolled off Kaelin's tongue, in the awkward phrasing that she had come to love with the hint of Kaelin's accent and unfamiliarity of the syllables. "What if I don't want to go home?"

She was about to answer when Kaelin's mouth was against hers. Kaelin's hand was wrapped around the back of Zendalia's neck, tugging her in close. Heat poured through Zendalia's body, warming her as she pressed in and took. If this was going to be the only kiss she got, then she was going to make it the best damn one she ever had. Threading her fingers into Kaelin's hair, she pulled Kaelin in closer, their chests brushing as the moment heated even more.

Zendalia swallowed, taking in a sharp breath as she kept their mouths together. This was pure, loving, so simple and yet so complicated. She ached at how much it would hurt for Kaelin to never be able to return to her tribe, for the pain that she would inadvertently cause simply by loving her. Clenching her eyes tight, Zendalia held on. She wasn't going to let go.

Their mouths moved against each other, Kaelin's tongue dashing out for the first taste. As soon as she had permission, Zendalia pushed in, sliding her tongue against Kaelin's, nipping at her lower lip, sighing into the touches. She fell down as Kaelin pulled her, her slighter form resting on top of Kaelin's. Kaelin's hands slid down her back and then up, nails digging into her flesh and dragging.

Zendalia gasped, pulling back slightly as her entire body shivered in anticipation. She wouldn't give this up for anything. Diving back in, Zendalia kissed Kaelin with raw desperation. Soulara had been right. Damn her for picking up on shit that way. Zendalia refused to slow down as she pressed harder, moving her hand down to cover Kaelin's breast and find her nipple, flicking it hard.

Kaelin grunted and broke the kiss, staring wide eyed up at Zendalia. "Not yet."

"Okay." Moving her hand away, Zendalia went back to kissing her. They had time—at least for now they did. What happened when Soulara figured out the box, when they finally convinced King Pregtox that there was an imminent threat, was something else entirely. For now, Zendalia would take what Kaelin so freely gave.

Kaelin broke the embrace again, her hands holding on tightly to Zendalia's back, wrapping around her as if she was her life source. Zendalia pressed her lips to Kaelin's neck, gently nipping at her skin before moving to the other side.

"My head is spinning," Kaelin stated, her voice clear instead of wispy like it had been.

Zendalia chuckled. "Normally I would take that as a compliment, but I'm betting it has something to do with the thin water up here and your lack of breathing for the last few minutes."

"Yeah." Kaelin's voice sounded so soft.

Slowing her teasing, Zendalia pressed her nose into Kaelin's neck and breathed in her scent deeply. She smelled like the earth beneath the sand, hearty and pure. Zendalia wasn't sure she would ever find anything else like it.

"Zendalia?" The drawl on her name was longer this time, and it kicked up fear in Zendalia's chest. "I'm dizzy."

"Come on. It's time to rest." Zendalia shifted off of Kaelin's long form to give her extra space to breathe. When she pulled back, Kaelin's companion was squished against the ground, but they looked oddly pleased—at least that was the sense Zendalia got from them. She narrowed her gaze at them before gripping onto Kaelin's wrist and pulling her up.

Instead of swimming off, she held her arms around Kaelin's shoulders to settle her before they moved to the bed of moss. Kaelin took deep steadying breaths, her eyes clenched tight. Zendalia did everything she could think of in the moment to ease Kaelin's discomfort. When Kaelin finally moved her nose into Zendalia's neck, that was her sign.

"I'm ready. I think, anyway."

"We'll go slow, I promise." Except Zendalia wasn't entirely sure if she was talking about moving to the bed of moss or if she was talking about whatever was between them or perhaps both. She tightened her grip around Kaelin's waist as they shifted and swam slowly back to the bed.

When Kaelin was settled, her companion curled up against her side and the vibrations started. At first Zendalia wasn't sure what to make of it, but when she saw Kaelin relax even more, she let it be for a bit. Settling down onto her side, Zendalia draped an arm across Kaelin's belly and tugged her in, so they were lying against each other.

"Just rest for now. Soulara works quickly, and she'll have a solution for the light soon."

Kaelin hummed, turning her chin to the side and somehow finding Zendalia's lips without opening her eyes. Zendalia gave in and kissed her again, the same comfort and rightness flowing through her that she'd found before. Instead of deepening the embrace, she pulled away.

"Rest, Kaelin."

"I heard you the first time."

Snorting slightly, Zendalia closed her eyes. Rest sounded like the perfect idea.

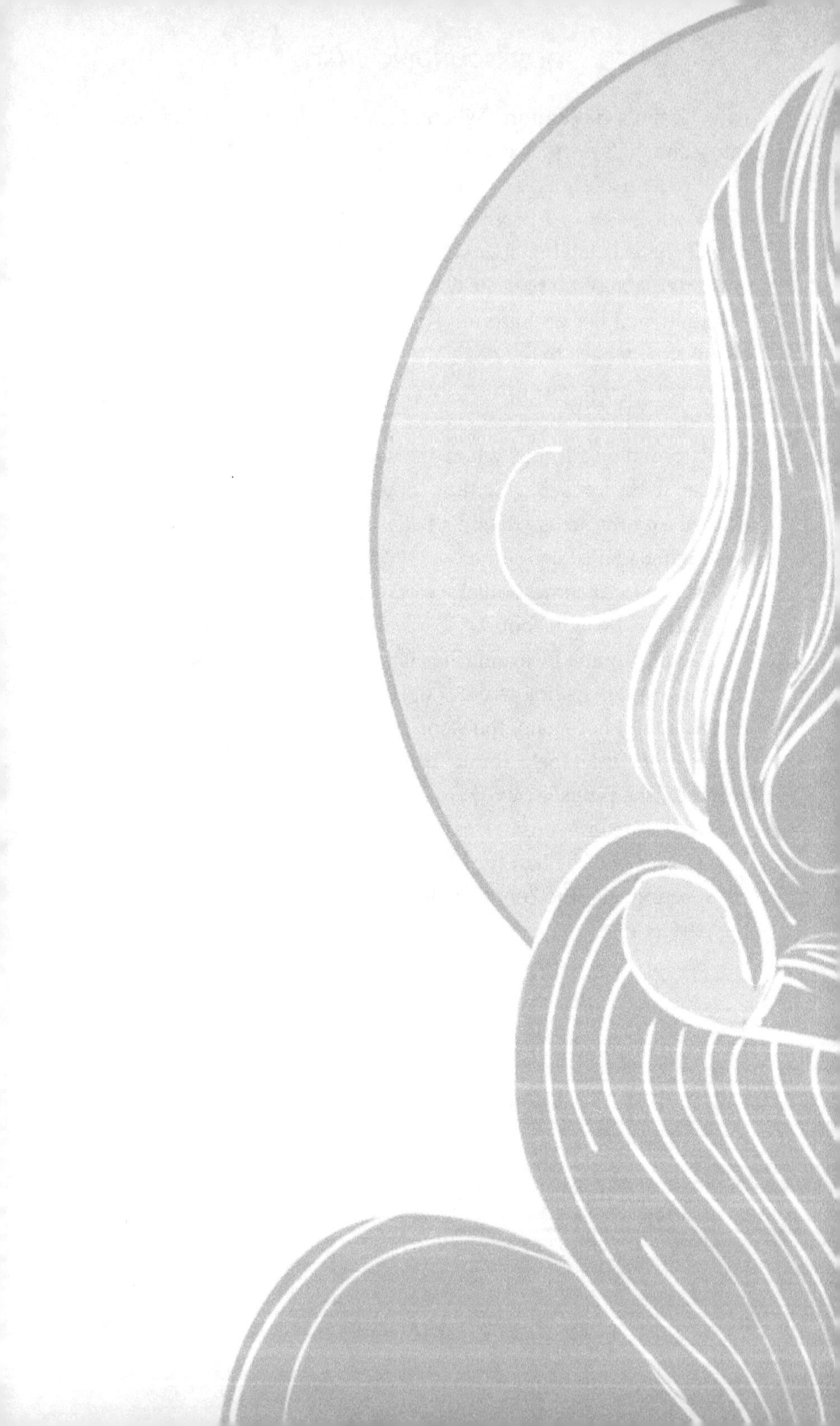

20

Kaelin woke with the warm pressure of another body half resting on her. The sensation was comforting while the pressure reminded Kaelin of exactly what she had missed during her seasons in exile.

She kept her eyes closed, turning her mind away from the more distant and sad memories to far more pleasant ones. She remembered Zendalia's kisses and how her body curled and curved on top of her. Kaelin's breath quickened, and her chest rose and fell a little higher and a little faster. Neyon vibrated against her skin, and she received images of the make-out session from the perspective of an amused and arrogant octopus. She wanted to scold the obnoxious jerk, but she stayed as quiet and still as she could, not wanting to ruin this moment before the pain returned and her inadequacies were once again brought to the light.

Besides, if she woke Zendalia now, the blush she could feel in the heat of her cheeks would be like bright lights in the deep soundings. Kaelin wanted to stop herself from thinking, from moving away from this perfect moment. But she had spent so many seasons when all she had were her thoughts, and they had just about mastered the skill of the deep overthinker.

Zendalia wriggled beside her, her tail brushing against some more delicate parts of Kaelin, sending her into another spiral of fast breathing and heated cheeks.

"Z?" A voice called out from too close by, and all thoughts of having moments and touching Zendalia vanished.

"Zendalia," Kaelin whispered, searching blindly with her webbed hand to find Zendalia's shoulder and shake her. "Zendalia, wake up. Someone is here."

"Urgh, tell her to fuck off until at least third rise." Zendalia groaned and shifted against Kaelin, the movement rocking pleasurable sensations through her body.

"Third rise has come and gone." The voice had entered the room. It was so close, Kaelin wondered if she lifted her arm, would it brush the visitor? Or was it an intruder? Zendalia didn't seem disturbed by whoever it was.

"Fuck off, Soulara, I haven't slept properly for days. Let a bitch sleep."

Kaelin eased up slightly. So this was the infamous Soulara, the woman Zendalia had gone to for help, and royalty. She knew she should have some reverence, but she didn't. Kaelin stayed put, not sure whether to move or stay just yet.

"Oh, all right then." Something in Soulara's tone told Kaelin this wasn't over yet. "I guess you aren't interested in seeing the different pages of the little black cube."

"Pages?" The weight suddenly lifted from Kaelin's chest and tail, replaced by an instant coldness.

"Ha, thought that might get you up." Soulara laughed. "I'll go make myself something to eat while you two get, well… I'll be out there."

The silence settled, and Zendalia's gentle palm cupped Kaelin's cheek. Their lips met in a tender, warming kiss. Kaelin sighed, parting her mouth out of pure instinct to reach out and taste. Zendalia pulled away, and Kaelin forced her eyes open. She had to admit the pain was significantly more bearable with the additional sleep. Her gaze met the piercing amber eyes she was certain she had also dreamed about.

"Good morning."

"I would agree with that assessment." Kaelin returned the embrace, not wanting this moment to end or be disrupted by anything. She finally had found her tail and felt that she could give as good as she got.

"If you fuck in there while I'm waiting, I'm not only going to record the sounds for posterity to show that whales aren't the only loud ones, but I'm also going to take this to the family now and get all the credit for myself," Soulara called from the other room.

Kaelin's face burned, and her eyes widened.

"I'm sorry. She's a princess and doesn't really understand what manners are." Zendalia leaned in for one more kiss before pulling away fully.

"I heard that," Soulara singsonged

"I meant for you to," Zendalia replied in kind.

"I guess that means we need to get up?" Kaelin winced at the very thought. The last time she had tried to get up on her own, she'd barely made it off the floor. She was still lightheaded, but at least the dizziness had stopped making her feel as though she was in a vortex.

"I'll help you."

It took a little longer than Kaelin had wanted and each subsequent minute of still not having it sorted out made her blood pump harder. They made it to where Soulara lounged, and Kaelin finally got her first full look at this stunning mer. Her hair was a silvery white, her eyes like ice, and bright. Kaelin had to squint to see her fully, but there were dark streaks that ran down the sides of her neck and over her shoulders, widening as they made their way down her body to her navy-blue tail. Of all the mers Kaelin had seen in the upper soundings, she'd never seen one with quite this coloring.

"Finally." Soulara opened her arms dramatically as she rose from one of the moss-covered stones, but there was a sparkle in her eyes and a quirk to her lips that Kaelin couldn't help snickering at.

"Whose side are you on?" Zendalia muttered to Kaelin.

"I'm not sure yet. I'm waiting to see what this mer has to offer." Kaelin smirked, though she suspected she looked more like an inebriated squid.

"Oh, I like this one, Z." Soulara gave Zendalia a wink before stopping in front of Kaelin, offering her hand. "Hi, I'm Soulara. Pleasure to meet you."

"Hi." Kaelin hesitated. There was so much touching casually offered with these people, and Kaelin wasn't certain how to handle it. Even in the tribe, touching was not something mers did so readily. She took a deep breath and touched Soulara's hand.

"Oooh, webbing." Soulara stared at their clasped hands, mesmerized by Kaelin's differences. Unlike the way Zendalia looked at her, Kaelin had the distinct impression of being a scientific curiosity, not something beautiful to be admired. "So you must be from the extreme deep soundings."

A look crossed Zendalia's face as she stared at her friend, a look Kaelin didn't understand.

Wait, beautiful? Kaelin had never felt beautiful in her life. Was that truly how Zendalia made her feel? Her head spun a little at the thought of unpacking that one.

"Soulara, I've not had anything to wake me up properly, and you're already being a jerk to my guest."

"I'm not." Soulara pouted, and Kaelin laughed, unable to entirely dislike this woman who, if the ease of their conversation was anything to go on, had known Zendalia a long time and in a capacity Kaelin was certain she didn't want to know the details of. Or did she have to know for peace of mind?

"So, did you get it working?" Zendalia steered the conversation.

"I did!" Change of topic accepted, Soulara held out her other hand to reveal the small black box.

"All right, show me the magic."

"I can't."

"What?" Zendalia snapped.

"It only works in certain places. That's why it didn't work when we tried to show the family."

"What the hell kind of tech only works in certain places?"

"A very special kind of tech, that's for sure." Soulara beamed down at the box as though it were her child.

"All right, well if it's not going to work here, why didn't you just send someone to fetch us?"

"Oh, because of these."

Kaelin hadn't noticed the goggles hanging from Soulara's arm until she grabbed them and held them up triumphantly.

"Are they them?" Zendalia asked.

"Yep." Soulara nodded a sharp single nod, her eyes radiating pride. "Prototype number three."

"Three?" Zendalia's eyebrows rose.

"Hey, I had very little to go on, but I'm certain these ones will work." Soulara held them out toward Kaelin.

Kaelin cocked her head, trying to examine the strange, twisted metal with two round holes. She didn't particularly understand them, but she wondered if they were waiting for her to try?

"Are they for me?"

"Of course." Soulara beamed, and Kaelin wondered what would possess this royal to help her.

"It's okay," Zendalia chimed in. "I trust Soulara with my life. Let's try them on."

Kaelin took the item dangling from Soulara's finger, careful not to touch any skin to skin. They slid on easily, and Kaelin blinked at the sudden darkness the glasses offered. Kaelin felt like she was seeing through a layer of old thinned seaweed, and she'd never smiled so easily. At least not in the last few seasons.

"These are amazing."

Soulara clapped, making happy noises that might have been words, but Kaelin didn't understand a thing that came from Soulara's mouth.

"Okay, so why again can't the box open here?"

"Because I'm not sure how long it's battery will last, and this way you can talk to the family immediately."

"Wait, you want to take us back to the family and open it there? What if it doesn't work again?"

"Trust me, it will." Soulara's confidence in herself and her work was just about to blow Kaelin's mind. "Time to move it, kiddies. I can't wait for Makryn get a hard-on once he sees what's inside this baby."

"Do you want to come with us or stay here?" Zendalia asked, and Kaelin felt the warmth in her cheeks once more. How could such a simple question make her feel like she had more worth up here as an individual mer than she had ever felt seen in the deep soundings?

"I am coming with you," Kaelin answered, more confident than she realized until she heard the strength in her own voice.

"Excellent, let's get our fins flapping."

Kaelin didn't know what to expect as they made their way out of Zendalia's home. Several mers bobbed around, some even tried to pretend they weren't interested in the convoy of merwomen leaving their cave. The world outside of Zendalia's suddenly exploded in size.

Kaelin flinched at the colors that while dulled, still seemed far too bright, and waited for the pain to sear through her head. It didn't come. She laughed, and the other two looked at her, Zendalia with a smile tugging at the corners of her lips and Soulara with knitted brows. But neither asked and Kaelin offered no explanation.

Everything was so alive and vibrant around them. And mers, there were so many mers swimming around doing their thing.

Sure, as soon as they noticed the three, they stopped what they were doing and stared at the odd group.

The swim itself was slow and sparking with electricity between the three of them. Kaelin's impatience tingled at her skin, the pain wanting her to get things done, and the fear of the goggles only working temporarily rested heavier on her shoulders then Neyon did. Her lungs however were grateful for the slow pace. The water was so thin, and if she looked at her companions too quickly her vision blurred, and the world seemed to tilt as dizziness overtook her.

When they made it to the castle neither of her traveling companions had to tell her. The place did not belong in Kaelin's world of the sea. Bubbles larger than the tribe's entire camps clumped together, so many of them Kaelin couldn't begin to count them. Her mouth gaped, and she didn't care. How could they have such a large construct, permanent and obvious, and not have any creature threatening them? The idea seemed entirely alien.

"It's okay. Surprisingly you do get used to it," Zendalia said, her fingers brushing ever so slightly over the back of Kaelin's hand.

"I don't think so." Kaelin smiled and wondered if it looked as deranged as she felt.

Both Zendalia and Soulara gave small chuckles, but Kaelin felt no hostility or mocking from either, and that alone helped her relax as she followed them through a gaping hole and between two mers dressed all in shining metal which reminded her of the goggles she had attached to her face.

In silence she followed, her mind trying to take in the colors and details that changed with each turn of the corridors. It was overwhelming, though after three turns she could see a kind of beauty in the delicate designs and patterns. Some of the paintings on the walls even reminded her of her own cave wall, and the loss was a knot in her chest once more.

"Let me speak." Soulara's gaze flicked over Kaelin and seemed to bore into Zendalia as they stopped outside a large metal plate, more of the armored men standing guard.

"Fine." Zendalia finally conceded, and Kaelin pressed her lips together, stifling a chuckle.

21

The room was silent while Soulara set the box on top of the table with a small dome over the top of it. She hit a button on the dome and then moved her hands into the bubble to press the buttons on the black box. Zendalia held her breath, curious as to what exactly Soulara had figured out about the box that was so interesting and would be enough to convince King Pregtox that they needed to do something about it. She had no idea what they could do, though. Fighting the kraken had been outside of anything she had trained for.

"Quiet now," Soulara ordered.

The water in the room stilled. Zendalia reached out for Kaelin's hand, holding it firmly in her own as she held her breath. Kaelin moved closer to her side, the warmth of her side fins brushing against Zendalia's. She wasn't going to give up being this close to Kaelin if she could help it. What they'd begun to find together was more than she expected, but it felt so natural.

The box opened. Pregtox's jaw tightened. Makryn glared at it. Zendalia held her breath tightly in her chest. This was the moment. Without this, she wasn't sure how they'd be able to convince Pregtox to listen to them.

"This is where the kraken is." Soulara pointed to the red dot that appeared on the map. She glanced over her shoulder at the two of them.

Kaelin swam forward and pointed to the map itself. "This is the ocean floor where my tribe is located. Right here is where we settled for the winter seasons, but we had to move when the warmer waters came in."

Zendalia kept her mouth shut and let the two of them explain everything. Perhaps that was the best way to do this, only answer questions when asked and let those who had more pull be the ones to try and convince him.

"And here." Soulara hit another button and the image projected changed. "Is an explanation of what they're doing."

Pregtox leaned in. "You know I can't read this garbage."

Soulara snorted lightly, pointing her finger along the first page. "It's a manual for a machine, Daddy. The machine is designed to collect water and siphon it somewhere. I haven't figured that part out because there's some degradation in the device, and I suspect it's an older device."

Degradation. That word rang through Zendalia's ears. She hadn't thought about that, or how old the box could truly be. All she'd wanted was to prove that her father had been right, that his ideas weren't outrageous, and that the royals needed to listen to her. "I've seen what it can do with my own eyes."

Kaelin shot Zendalia a look of sarcasm. True, Zendalia hadn't been able to see well in the deep soundings, but she had been able to see enough to know what was happening. Kaelin turned back to the table. "I've studied the kraken for seasons. My introduction to it was through Zen."

Zendalia's heart warmed at the mention of her father, and that he would get credit for this discovery, even if it was one that would lead to everyone's demise. He wasn't wrong, and that had to be enough for Zendalia to grasp onto. What happened from there on out wasn't something she could control.

"The kraken has been changing the entire system in the deep.

It's destroying the landscape, which is making it difficult to find food, but what I've been informed of up here is worse—at least for now." Kaelin straightened her shoulders, as if she was made for this. The confidence in her voice was something Zendalia had rarely seen from her except when dealing with the kraken issue. It was damn sexy, too.

"The water, Daddy. We can't ignore it any longer."

Pregtox blew out a breath, bubbles rising to the ceiling in the small room they were in. He crossed his arms, eyeing each of them and then landing his gaze on Makryn. "Leave us."

"But Father—"

Pregtox gave Makryn a hard look and was obeyed without another protest. As soon as he was gone, he turned on Soulara. "What do you know?"

"They're not lying." Soulara's eyes shone brightly. There was an undercurrent to the conversation that Zendalia knew she wasn't privy to. They were talking about something beyond the black box and Zendalia's story of the kraken. "It's real, and it's destroying the deep soundings."

Pregtox's skin sheened, sliding into a paler color before he turned his eyes on Zendalia and Kaelin. "Your people are aware?"

Kaelin stiffened. "They don't understand it, and for now, they have chosen to move rather than face the kraken. Probably wise, considering I don't think they would survive a direct attack."

Soulara put her hand up. "It's not a direct attack. They're siphoning our water and stealing it. They aren't here to harm us, although that *is* what they're doing."

"Who is *they*?" Zendalia leaned forward, hoping she would get some sort of an answer to the unasked question. Soulara and Pregtox clearly knew what they were talking about, but Zendalia was left in the dark, and she suspected that Kaelin was as well.

Soulara faced Zendalia, a slight shake to her head before she turned back to her father. "We need to speak with the deep sounding mers."

"You know how I feel about them."

"I do." Soulara put her hands on her hips, rising to her full form.

For the first time, Zendalia saw the connection that she'd ignored before. Soulara was sought after by many mers in their city, lusted after. She'd been lucky that Soulara had given her the time of day when she had, but it hadn't been because Zendalia had made advances. In fact, she'd treated Soulara like she would anyone with a brilliant mind and insatiable curiosity. But Soulara looked exotic, at least that was the word whispered around the back alleys of coral. Her tail had a darkening to it that no one had seen before, and it nearly matched Kaelin's in length.

"I won't let them die," Soulara stated, her fingers curling into fists. "We all descend from the same mers, Father, and it wouldn't do us well to ignore our family."

Again, Zendalia felt as though there was a conversation happening that she wasn't hearing. She raised her chin and looked Pregtox directly in the eye. "I'll go back down there and speak with them, see if they're interested in forming some sort of alliance or at the very least giving us information they may have that we don't."

Pregtox flicked his gaze from his daughter to Zendalia. He pointed at Kaelin. "She is from the deep soundings. She can give us what information we need."

"I can't." Kaelin shook her head, her hand in Zendalia's tensing. Zendalia didn't have to be any closer to see how fearful she had become. "I don't know more than what it's doing. I'm not a scientist like Soulara, and I'm not a warrior like Zendalia. I'm merely a mer who had a run-in with the kraken."

Zendalia knew Kaelin was skirting around the fact that she was banished, that she couldn't return even if she wanted to, and that despite her hopes that the elders would listen to her about the kraken issue, they'd sent her on her way to suffer alone. Zendalia's heart broke again at the thought, about the disrespect and undeserving punishment.

"I can go back down and see where it's at currently, but I'm afraid I won't be able to convince my people to give you information they likely don't have."

Pregtox stayed still, his hands at his sides, and that practiced glare pointed in Kaelin's direction. "I'll offer you asylum for what information you have."

Kaelin shifted, her shoulders rounding as she moved from confident to defeated. Zendalia parted her lips, looking directly at Pregtox. "Kaelin has given you all the information she has, freely, without request of asylum or payment. I promise you that she has nothing else to share."

"And you." Pregtox pointed his finger at her. "You shouldn't even be here. Your father—"

"My father risked his life to discover what you ignored, and it cost him exactly that. I'm here to take his place, to stay here until you listen to me. I'm not backing down because you think you have some sort of power over me." Zendalia's heart raced. She couldn't believe she had spoken to the king like that. Soulara, yes, maybe when they were in a heated argument, but never the king.

Pink tinged his cheeks, his eyes narrowing as anger was about to burst. Zendalia knew she deserved it. She'd been rude, and she'd disregarded any traditions they had about how she should treat him. But she didn't care. She was tired of him bashing on her father. Pregtox slid forward sharply, but Soulara moved between them, her hands at her sides.

All Zendalia could see was the back of Soulara's head, her long silvery hair swaying in the water from the sudden movement in the room. Kaelin pulled Zendalia back slowly, as if she was going to protect her. But Zendalia wanted to hold her ground. She wanted to stay right there and defend her father's honor and memory as much as she could. Her heart thrummed, ready for the next volley.

"Zen was brilliant, but he was also a very stupid mer. He defied my orders to remain here, and it cost him everything."

Pregtox looked over Soulara's shoulder at Zendalia. "Don't be so stupid as to follow in his path."

"My father wasn't stupid." Zendalia jerked forward, but Kaelin held her back, not only by the firm grasp on her hand but with the end of her tail wrapped around Zendalia's. When had that happened? "My father risked everything to prove to you that we're all in danger. And you need to believe him, because if you don't, you'll be the cause of all of us dying."

"She's right, Daddy." Soulara's voice was soft, gentle, pleading. "The pages in this box prove that."

"You know I can't read that."

"Then trust me, because I can. They are stealing the water from the deep soundings because it's exactly the chemical makeup that they need. They steal that water, and it lowers our water. I can almost see the surface from here." Soulara stayed between them, putting herself in the line of fire. "Trust me, Daddy. Let me do this."

Zendalia's heart was in her throat. She wasn't sure what they would do if he didn't agree with them, if he resisted like he always had about this issue, about anything to do with the lower soundings. Zendalia stopped, her lips parted in surprise.

"King Pregtox," Zendalia started, pulling Kaelin closer. "I think Kaelin needs to share her full story with you."

Kaelin's eyes were wild with fear.

"Because the lower sounding tribes share a history with us. We come from the same mers way back in time, and while we've gone our separate ways, we are still one and the same." Zendalia's chest tightened with nerves. "Kaelin has been on her own for many seasons, since my father died, and she doesn't have the most up-to-date information about her tribe. They may be amenable to discussions."

Kaelin interjected, her voice wavering with each word. "I was banished for murdering Zen, but it was the kraken. I wasn't able to save him."

"It's not her fault," Zendalia added. "And I don't blame her for it. We all know my father took risks for information, and this was no different than that. This time he paid the ultimate price with his life."

"Please listen to us," Kaelin begged. "The kraken is an enemy to our people."

The king frowned, looking each of them over. "I will permit you two to travel to the deep soundings and request more information."

"I'll go too," Soulara's voice was firm.

"Absolutely not." Pregtox crossed his arms. "You'll stay right here where I can make sure you won't be defeated by an enemy."

Soulara's shoulder tensed, her arms flung out to her sides, and the muscles in her neck tightened. Soulara was about to rage. Zendalia reached in and grabbed her arm, jerking her back. They couldn't risk Soulara's outrage turning the king's decision.

"Thank you. I'm sure Princess Soulara will provide me with more tech to travel."

"You'll take a convoy with you," he said, turning his back toward the desk with the black box on it. "Soulara, you'll translate this and get it to me as soon as possible."

"Yes, Father."

Kaelin tugged Zendalia closer, but they left the room quickly, Soulara following them. Zendalia grabbed Kaelin by the cheeks and kissed her hard. She wanted this to feel like success no matter how much they had been through. She knew they still had a long road ahead of them, but she couldn't stop the excitement that for once Pregtox had listened.

"Yeah, yeah, get a room, you two." Soulara's voice didn't have the same joyful sting it normally did.

Zendalia moved away from Kaelin and faced her ex-girl-friend. She'd heard that tone before, but she'd never been able to pin it down to exactly what caused it. "Did you really want to go with us?"

"I always want to go to the deep soundings." Soulara looked

Zendalia straight in the eye before shifting her gaze to Kaelin. "I wish you luck. Z, I'll have a new mask for you when you're ready to leave. It'll be with the alliance party. You'll leave in the morning."

"Soulara." Zendalia reached forward to touch her shoulder, but Soulara jerked back.

"I'll be fine." She swam away, dejected.

Zendalia grasped Kaelin's hand again, holding firm to the last strength she had and using it to keep herself steady. They didn't have time to make plans, and she didn't have time to find out what had crawled up Soulara's butt. They'd gotten exactly what she wanted, so she couldn't figure out why Soulara seemed so despondent.

"Give her some time," Kaelin murmured. "She made a stand today."

Zendalia turned her chin up to look into those violet eyes. "What do you mean?"

"I don't think she's spoken to her father like that before."

"She never wanted to be a princess," Zendalia commented, her eyes trailing back to where Soulara had once been. "But it seems she's working her way into that role, doesn't it?"

"Perhaps, or perhaps she wanted to see the deep. Its call is strong."

Zendalia's heart thudded before tearing. "It hurts not to be with them, doesn't it?"

"Every breath I take."

22

Zendalia led the way to her home, and Kaelin couldn't get herself out of her head. She couldn't go back to her tribe. She wouldn't be allowed in, and the king thinking that his orders had any weight with her people was laughable. The weight on her was heavy, and by the time they got to Zendalia's, she wasn't sure she could turn around and leave the next morning.

Kaelin wanted nothing more than to go home, but she couldn't see her people opening their arms and accepting her in—a warm welcome was absurd. Not before her banishment was over and not openly anyway. She would always carry that stigma with her. She would always be the outcast.

Shuddering, Kaelin swam her way to the mossy bed. She wanted to curl into a ball and stay there until they had to leave again. She wouldn't defy the king, but she also couldn't see it going according to his plan either. She swam blindly and pulled off the goggles Soulara had given her in the process, Neyon holding close to her hip. They were the best companion she could have asked for.

"Kaelin?"

She'd just managed to lie down when Zendalia's voice

reached her. She was so gentle and soft. It broke Kaelin's heart. She wasn't someone Zendalia could be happy with. She was an outcast, not allowed back into her own tribe. If her own people didn't want her, Zendalia wouldn't either.

"Kae." Zendalia's voice dropped, pity leaking through her tone.

Kaelin hated it. She shivered and clenched her eyes, turning her face into the soft moss. She couldn't stand to turn around and look Zendalia in the eye. To see the look Zendalia no doubt was giving her would fill her with so much shame she wouldn't survive the night. Kaelin clenched her eyes against the tears.

Zendalia's fingers trailed over her shoulders and down her sides. "Kae, look at me."

"I can't," Kaelin whispered. It was all for her own protection, but she knew Zendalia wouldn't see it that way.

"We just won. Aren't you happy about that? Pregtox listened."

Kaelin nodded, still keeping her eyes shut like the world depended on it. "I know."

"Then what's wrong?" Zendalia sounded so concerned.

Kaelin's heart sank because she was the cause of the worry. She couldn't control herself enough to make it through one night and work through her own demons without falling apart. The last thing she wanted to do was to show this side of herself to Zendalia—a warrior, someone who was far stronger than she ever could imagine being.

"Oh, Kae, talk to me." Zendalia pressed up behind Kaelin, wrapping an arm around her middle.

Neyon detached themself from her side and swam off. The emptiness that Kaelin expected didn't arrive because Zendalia was there, and that should have told her something, but she chose to ignore it.

"It went so well. Better than I expected. I'm sorry I made you share about the banishment." Zendalia stroked her again, those fingertips spreading in ways Kaelin's never could as they trailed back and forth against her skin. It was so distracting but also exactly what she needed.

Kaelin wrinkled her nose and focused on the touch, centering herself so she could answer. "It's not that. You were brilliant."

She could barely make it through the words without crying. Putting her fist up by her face, Kaelin worked hard to steady her breathing, to hold back the tears.

"Look at me, Kaelin."

She shook her head. Zendalia sighed and shifted again, moving slightly on top of Kaelin's side so she could look over. She took Kaelin's chin in her hand and turned her face upward.

"Please."

Swallowing hard, Kaelin pried her eyes open.

"What's wrong?"

"I never…" She sniffled. "…I never thought this was how I would go back."

"As a hero?"

Snorting, Kaelin shook her head. "I'm no hero, and the only thing I'm bringing them is news of a potential war, and outsiders."

Zendalia's features softened, her jaw going slack and her eyes closing slowly before opening again. "You may be bringing them news of an attack, but it's with reinforcements in tow. We're all in this together, finally, and they believe us."

"They believe you," Kaelin whispered.

"You don't think the elders will believe us?"

"I don't know." Kaelin frowned. "I'm not someone who held any position within our community. I was always just outside of it."

Zendalia moved her fingers, brushing them along Kaelin's cheek gingerly. "Kaelin, you've found a place in my heart. I know we haven't known each other very long, but I haven't been able to stop thinking about you since I found you."

"Since you wanted to kill me?" Kaelin raised an eyebrow, her lower lip poking out. "I don't exactly think that's a very good declaration of love."

"Love?" Zendalia's cheeks reddened, her eyes widening.

Kaelin bit her lip, a rush of embarrassment coming over her. She hadn't meant to say that. They were nowhere near that—at least, they shouldn't be. But Zendalia was right. The connection between them was stronger than she'd ever felt with anyone before, and that scared her. She wasn't worthy of that kind of connection, and she certainly wasn't worthy of anyone near Zendalia's levels.

"I don't know about love, not yet anyway, but I do know that I found you incredibly sexy today. You stood up to Pregtox, you held your ground, and you were confident in a way I saw you be when we were dealing with the kraken. That is *damn* sexy, Kaelin."

Except Kaelin wasn't that person. She never was that, and they were dealing with a crisis at the time. It'd been the only way to get through it, and afterward she'd closed in on herself.

"You're creative, artful, beautiful." Zendalia moved in, her lips brushing the edge of Kaelin's jaw in a light kiss. "Everything about you is a wonderful blend of beauty and mystery. All I want is to get to know you more."

Kaelin's breath was raspy when she dragged it in. Her chest rose sharply, her breasts bumping into Zendalia's. Her nipples hardened unexpectedly. She wasn't sure she believed everything that Zendalia told her, but she wanted to.

"You're much stronger than you know." Another kiss to Kaelin's jaw, then another against the underside. "You survived out there all on your own."

Kaelin swallowed, turning onto her back slightly. Zendalia floated above her for an instant before lowering fully down on top of her. The gentle kissing resumed. Kaelin pressed her hands to Zendalia's hips and held on. "Why would you want someone like me?"

"Because everything I have seen about you has caused me to

rethink my life. You never once hesitated in your goodness, and I do love that about you." Zendalia made her way to Kaelin's collarbone, the very same place she had been when they were kissing before.

Kaelin closed her eyes, remembering the feel of Zendalia against her then, the inciting touches, the tweak to her nipple. She gasped at the memory and just how much she had wanted it. Her clit tingled in anticipation. Pulling Zendalia closer to her, Kaelin swallowed a moan and slid her hands up Zendalia's back to her shoulder blades.

"I'm not the mer you think I am," Kaelin whispered, but it was next to impossible to hear her own voice over the thundering of her heart. "I'm not kind or good."

"You're honest." Zendalia breathed, the water moving against Kaelin's skin like a caress all its own. "You can't hide from your own honestly, and not once have you tried to hide from me."

Kaelin shivered. She tilted her chin down, locking her gaze onto those fiery amber eyes. They paused, holding the moment of tension between them. Kaelin had no idea what to do next, whether this was the right decision or not, but fuck, she wanted it. No one had touched her like this before, with a simple reverence like she was the most precious creature in the ocean.

"I don't know if we should do this." Kaelin moved her hand, skimming it from Zendalia's chest and over her full breast, against her hard nipple. She moved her thumb across the nub, back and forth. Zendalia hissed slightly, settling her forehead into the crook of Kaelin's neck.

"Then you better stop doing that."

Kaelin hummed, but she didn't stop. She kept the slight teasing, the tender touch, prolonging the moment as she processed her thoughts. Zendalia's breathing steadied, her lips brushing against Kaelin's neck in a gentle kiss. Kaelin had longed for this. She'd always wanted someone to look at her the way Zendalia had been doing in the last few days. She closed her eyes, palming Zendalia's breast fully and squeezing gently. Her clit throbbed, begging for someone to touch it, either herself or Zendalia. She hadn't felt this physically attracted to someone in a very long time.

"I don't want to stop," Kaelin murmured, opening her eyes as the decision reached her.

"Thank fuck," Zendalia said on a laugh, her kiss turning into a sharp nip.

Kaelin squeaked. Zendalia moved swiftly, her mouth against Kaelin's breast in an instant, her nipple pulled between her lips, and her tongue swirling circle after circle. Kaelin groaned loudly, her full hand on the back of Zendalia's head to hold her firmly against her chest. Her hips bucked up, starting a slow pattern in the water that she couldn't stop.

Zendalia groaned sharply, moving to the other breast. Kaelin held her with everything she had, her hips still undulating against Zendalia's. Each thump hit her clit underneath her slit. It was like heaven, pleasure soaring through her nerves and spreading throughout her entire body. She could only hope Zendalia was getting as much pleasure from it as she was. With a rasping breath, Kaelin shifted. She used all her strength and flipped them quickly, smooshing Zendalia between herself and the mossy bed.

Kaelin kissed Zendalia hard, their tongues moving together. She spread her fingers as far apart as they would go and trailed her hand down with a firm motion. Zendalia whimpered when she brushed over her nipple but didn't stop. Breaking the kiss, Kaelin slid down Zendalia's body. The brushing of their scales set her nerves on fire. Her heart moved rapidly as she nipped gently at Zendalia's breast. Her hand moved down to Zendalia's slit, finding it already slightly parted.

Using the edge of her thumb, she brushed the opening line of Zendalia's slit back and forth in a steady pattern while using her tongue wildly against her breasts. Zendalia cried out, her back arching off the moss as her eyes closed.

"Yes," Zendalia murmured. "Fuck."

Kaelin smiled to herself as Zendalia settled back down. Moving down her body again, Kaelin pressed kiss after kiss in a trail along her path. Her cheeks were flushed, her body ready for anything that might happen between them. She dipped her chin down, replacing her thumb with her tongue.

"Gods, what are you doing?" There was curiosity along with pleasure in Zendalia's voice.

Raising her chin up again, Kaelin looked at her until their gazes locked. Something in the question seemed so real, and that was confirmed in her look. "Using my mouth."

"You're what?" Zendalia breathed out, barely catching her breath.

"I'm using my mouth. Haven't you…?"

Zendalia shook her head. "No, we don't…oh gods."

She flung a hand over her eyes as she dragged in a solid deep breath. "Whatever you're doing, it feels amazing. I don't want you to stop."

Kaelin hesitated only for one moment, but when Zendalia snuck a second look at her, she glanced down at the bronze scales and blew water across Zendalia's slit. She was going to have to start again, and she was going to have to do this slowly. She hadn't realized their cultures would be that different in this way, but since they were, she was going to have to take her sweet time to make sure she did this right.

"Kae." Zendalia groaned, her hands reaching up above her head as she stretched out. "Gods."

Kaelin chuckled as she dragged her tongue across Zendalia's salty scales and back to the opening in her tail. She was going to enjoy this more than she originally thought, and that was something to be celebrated. This was the right decision. Kaelin used the tip of her tongue to tease Zendalia's body until she was open, until the nub of her clit shone brightly in the dim light of the room. Kaelin resisted diving straight for it and continued to tease around her, circling the one place she knew Zendalia would want her to go.

"Fuck," Zendalia murmured again, bucking her hips up before dropping them back down sharply. "Fuck, Kae."

Laughing, Kaelin sucked in a sharp breath and covered Zendalia's clit with her mouth. Her heart hammered in her chest, pleasure surging throughout her body as she listened to every sign from Zendalia that she was doing the right thing.

Zendalia jerked her hand down, clasping Kaelin's hair sharply and tugging hard. Kaelin pulled away, looking directly into Zendalia's eyes. "What's wrong?"

"Nothing. Oh gods, nothing, don't stop. I never imagined…" Zendalia swallowed hard, catching her breath. "…I never thought. Fuck, I can't think. Don't stop. Do that again. Do that— do that until I'm finished."

Kaelin grinned broadly, her chin resting on Zendalia's hip. When she didn't move fast enough, Zendalia tried to push her face against her slit. Chuckling at the insistence, Kaelin did as she was told. She sucked, she teased, she brought Zendalia as close to the edge as possible before backing away and slowing down, only to have Zendalia groan and whine before she started up again. When Zendalia finally couldn't stop, she writhed wildly under Kaelin, jerking up and holding Kaelin firmly against her as she cried out her release.

Continuing her sucking, her licking, her pleasurable torture but more slowly than before, and easing away, Kaelin smiled not only to herself but to Zendalia. Lazily she moved back up Zendalia's body, teasing gently here and there while she could before Zendalia pulled their mouths together and relaxed into the bed of moss.

Before Kaelin knew what was happening, Zendalia's hand was at her own slit, which was already parted and fully ready for whatever Zendalia was going to do to her. Zendalia nipped at Kaelin's lower lip and dragged in a deep breath.

"I have never experienced anything like that before. We don't use our mouths up here."

"Pity," Kaelin murmured.

"But we do use fingers." Zendalia slid two fingers inside Kaelin's warm opening, her thumb on Kaelin's clit. No one in the lower soundings could manage this position, not without another hand or a mouth.

Zendalia swished her thumb back and forth wildly. Kaelin's hips jerked as a lightning bolt of pleasure shot through her. She understood now exactly what Zendalia had experienced, the pleasure of something new, something exciting, something that was so different from any other experience that she had nothing to compare it to. Kaelin gasped, digging her fingers into the moss and sand underneath it to hold herself still and above Zendalia while she rocked up and down.

She pressed their mouths together hard, the kiss brutal and messy. She could barely catch her breath before the rapid movement pulled her through an orgasm that ricocheted throughout her entire body. Her skin was alive with touch and pleasure, with hope and dreams that she could ever experience something like this, not once and maybe never again.

Collapsing against Zendalia's chest, Kaelin closed her eyes and took deep gulping breaths as she calmed down. She caught her breath, shifting to lie next to Zendalia on the bed of moss and stare up at the water above them.

"We should definitely do that again." Zendalia laughed as she spoke, her hand curling around Kaelin's in a gentle embrace.

"Yeah," Kaelin answered, not sure what to say. She wanted that to happen again, but at the same time, she was pretty sure it never would. Her heart still hammered in her chest as she tried to catch her breath, as the dizziness from overexerting herself in the thinner waters took over her head. She shouldn't have done that, at least not without slowing down first.

Zendalia turned into her side, pressing a kiss to her neck. "I really liked that."

"Me too," Kaelin answered, closing her eyes against the spinning water. She couldn't help the thoughts raging back into her mind, of what to do and what was going to happen next.

They were going to leave in the morning, and she would have to face her tribe. She'd have to beg for them to let her in and not turn her away just so that maybe they would listen to her. The lump in her throat grew instantaneously, and it hurt. Zendalia settled against her side, holding onto her arm and nuzzling her face into Kaelin's shoulder.

"That was amazing," Zendalia whispered.

Kaelin wanted to agree. She wanted to tell Zendalia everything she was feeling from the last of the pleasure rippling through her to the worries that berated her, but she couldn't form words. Instead, she closed her eyes and held back everything. Zendalia wouldn't care about that stuff anyway, not in the long run. They wouldn't be together much longer. As soon as Kaelin had her people on board, she would return to her banishment and Zendalia would come back to the upper soundings. They would go their separate ways and that would be that.

Blowing out a slow breath, Kaelin closed her eyes and swallowed. They fell into a comfortable silence for what seemed like hours. When Kaelin opened her eyes, half the day had passed. She shifted, moving away from Zendalia slightly.

"Where are you going?" Zendalia asked, noticing the change. Her eyes said everything, and Kaelin very nearly leaned in for another kiss.

Pursing her lips, Kaelin said the only thing she could think of. "We should get ready to leave."

"Kae…" Zendalia trailed off.

Shaking her head, Kaelin pushed herself up and grabbed the goggles Soulara had given her. "We don't have much time."

"We should talk about this," Zendalia pushed.

"No," Kaelin responded, sadness filling her chest. "There's nothing to talk about."

"Are you ashamed by what we did?" Zendalia's voice rose.

Kaelin stopped sharply. She shook her head, looking deeply into Zendalia's eyes. "Nothing about what we did is shameful."

"Then what is it?"

"We need to leave soon. It's a long journey to reach my people."

"Kaelin—"

"No." Kaelin put the goggles on. "We have a lot of preparations to make."

Zendalia touched Kaelin's arm. "I want to talk about this."

"Not now. We'll talk when we travel. Right now, we need to prepare." Kaelin didn't give Zendalia another chance. She moved out of the bed and into the other room, grabbing anything she could think they might need.

23

It had been less than two weeks since Zendalia last left Reine to find her father's killer, but this time couldn't have been more different than if she had been an entirely different mer. Instead of anger and revenge squeezing her heart, hope and euphoria buoyed her.

She had wanted to talk to Kaelin, find out what had happened that made their night together become an awkward interaction this morning. But she knew better than to bring it up while the two of them were surrounded by a convoy of her king's soldiers. And to be honest, she had grown more excited about this adventure as time had ticked down. The convoy had shown up not long after the frantic collection of items from Kaelin had settled into a calmer distracted conversation about needs and what they might expect going back to the deep soundings.

She reached over and took Kaelin's hand, her fingers stopping at the top of the webbing. Such obvious differences, and yet last night had been the most incredible sexual experience of Zendalia's life, bar none. Heat warmed her cheeks, and she squeezed Kaelin's hand harder. From the corner of her eye, she caught Kaelin's grin.

"Not sure why you are so proud of yourself." Zendalia smiled, belying the sting of her words as she lifted Kaelin's hand to her mouth and kissed it.

"Oh I know exactly why I'm proud of myself, and don't worry, I can teach you how to use your mouth for a lot more than that." Kaelin spoke so low Zendalia was certain no one near them could hear, and yet still she spluttered at the unexpected directness.

Kaelin laughed, bubbles floating up over her beautiful curvaceous body, dissipating as they reached the fins of her tail, and Zendalia breathed a little easier. No matter what was happening in Kaelin's mind, whatever had shut her down, Zendalia could wait and give Kaelin the time she needed.

The thought hit Zendalia like a zap from Kaelin's companion. Blinking, she stared at the backs of the mers ahead of them.

She wasn't scared about waiting, that didn't scare her in the least. What scared her was losing Kaelin entirely and waiting for her warmed her heart instead of freezing it. She knew she could wait lifetimes for Kaelin, but since when? She had never been good at waiting in the past, not for anything. Not with any previous relationships, not with exacting her revenge for her father's death. Waiting now seemed the most natural thing in the entire ocean.

"Where did you just go?" Kaelin asked, her voice soft and husky.

"I'm not sure you want to know."

"Really?" Kaelin dipped her voice down, doing all kinds of crazy things to Zendalia's clit, making it twitch and pulse in memory of last night's pleasure.

"Not that." Damn, if Zendalia didn't get control of herself, her cheeks would light up all the deep soundings.

"Oh." Kaelin's head dropped forward.

"I adore you, Kaelin." The words almost stuck in Zendalia's throat, though she didn't know why. She could hazard a guess, but it couldn't be that the words weren't enough. Not enough to express her feelings, not enough of the truth that throbbed in her heart.

"I like you too, Zendalia."

The words were sweet, they filled Zendalia with a warm relief, but they also sliced a little into her heart, carving out a chunk that was raw and bloody. She sensed the *but* that Kaelin didn't say.

"Hey." Kaelin smiled, and the worry that still clung at the edges floated away from Zendalia's mind. "I really like you, Zendalia, and I can't wait until we make camp tonight."

"Really?" Zendalia smiled back. Now was all that mattered, and she would take whatever this brilliant angelfish offered her.

She nodded to herself, fingers reaching for the stone around her neck. The sensations washed over her, feelings of adventure and rightness. And such clear images of Kaelin, ones Zendalia had never seen before. Zendalia squeezed her eyes shut against the images in her mind. They made no sense, and right now they were heading into dangerous territories. She had to keep her mind clear and her focus on the task at hand.

"Really." Kaelin looked at her from beneath half-lidded eyes, making Zendalia's core clench and her slit shiver. Zendalia had never been so grateful for the armor that wrapped around her chest as her nipples hardened.

"Unless you are up for an audience, you are going to have to stop looking at me like that." Zendalia leaned in closer to Kaelin, their fins brushing, sending bolts of energy through her scales.

"Ahem." The false cough came from too close to Zendalia's other side, making her flinch, a very different kind of heat rushing through her chest and spreading down through her arms and up her neck.

"Yes?" Kaelin asked, a small squeak ended the word.

"We are nearing the first league into the middle soundings." General Honour was strong and fierce. Her fluke was slightly wider than Zendalia's own but still narrower than Kaelin's. "I would suggest you consider putting on your mask shortly, Zendalia."

"Oh, of course." Zendalia's pulse thumped at her wrist as she pulled the newest mask Soulara had given her over her face. Only then did she look around and realize that this woman, the leader of the convoy, was the only one of their people who had yet to don a mask.

"Will you also be putting your mask on?"

Honour tilted her head, a small smile tugging but not quite successfully pulling up the corner of her lips.

"You needn't worry about me. I have never faltered in my duties to our king. I will don my own when necessary. Perhaps not until after we make first camp."

Zendalia could have sworn Honour gave her a small wink, but it was entirely too fast for her to be certain.

"Did she hear us talking? Is that what she just hinted at?" Zendalia turned to face Kaelin as they continued their down-ward trajectory in the water, her smile dropping and the chuckle that had worked its way up from her stomach stopping like a bubble pressed against her chest. The mask couldn't help her with this kind of breathing problem.

Kaelin's face was as still as dead coral, frozen and serious.

"I think so." Kaelin's voice was as cold as the chill Zendalia remembered too clearly of the deep soundings.

"Are you okay?" Worry etched through Zendalia. She had seen Kaelin pull in on herself more and more as the day wore on, and she desperately wanted to pull Kaelin out of that black hole that she was drifting so dangerously close to. But they hadn't known each other long enough, and Zendalia was at a complete loss as to how to do that.

"Of course." Kaelin faced Zendalia and her lips curled upward, but it held nothing compared to the smiles she had given Zendalia before they were interrupted. "I just haven't been through here when I've been able to see."

Zendalia mentally cursed herself. It did make sense for

Kaelin to be intrigued by the world around them, but it rubbed like sand caught under her scales. There might have been truth in what Kaelin said, but there was so much more than that on her mind. It was almost as though Zendalia could see the bubbles forming and popping behind Kaelin's eyes. It was a pure and simple excuse for what she was really feeling, and the question remained as to whether Zendalia would have guts enough to push for an actual answer.

Holding that tension, Zendalia watched as Kaelin swam next to her, chin down, shoulders drawn, and her hair trailing behind her beautifully, beginning to blend into the darker waters. Ultimately, she allowed Kaelin her quiet and found herself looking around at the beauty she hadn't noticed before, despite having been through here twice before.

With enough light still filtering through the water, Zendalia could see the life and beauty that teemed around them. Rocks shifted to reveal themselves as animals, tentacles thickening and thinning as they moved in darker corners that Zendalia's eyes couldn't penetrate. There were schools of fish that turned as one the moment they noticed the group of mer heading their way. Water rippled and tickled against her skin and tail, and she thrived on the adventure of it all.

As still as the waters were currently, anticipation built in her chest. They were really doing it. They were going to save their people because her father had been an incredible scientist, passionate about his discoveries and his people. If only he had been as passionate about his own life or his daughter's. That had always stung no matter which way she looked at it. Zendalia had spent most of her life trying to prove to him that she was worthy of his attention, and in the end, he hadn't cared enough to think about the consequences of his actions and the repercussions they would have on her life. The lump formed in Zendalia's throat, and she was suddenly grateful for Kaelin's desire for a quiet companion.

The convoy slowed their pace, and Zendalia wondered if any

of them bothered to look at the beauty around them. She was a warrior of her people, and she doubted she would have bothered turning her head if she were on this mission in that role, but in this capacity, she had been relegated to no more than a diplomat. The idea made her snort, which earned her a furrowed brow from Kaelin.

"Sorry, just thinking how much Father would have laughed thinking of me as a diplomat." For all she knew, he might have actually been proud of her for once. He'd been to her pinning ceremony when she'd completed her training, but he'd been less than lackluster in his support of her career decisions. Then again, he had always told her she knew how to fight dirty.

"Why?" Kaelin smiled. It wasn't quite the warmth Zendalia craved, but it wasn't as cold as her previous effort.

"You might not have noticed…" Zendalia's lips twitched as amusement floated through her "…but I may be a little bit of a hot tail at times."

"Only at times?" Lines formed around Kaelin's eyes and lips. She was trying, of that Zendalia was absolutely certain.

"Perhaps." Zendalia winked, knowing that her temper had gotten her into trouble more times than she ever cared to admit.

"Will you tell me more about him?"

The question knocked the breath out of Zendalia's lungs. That had been the hope she'd been vying for, and Kaelin had handed it to her so simply. "I will, but not right now."

"Okay." Kaelin reached again for Zendalia's hand and squeezed gently as she curled her tail sweetly around Zendalia's for just a moment.

They didn't speak as they crossed into the first league of the middle soundings. Their fingers & remained connected, though Zendalia suspected she was holding on tighter than Kaelin now.

Around her, life continued to swim, moving the water and keeping it warm against her skin and scales. A tension floated back to them as the convoy took in their surroundings. Most likely none of them had ever been this far down before, and

Zendalia's own curiosity raised its head as the water thickened around her. Without the adrenaline of righteous indignation and the fury of revenge, she was almost painfully aware of the changes in her body. Her tail slowed, heavier with each flap.

It was harder to keep up with Kaelin, and each stroke of her tail meant that she fell farther behind. Kaelin's hand tugged at hers, pulling twice in succession before she slowed and came to Zendalia's pace.

"Are you okay?" Kaelin asked, her voice quieter than when they had spoken of sex and pleasure.

"Just feeling the changes in the water." Zendalia couldn't quite describe the effects it was having on her. She must have ignored it before, but now in the quiet between them she couldn't feel anything but.

"Hmm." Kaelin nodded, concern lighting in her eyes, but at the same time, it seemed so far away, as if she wasn't truly thinking about that.

Taking a risk, Zendalia floated in closer, needing to know what was happening. "You know you can talk to me, Kaelin, about anything."

"Of course." Kaelin's fingers slipped out of Zendalia's hand, and though the movement was minimal, cold instantly seeped between their shoulders as Kaelin no longer pressed against her side.

"Kaelin." Zendalia hesitated, not entirely sure what she would say next. Desperation clung to her like a bad stench. "Please talk to me. Tell me what's going on."

"I'm going to go see if Honour needs any help with where to go."

"Honour." Zendalia wasn't sure if she repeated the name for herself or as a question for Kaelin.

"Yes." Before Zendalia could say anything more, Kaelin slapped her tail hard and fast, leaving Zendalia in a cloud of bubbles that tickled her skin and made her feel all manner of stupid, unsure about what had happened.

Alone with her thoughts Zendalia tried once again to focus on the mission at hand. Kaelin's distance kept interfering with her thoughts, and she hoped before they got to Kaelin's tribe she would be able to see Kaelin smile once more and perhaps break through some of the barriers that were appearing seemingly out of nowhere between them.

The world darkened around her bit by bit as the colors drained from the sea life they passed. Zendalia sucked at her mask as the water thickened. What she wouldn't have given to have it just be her and Kaelin, like it had been on the journey home.

"We are going to make camp shortly. I've helped Honour find a safe outcrop where we can all camp." Kaelin's voice was soft and gentle. And while Zendalia's breath eased just a little, a knot tightened in her guts hearing the tentativeness in Kaelin's voice.

"Our outcrop?" Zendalia tried to speak calmly but anger permeated the air around her.

"No." Kaelin's eyebrows furrowed, and Zendalia could almost taste the truth in the word.

"I'm sure the General is very grateful for your help." Why was she creating distance now? That was the last thing Zendalia wanted to happen, but she couldn't avoid getting defensive. She hated herself for it.

"At least I can help with something." Kaelin shifted as though preparing to swim away again.

"Please." Zendalia brushed Kaelin's arm lightly, wanting to grab her but suddenly afraid because of the strange fragility she sensed in her formidable lover. "Won't you stay with me?"

"I can't." Kaelin gave a small smile, one that didn't even come close to her eyes, though the sadness covered her entire face.

Zendalia didn't hold on or try to stop Kaelin again. She would wait until they made camp, and hopefully she could work through that distance and find Kaelin and that cheeky smile once again.

24

The campgrounds were ones Kaelin had used before, but they were not the small outcrop she had taken Zendalia to previously. Her chest had warmed at Zendalia's claiming the outcrop as theirs, but just as quickly, dread settled into the pit of her belly.

She shook her head and led Zendalia behind a natural coral growth, allowing it to act as a barrier between them and the half a dozen convoy members who had half-led, half-followed her this far into the soundings. Sucking her bottom lip into her mouth, she focused on helping Zendalia unroll the moss travel bed out onto the flattest part of the smaller area.

"We don't have to camp over here if you don't want." Kaelin wanted to break the tension, though fear gnawed at her. "Or if you would prefer to camp alone, I can join the convoy."

"Come here." Zendalia reached for Kaelin's webbed fingers, running her own fingertips over the webbing, tracing it between each finger, tip to tip.

Kaelin shuddered at the sensation but didn't pull away, though she knew she should. It would be hard enough for her to leave as it was, but they needed the tribal elders to listen. And she couldn't be a part of that. If only she could explain that to

Zendalia. If only Zendalia would listen instead of insisting Kaelin had been wronged by them. They were from two entirely different worlds.

"Hey, come back to me." Zendalia's voice was the perfect mix of soothing and enticing. She always seemed to know how to draw Kaelin back to her when she got lost in her own thoughts.

Kaelin raised her gaze, meeting those beautiful amber eyes in the moment they were in, a moment where fears and worries blended and mixed to the point she could decipher where they started or where they ended. "I'm here."

"Maybe." Zendalia traced a circle around Kaelin's temple, above the strap of her goggles. The touch was so tender, and Kaelin closed her eyes at it, reveling in the closeness she had found. "But up here, you keep going where I can't find you."

"I…" Kaelin opened her mouth and then shut it again. Shame rose inside of her, and she shoved out of Zendalia's gentle embrace. She didn't deserve it, the kindness or the affection. She most certainly didn't deserve the touch. Her movements became rigid as she went back to setting up the camp area. It probably would be a better idea for the two of them to sleep in separate areas that night.

"Kaelin?" Zendalia's eyebrows pulled together, while her eyes shone over the top of her face mask.

"You need to stop." Kaelin's voice wavered as she reached for the last of her resolve. She had to be the one to draw this line, to make it clear since at this point it was obvious Zendalia wasn't going to figure it out.

"Stop? Stop what?" Zendalia's eyes widened as she swam closer, her hands reaching out to touch.

Kaelin jerked away, her eyes stinging with tears. "Stop acting like this can ever work."

"What do you mean?" But the words came out hard and raspy, and Kaelin knew she had hurt Zendalia. The same pain squeezed her insides. But she had to do this.

"I mean, stop acting like there are feelings that go with the fucking." She forced the words out, powered by her own disgust in her weakness. She should have never allowed that to happen, but she'd been seduced by the closeness Zendalia gave her, the intimacy of touch and presence. That's all this was. "I needed contact. I was weak and stupid. I deserve my sentence, Zendalia. I didn't listen to your father, and because of me he's dead. He died suffocating while I carried him in my arms, not helping or listening to what his body screamed for."

"Stop." Zendalia's voice was hard, pushed between clenched teeth as she waved water from in front of her eyes that now looked red veined.

More proof that Kaelin was not a nice person. More proof that they should never have even started this. Kaelin was weak, and she wasn't someone who could be trusted. The king shouldn't have allowed her to lead them to the lower soundings.

"But you wanted to know the truth. Well, here it is. He clawed at my arms, and I shushed him. He looked at me with your eyes, and I looked away. I killed him. Stop acting like I'm innocent."

"You didn't kill him." Zendalia's voice was so obtusely calm it irked Kaelin.

"I did!" Kaelin fisted her hands and shoved them down to her sides, afraid she might do something stupid if she didn't get control of herself. Every time Zendalia pushed back on this one truth, it made it hurt even more. Kaelin breathed heavily, blowing out bubbles as she tried to calm herself by taking deeper breaths. It wasn't working. Everything about herself clashed with Zendalia. They had found a nice break and some calm in the middle of the storm, but now Zendalia had to see the real her behind everything—the coward, the murderer, the one who wasn't even welcomed by her own family. It was only Kaelin's weakness that made her ignore everything, made her crave the affection, the contact with another mer.

"You didn't kill him." Zendalia pushed herself back toward Kaelin and took her fist tenderly. "I don't know what's happened. Did Honour or the convoy make you feel like you shouldn't be here?"

Kaelin wanted to keep the rage in the center of her chest, but each passing moment made that more difficult than the last. Zendalia was so damn good at that. She hated it. Someone she had known for such a short period of time shouldn't know how to disarm her that easily. Taking a different tack, Kaelin settled herself.

"I don't belong here. You're arrogant assholes, your entire people. You think you can just send a convoy of warriors down into the deep soundings and think *my* people, *my tribe,* are just going to ignore our culture, our entire way of being to help you? You who left? You who abandoned your people? You're not better than us. And you won't change their minds."

Zendalia's eyes widened, her lips parting in shock. "I'm not better than you. I never thought that."

Kaelin scoffed. The calmness in Zendalia's tone made her want to scream, but it also stopped her raging. It felt as though they had flipped on each other. Kaelin was now the one so angry that she couldn't control herself, and Zendalia was the voice of reason.

The anger that burned inside of Kaelin threatened to engulf her at any time, and Zendalia, her little spitfire, simply held tighter to her hand and stared into her eyes. Zendalia, the only woman Kaelin foolishly let herself believe she could fall in love with, didn't move or flinch, simply stayed buoyed in front of her, staring. No, Zendalia didn't stare at her, she stared entirely through her, and Kaelin pulled her hand back with as much force as she could.

"I can't stay here. I am in exile. I'm not welcome to return no matter what. I have a sentence to live out, and that's what I'll do. Tell Honour good luck."

"What?" Zendalia darted toward Kaelin, but she easily avoided the reaching hand. "Kaelin, please no."

"I have to."

Kaelin didn't try to stop the tears or the sobs from escaping as she swam as fast as she could away from the campsite. She had chosen this spot for the convoy for one reason and one reason alone—the caves that were hidden in the darkness of the coral shelf nearby.

She swam for them, her tail beating against the water faster than she knew any of the convoy would be able to follow. During the travels, she had studied each mer. Without a doubt General Honour would be the closest to catching her, but Kaelin knew her own strength and power overtook all of theirs. Even while still needing to wear the goggles, she could find her way and hide out. Once there, she would catch her breath and thank the waters for her safety by being still and allowing her body to heal and rest.

There they were—just a few more movements of her tail and she would be in their protection. A smile, without happiness, pulled the corners of her lips upward. But before she could feel the coolness of the cave around her, Neyon appeared directly in her path, too close and obviously pissed off, tentacles thick and flicking.

Kaelin cursed and flung her tail as quickly as she could. She had to avoid them, because she knew exactly what they were going to tell her—that she was an idiot for running away. That being on her own in the depths of soundings she wasn't familiar with would most likely result in her death. That she'd made a mistake.

What in the seas is the octopus playing at?

Bubbles and foam frothed around Kaelin as she used all her strength to slow her trajectory, her powerful tail now in front of her moving against her previous path.

"Kaelin," Zendalia's voice was muffled from mask and exertion.

Kaelin narrowed her eyes at her small luminescent companion who appeared to tremble and vibrate, pleased with their efforts. She cursed them silently and refused to turn around and look. She couldn't bear to see what she'd done, how she'd hurt Zendalia. And she knew she had.

"Kaelin," Zendalia huffed out again as she came to a stop next to her.

Kaelin watched as Zendalia looked at Neyon and back to her, a smile spreading over her face. Great, now they really were ganging up on her.

"Thanks little dude." Zendalia poked her finger out toward Neyon, and their tentacle flicked up to touch the tip of Zendalia's finger with a bright burst of electricity as if giving her a high five.

Kaelin turned her eyes away from Neyon and focused solely on Zendalia. The warm anger that had fueled her words earlier had disappeared in an instant. Relief and sadness washed over her, mixed with a good old serving of the more familiar self-loathing that, other than Neyon, had been her only companion over the last few seasons.

"What do you want, Zendalia?" Kaelin had to work hard to keep her voice from wavering and her words strong. She needed to have resolve in this.

"Haven't you worked that out yet?" There was no anger or judgment in the words, but a rawness that grabbed Kaelin by the tail fins.

"No."

"I want you, Kaelin. You deserve to be the one to go to your people and tell them you have found a way to save them."

Kaelin had no words. She ground her teeth together, running her thumb along the tips of her fingers as far as the webbing would allow. They would never let her back in, not even for that. While she was banished, they had zero trust in her, and she must not have properly explained that to Zendalia. Bringing the convoy there would put her even more on the outs than before.

"Please don't leave us. We need you," Zendalia pleaded, her voice gentle through the sucking of the mask.

"You need me to find them, nothing more." Kaelin closed her

eyes, annoyed at her neediness and desperation. Of course that's what Zendalia needed. She didn't want Kaelin at all. Zendalia needed her for the mission.

"General Honour has an idea where it is, I've no doubt. But it would be easier with your help." Zendalia kept her tone light, and Kaelin knew she was trying to coerce her back to their makeshift camp for the night.

"I know."

"Okay? So you weren't just about to abandon us, to abandon me?" The tone in Zendalia's words had started light and teasing but there was something behind them, an edge of fear or perhaps it was pain that Kaelin couldn't quite put her finger on.

Kaelin shook her head, though that had been her exact plan after recuperating. She wouldn't help them if she didn't have to, but Zendalia had been faster than she'd anticipated, and Neyon's little barrage didn't help matters. It was her own wishful thinking to hope that Zendalia had ulterior motives for keeping her around, which told her everything she had thought at first had been exactly true.

"I just needed a swim to clear my head a little," Kaelin lied, unable to look Zendalia in the eyes.

Neyon's smooth vibrating touch on Kaelin's shoulder almost made her lose what little control she had remaining over her emotions.

"Kaelin, please talk to me."

"It's okay. I'm fine. Let's get back to camp."

Kaelin turned her back on the safety of her hidden caves and swam to the campsite. Zendalia tried another few times to reach her, to engage in conversation but gave up long before they made it to camp.

"You don't have to stay here with me." Kaelin reached the small moss bed she had helped Zendalia lay out earlier behind the coral barrier.

"Kaelin, please stop." Whatever emotions hid behind Zendalia's words made Kaelin do just that.

She met Zendalia's eyes for the first time and felt her own heat up with unshed tears. She wished it didn't have to be this way, that she was a mer who could love Zendalia for everything she was worth. Her past and her mistakes tainted everything going forward, and she needed to accept that. Zendalia had been a distraction, a physical connection, nothing more, and she had to keep reminding herself of that. Zendalia would never understand until they got to her home and met the elders. Until she witnessed them turning Kaelin away because of her crimes.

"I'm sorry, Zendalia." Several betraying tears fell from her eyes, warming the water in front of her. In a moment, Zendalia's arms were around her, holding her close, and Kaelin gave into her weakness once more, sobbing into the arms of the woman who made her forget what a worthless mer she was.

25

Zendalia missed the first signs that they were close to Kaelin's tribe. Kaelin had gotten quieter as they'd neared, but that was the only outward sign. It wasn't until Kaelin swam next to her and whispered something unintelligible that Zendalia realized they were nearly at the edge of the camping grounds.

"How many are in your tribe?" Zendalia's heart thundered. Honour had asked most of the questions, but she should have been curious about the situation they were swimming into.

"I imagine as many as in your tribe, but we're broken into factions to make it easier to move."

"Factions?" Zendalia should have known this before. She should have pressed more. Kaelin was right—they didn't know nearly enough about each other or where they came from.

Kaelin nodded and pointed to their left. "This is my tribe, the main one where the elders reside. We're the largest of the groups. The others live nearby, enough to get from home to home within a half day."

"Half day? I didn't realize you were so spread out."

Kaelin gave a half shrug, her lips closed tightly as they swam at a leisurely pace. Zendalia wanted to reach out and touch her hand, anything to make some sort of connection between them again. She knew Kaelin was nervous, but she wanted to be there so Kaelin could lean on her.

"When will we speak with the elders?" Zendalia asked, trying to get a sense of what was going to happen now that they were there.

Kaelin looked over her shoulder. "I imagine almost right away. They don't like outsiders, so the more swiftly they can deal with us the better."

It didn't go over Zendalia's head that Kaelin included herself in that group. She hated that Kaelin thought of herself that way, that she felt she deserved the punishment and exile at all. It hadn't taken much to shift Zendalia's thoughts on that, and she knew these budding feelings for Kaelin were part of that. Speeding up, Zendalia swam next to Kaelin at the front of the convoy as she led the way.

Now that they were closer, Zendalia saw the signs that merpeople lived nearby. Some of the rocks were moved, and the vegetation that grew this deep had been bent in certain places. If she put herself in a warrior's position, she was surprised she had missed the signs earlier, and she wondered briefly if General Honour had. She should do better if she wanted to move up in the ranks instead of being a peon.

"What are the customs with the elders?" Zendalia breathed out her question as though her entire life rested in the answer.

Kaelin shot her a sharp look, every muscle tight in her face. "They won't expect you to know them."

"But I would like to know them," Zendalia fired back. "So I can show them respect."

Kaelin hesitated, her body rigid as they continued to swim. She tilted her chin down toward the ocean floor, her goggles long since abandoned. As much as Zendalia appreciated being able to see into her gaze unobstructed, it was still a struggle to get a read on what Kaelin was thinking and feeling. She wished she was in the know.

"They'll know who shared that with you," Kaelin mumbled.

Zendalia was about to respond when she caught the electric blue lights from Kaelin's companion warming up. They were wrapped just behind Kaelin's neck, burrowed deep in her hair, but the warning was there. Shutting her mouth, Zendalia swam forward. They moved through the ridges in the ocean floor, between craggy rocks, until Kaelin came to a stop in the deep center. It was so dark that it was next to impossible to see, and she wished Soulara had been able to come up with goggles for her that did the opposite of Kaelin's. Being able to see would be a godsend just then.

"Wait here," Kaelin said, loud enough for Honour and Zendalia to hear.

Zendalia did as she was told, having to trust that Kaelin knew what was going to happen and would let her in on the secret as soon as they were there. The slam came out of nowhere. Kaelin's limp form shot back toward Zendalia, nearly folded in half as she flew through the water. Reaching up instinctively, Zendalia grabbed hold of Kaelin to stop her backward motion. When she took her next deep breath in, all she tasted was blood.

"Kaelin…" Zendalia's voice trailed off as she fluttered her fingers over Kaelin's face, trying to find the source of the injury.

Honour shot forward, putting herself between Zendalia and whatever was attacking. Zendalia's heart raced, and she lifted her chin up just as a light appeared in front of them, lighting up the face of what could only be an ancient mer.

"We come from Reine," Honour stated, her entire body ready for battle.

Zendalia cradled Kaelin against her chest even as she started to move and shift within her grasp. Her breathing was raspy as she tried to collect herself. Glancing to the rest of the convoy, she caught the formation they made around the two of them. Her body was tight with anticipation of what was going to happen next.

"Your people are not welcome here." The voice was fried

with age, and the words slow, that same rounding that Kaelin had in her tone every time she spoke.

"We have information about a threat to both our peoples," Zendalia spoke, needing to mend this, to make everything right.

In an instant, the ancient one was in her face, their noses almost touching. When the hell had they moved so fast? How had they done it? But from here, Zendalia could see the deep lines in their skin, wrinkled with age, the pure dark black of their gaze as they flicked it from Kaelin to Zendalia.

"She is banished from our people and not welcome."

"We needed her to show us where to go."

The ancient one snorted, looking fully into Kaelin's face. "We will add seasons to her punishment for this."

"What? No!"

Kaelin flipped over in an instant, her chin down as she slowly backed away with her hands folded together. As soon as she was out of sight, Zendalia knew Kaelin was gone, that she had swum and escaped from her home without a second glance back. Zendalia wanted to follow her, wanted to make sure she was okay and tell her that she didn't deserve the punishment at all. Reaching up out of habit, she grabbed the necklace and stone at the hollow of her neck. She was greeted with an image of Kaelin pistoning her way out of the clearing.

"You are the leader?" the ancient one asked.

"I'm the diplomat, yes." Zendalia raised her face, narrowing her gaze with a determined look. She wasn't going to let this go so easily. Kaelin deserved more than what she'd been given. It was out of desperation that Zendalia stayed put. She didn't have a choice right then. She had a job to complete, and the threat of the kraken weighed more than Kaelin's banishment and current injuries. The threat was real.

"Speak now."

"I would like to speak with *all* the elders." Zendalia would use this opportunity as best as she could, not only to speak of the threat but to fight for Kaelin—the mer she loved. She stuttered at that thought, the realization fully hitting her in an instant. She forced herself not to look over her shoulder as she stared into the ancient one's eyes. "I am Zendalia, daughter of Zen, and I come on behalf of King Pregtox and his people to bring you news of an imminent threat."

Zendalia's hands shook as she waited for some kind of response, some answer that they would be listened to. When she was greeted with silence, Zendalia licked her lips and started again.

"There is a kraken—"

"Our lost sister has confused you," the ancient one spoke.

Zendalia shook her head. "She hasn't. I've seen it. I've been attacked by it, but more important than that, it's stealing our water."

Silence reverberated through the convoy. She was sure no one had told her people why they were going down there. Zendalia clenched her fists tightly and moved forward a little, hoping that they would listen to what she had to say.

"We've noticed over the past year that the water level has fallen drastically. It's so bright in our city, but it's changing the entire ecosystem and it's killing our plant and animal life, or they are moving to seek better water."

"This is the problem with permanent residences."

Zendalia's lips parted in surprise. So they clearly knew more than Kaelin did about the upper soundings and their way of life. Swallowing hard, Zendalia straightened her shoulders. "Yes, it is, but that's what my people have chosen to do for generations, since our two tribes split from each other."

The ancient one didn't respond. The silence was deafening, and Zendalia did the only thing she could think of and continued with her explanation.

"The kraken is taking water from the deep soundings, however, not from us directly. It is stealing what you hold so holy and pure."

The ancient one frowned. "I see the banished child of ours *has* taught you something."

"Yes, she has." Zendalia would do anything to give Kaelin a leg up on returning to her people. She knew that was all Kaelin wanted, even if it prevented the two of them from being together. "Kaelin, a daughter of your people, has been very gracious with us, and she has done nothing but try to protect our people and save us from the detriment the kraken is bringing on us."

The ancient one hummed, and Zendalia hoped that it was a good sign, that her praise of Kaelin's actions was making some sort of dent in this thick mer's skull. Kaelin didn't deserve any type of punishment. Zen was dead anyway.

"If we don't stop the kraken, the entire ocean will suffer. We need to work together on this."

The ancient one looked from Zendalia to Honour. "Why would you bring warriors with you?"

"I am a warrior," Zendalia responded. "Though not as decorated as General Honour. I brought them by request of my king, but mainly for protection as we traveled here. We're not attacking you."

"Never have our peoples attacked each other." The ancient one breathed the words into Zendalia's ear, the intimidation tactic working. She was unpredictable, and nerves fluttered through Zendalia's belly. If this was the reign that Kaelin had grown up under, it was no doubt why she was so fearful of returning to her people.

The ancient one stilled, leaning back slightly as if her eyes caught sight of something. One single finger reached forward and touched the stone at the hollow of Zendalia's neck. "Where did you get this?"

"Princess Soulara fashioned it for me." Zendalia shivered, instantly seeing Soulara handing over the gift with a gleeful look in her gaze. It wasn't only a pretty bobble, but it had a purpose, one that she had shown Zendalia how to use. It was the connection to the familiar she kept with her always, the guide that was so angry for her coming down here.

"Do you know what it does?" her voice slithered, and goose-bumps ran along Zendalia's arms in response.

"Yes," Zendalia whispered, her entire focus on the closeness of their forms and the underlying conversation that no one else would know about. She had to wonder if this mer was psychic in some form, able to read Zendalia's mind and mood at a glance. She shuddered at the thought.

"And have they found you?"

Zendalia hesitated, but she decided to answer. Perhaps this would be the in that she needed with these people for them to listen to her. "Yes."

"Then you are worthy in our eyes."

"Worthy of what?"

The ancient one turned around and clapped her hands twice. Lights flickered on in the dark gully, lighting up all around them. Honour jerked with a start, but Zendalia stayed completely still, the ancient one next to her.

"We will welcome Zendalia, daughter of Zen, into our homes tonight, and we will listen to the stories she has brought to us from her people. She brings with her a gift most precious to our people—one of the souls returned to us."

Zendalia's heart raced, her hand clasped in the ancient one's as her fist was raised above her head. She had no idea what was going on, but it must be good. Honour moved in to flank her as protection now that they knew they were completely surrounded. She couldn't even begin to fathom what was going to happen next, and all she wanted to do was turn tail and swim away to find Kaelin. She needed to know that Kaelin was all right, that she was unharmed.

The ancient one leaned in close to Zendalia's ear. "We will feast tonight."

"But Kaelin—"

"Our banished sister will survive, and she will return to our people. I trust the waters will protect her."

Zendalia quieted down, not sure what to say next. All she could think about was Kaelin, and the desperate need she had to find her. But she was stuck here, talking with the elders, feasting, and making nice. She didn't have a moment to think about Kaelin when the ocean's life was in her hands. The only thing she knew was that as soon as she got a chance and once the elders were convinced of the imminent danger, she was going after Kaelin.

26

Zendalia's head pounded as she finally managed to slip away from Kaelin's tribe. She fought for every breath she took as her tail pushed through the water as though she swam through a sandy ravine.

"Zendalia." Her name was called from behind her, and she squeezed her eyes shut. Should she ignore the call or not? Her mind warred between the two options but eventually her duty to her own people won out. She slowed, pulling her tail beneath her and turning around as she now floated vertically, waiting for General Honour to reach her.

"Yes, General?" Zendalia clasped her hands behind her back, hoping that the movement of respect would shorten this delay.

"You tried your best. You have done a great service to both of our tribes."

"Yes, ma'am." Though none of that felt true. The stab of failure was sharp, and Zendalia wanted to wallow in her shame while she went on her way.

"Don't think of this as a failed mission. You have succeeded. I will be speaking with their general tomorrow and plans will begin to reunite our tribes against this joint enemy." Honour seemed so pleased, a light in her eyes that Zendalia hadn't seen on their travels there.

Zendalia nodded. She had no words she could say. Not ones that would hurry this interruption up, nor ones she could bring herself to say to a higher-ranked warrior.

"Pass my appreciation on to Kaelin when you find her." Honour smiled, softly, as though she were just any other mer. "I hadn't realized what she knew she would face when returning."

"I will." Zendalia didn't try to hide the thickness in her throat as she spoke. She hadn't fully realized it either, and bearing witness to the abuse Kaelin had faced at the hand of her leader shattered her heart.

"At ease, warrior," Honour's voice was gentle, the permission finally given to allow her to leave.

Zendalia breathed out as best she could and unclasped her hands with a small nod to the general. Her muscles relaxed for an instant before tightening again as the weight of her next task settled into her chest.

"Now go find your girl." Honour turned and left before Zendalia could truly process the words.

Zendalia watched as Honour swam back, her troop mixed and half-hidden among those of the deep sounding tribe. After Honour disappeared among them, Zendalia shook her head and closed her mouth behind the mask. The question was, how the hell was she going to find Kaelin? Her focus had been entirely on her diplomatic mission—well, mostly on that. But now that she had finally earned her time away from the tribe, she had no idea where to start.

Her heart ached as she allowed herself to think more about Kaelin and her reactions to all that had happened. No wonder she had withdrawn as they dove deeper into the soundings. Zendalia couldn't even imagine something similar happening back at home. I mean, her father had often been ignored by the king, and she had lived through the mocking years and the clashes with others. But to be forced out of your home and the love and protection of all that you had ever known. Zendalia was glad she hadn't allowed herself to focus on these things while she was surrounded by the very assholes who put her Kaelin through this.

Yes, she was *her* Kaelin.

She just hoped Kaelin wanted her.

She swam with no idea where she was going except knowing that she was following their trails and bubbles back the way they had come. It had only taken a few hours to get from the convoy's camp to Kaelin's tribe, and that seemed as good a place to start as any. Her father had taught her that. When you are lost, retrace your steps and take a deep breath—the rest will find you. Zendalia's chest tightened in a way it hadn't since she had truly gotten to know Kaelin.

As she swam, Zendalia's fingers rose to the stone at her neck. It was warm, almost pulsing, as her fingers curled around it. Had Soulara known the familiar the stone called was what the deep soundings tribe called souls? Did she know the history of what she had fashioned for Zendalia? Had she known it would be the tipping point in this peace treaty between the two tribes? If so, how?

Images from her familiar played across Zendalia's mind's eye. They danced around happily in front of her vision, tentacles swimming wildly in every direction. Then there was Kaelin, curled up in the back of a cave, tail pulled to her chest as she sobbed.

Zendalia's chest squeezed as though the emotions she thought she could have only imagined Kaelin going through were her own as well. She struggled to breathe, though the mask didn't squeal with that horrific portent of doom like the too-small, cracked one had.

A cave.

While relief floated at the edges of her thoughts, seeing Kaelin unharmed at least physically, the image didn't exactly help Zendalia in locating her. It was dark in there, to the point that Zendalia could barely even see beyond Kaelin herself, and certainly not outside in order to get a better view of where she was.

Pursing her lips, Zendalia slowed her movement. Was she even seeing Kaelin in the moment? This could so easily be something else, couldn't it? Zendalia dropped her hand and the image vanished from her gaze. Taking slow breaths, Zendalia looked around. It was hard for her to see in the deep soundings in general, the blurred water so dark that she couldn't make out much. It was dangerous for her to be out there by herself, and General Honour probably shouldn't have let her go.

They would both pay for it if something happened. Gnawing on her lip, Zendalia looked from side to side, her head pivoting as she dared to try and figure out which way Kaelin had gone. But there were no signs, not that she could see. No change in the water, no rocks that looked recently moved. And with the mask on, Zendalia wasn't able to scent her way through the waters either, at least not as well as she wanted to be able to.

She wished she could huff properly in this mask. It would have been so satisfying. She never thought of her huffs as a release of her frustration or fear, but it was amazing the little things she had been learning to appreciate. Shaking out her hands, Zendalia closed her eyes and focused. Where would Kaelin have gone?

She didn't know the deep soundings well enough to navigate this on her own. Just like before, the first time she had come down here, Zendalia reached up to her neck and touched the stone. On her shoulder appeared a little blue octopus, her best friend in all the waters. She smiled at them, her eyes crinkling in the corners.

"Are you still mad at me, little one?" Zendalia's voice wavered. This was the first time they had appeared to her since she had run into Kaelin the first time, and then they had been trying to deter her from seeking revenge. For the first time, she understood why. They must have known, somehow, that Kaelin wasn't the one to blame. Zendalia had been blinded by her own rage.

"I'm sorry about before." Her voice was muffled by the mask as she spoke aloud, but she had no other option. Her little blue friend understood her thoughts well enough, but this was an apology that needed words. "You were right, and I was wrong."

The little octopus straightened their tentacles out sharply as if to say, "Damn straight!"

Zendalia giggled, finding a lightness she hadn't felt in quite some time. She had missed her friend, and she was glad they were speaking to her again, though words weren't exactly the way they spoke to her.

"Do you remember that mer? The one I was trying to kill?"

A tentacle slapped against her cheek, except it went straight through her skin as she knew it would and no pain echoed in her body. They couldn't touch, separated by the distance of soul and mortal flesh. Zendalia had never managed to figure that one out, but Soulara had assured her that was how it was to be. Squaring her shoulders, Zendalia nodded.

"I know, I know. I don't need the reminder. But have you been lurking since then? She's amazing, my friend. Beautiful, stunning. She's so strong, and she doesn't even know it. Not just physical strength but everything about her. She's survived on her own when she shouldn't have had to."

Her companion interrupted her rambling praise by swimming out in front of her eyes and spreading all their tentacles out wide in a giant *stop* motion. Zendalia canted her head to the side, her tongue dashing against her lips as she tried to figure out what was going on. They didn't have the greatest communication, but it was better than nothing, and over the years of being together, she had learned she needed to focus in order to understand.

"What is it?" Zendalia's gaze rested on their form, knowing no one would be able to see their brightness.

The small octopus swam straight at her, their tentacles

pushing together into a point before they moved straight into the necklace at the hollow of her neck. Instinctively, Zendalia reached up and covered the necklace again with her hand, tightening her grasp. The image of Kaelin stole over her mind again, stark, cold, hungry for touch and love. Zendalia's heart thudded hard, and she knew she had to find Kaelin quickly. They needed to talk, and Zendalia needed to soothe the hurt that had been caused.

"But where is she?" Zendalia whispered, closing her eyes as a tear slipped from the corner of her eye, the image not moving from her mind. "I have to find her."

Deciding to keep a hold of her stone, she swam, hoping her familiar would alert her if she turned the wrong way. Zendalia pushed her tail through the water and swam as fast as she could. The hair on the back of her neck stood up as the water around her rippled, a wave followed by a distant rumble. It was so cold down here that goosebumps running along her arms and chest made it hard to focus.

Fear pierced through her chest, the long tentacle legs in front of her suddenly not ones from her best friend and familiar, but those that were much more dangerous. Damage would be done with this. Zendalia tried to hide the panic that wanted to burst its way up through her.

The kraken.

Pushing her tail a little harder, Zendalia focused harder on the images that now streamed through her mind. It had to be some odd connection between her familiar and Kaelin, or perhaps they were simply trying to help her get there faster to save them both. Zendalia focused on the images while also keeping her eyes wide open to the ocean in front of her so she could navigate the terrain that confronted her. Her familiar had slowly shown Kaelin closer and closer, so that Zendalia could see the dark bruises beneath Kaelin's eyes. Tiredness and pain squeezed Zendalia's heart without any sign of easing up.

"Come on, help me find her. Please," Zendalia begged her

familiar, now fully understanding why she'd never been able to touch them. If they were a soul, that should mean their physical form was somewhere, shouldn't it? The knowledge had shocked her, to learn they were souls, while not surprising her nearly as much as she would have otherwise expected. Perhaps she really had always known.

The image in her mind changed, a path showing in front of her from a strange perspective, buoyed with the occasional flick of dark seaweed that blocked strips of the image but never for long. Zendalia had to pause for a moment to sort through it all and her memories, as she tried to recall exactly where the place was.

Zendalia's heart lightened, though her tail muscles ached from the extra exertion. She would find Kaelin, and she would tell her everything. The lightness disappeared. She would tell Kaelin what exactly? That she loved her? She had never told anyone that. It was not a word she knew well and had rarely ever uttered it in her life, even to her father. It had never even been a consideration where it concerned Soulara.

She shook her head and forced away the panic threatening to consume her because underneath that panic was a serenity she had never experienced before. Fear in that moment, in handing that power to someone else, was natural, but at the same time, this was absolutely right, and she wouldn't do that for just anyone.

As she rubbed her thumb over the stone once more, a familiar fluorescence took over the scene as the trail ended at the large opening of a cave. Zendalia stopped swimming, hovering in the water beside the same features that floated in her head. To the right was the same jagged boulder, shorn in half by a force that made Zendalia shudder, and to her left three oval weavings of coral, as though they were eggs waiting to be hatched.

She was in the right place, except in front of her stood a wall of darkness. There was no cave mouth, and no path leading into it. The image in her mind flickered again, filling with Kaelin's face devoid of any of the light Zendalia had grown to love. This couldn't be the end of the path. Zendalia wouldn't accept that.

"Oh Kaelin," Zendalia whispered and gently moved herself forward. She would find a way through this wall, through this barrier, even if it was the last thing she did before the kraken consumed her.

Her familiar had never led her astray, though she doubted the opposite could be said. She had to trust, just as she would have in the upper soundings. Kaelin was worth it.

"All right, help me out here, yeah?"

The cave bloomed up around her once she moved forward. A warmth floated around her, and as she swam a little faster, she could now see the change around her, the darkness of the cave walls that enveloped her.

Zendalia stopped short as she rounded the last corner. She blinked, and blinked again. Her fingers trembled against the stone she still held on to, but nothing would make her give up that grip. She doubted even death would have that amount of strength and power against her.

She cringed as her mask made her breathing sound like a scream inside the contained area.

27

Kaelin looked up, her heart thundering wildly as she gaped at the intruder. Her eyes adjusted quickly, and Neyon left her side, swimming to Zendalia. As much as she welcomed the sight of Zendalia in front of her, she was utterly embarrassed by what had happened, what she had known was going to happen. Zendalia's features softened, and she swam forward, stopping right in front of Kaelin.

Flicking her gaze just over Zendalia's shoulder, Kaelin focused on Neyon. They were a betrayer. Kaelin knew it deeply in her soul. Neyon had left her for Zendalia, and while they were fond of both of them, Zendalia would win out over her like everyone else did. She never stood a chance.

Slowly, Zendalia turned her head and looked to her right, right where the octopus floated, flickering lights across the dark bare walls as electricity zapped between all three of them. Kaelin was about to swim away while Zendalia was distracted, slide right by her and escape out of the cave's entrance. It was the perfect plan.

"Neyon?" The word slipped from Zendalia's lips on a soft breath.

Kaelin's head shot back to where the two of them floated, her

261

eyes wide with shock. She hadn't used Neyon's name once when Zendalia had been around. It was strictly forbidden to share her companion's name with anyone. She hadn't fucked that up too, had she? Rolling through every memory she had with them, Kaelin struggled to remember where she had messed up, where she had broken yet another rule and shared what wasn't hers to share. She cowered down again. The penance she would feel from this one would be worse than anything. They would take Neyon from her and leave her completely on her own to fend for herself.

Zendalia reached her hand out, and Neyon wrapped around her wrist and arm, their bulbous head settling into her palm.

"How do you know their name?" Kaelin accused. She wasn't going to take the blame for this one.

Zendalia's amber eyes flicked to Kaelin. The water rushed from Kaelin's lungs in a sharp exhale as recognition hit her. Neither of them had known. Zendalia's lip trembled. "My necklace…when we arrived at your tribe, she said my necklace was one for souls. I didn't understand what she was talking about. Soulara gave it to me as a gift so many years ago, but…is their name Neyon?"

"Yes." Kaelin's voice trembled with uncertainty. Her hands shook, her chest constricting. What the hell did this all mean?

Zendalia's gaze narrowed, focused on the octopus as her face formed into a glare. Kaelin was taken aback by it. Zendalia reached up and touched the stone at her neck, the one Kaelin hadn't seen her without in all the time they'd known each other. She'd honestly assumed it was some bobble that Zendalia refused to let go of, perhaps something her father had given her.

Zendalia rubbed the stone firmly with her thumb. Kaelin listed forward, her curiosity getting the better of her. Zendalia reached out sharply with her free hand and snagged Kaelin's, bringing it toward the necklace. Kaelin was so unsure of what was happening. Anxiety twisted in her stomach, nerves ratcheting up.

"What are you doing?" Kaelin whispered.

"Do you trust me?" Zendalia's eyes met Kaelin's, a firm and serious look in them.

Kaelin's lips parted, her heart in her throat. She couldn't form words. Instead she nodded her answer, hoping that she would get some sort of conclusion swiftly. Zendalia took her hand and brought it to the stone at her neck. They both held on to it. It vibrated under their touch, the stone warming and heating unexpectedly. Kaelin shivered as the heat moved through her body.

Blinking, Kaelin swallowed before opening her eyes again and blowing out a breath. A small ethereal octopus swam in front of her vision, right next to the real octopus in the cave. They spun around each other, their tentacles not quite touching as they danced in the water.

"What's going on?" Kaelin breathed out.

"I think my Neyon is your Neyon," Zendalia whispered. "I had their soul with me, and you had their physical form. This is them being reunited."

"I don't understand. All the legends..." Kaelin trailed off, unable to tear her eyes away from the beautiful homecoming in front of her.

Neyon shot toward Zendalia, tentacles still spread wide as they wrapped around Zendalia's arms and torso on impact. Their soul followed, melting into the body so they both burned an even brighter blue than Kaelin had ever seen before. It removed any last lingering doubt that might have resided within Kaelin, the image in her mind and the sense of home was so overwhelming.

"They're the same." Zendalia grinned and laughed loudly, bubbles exiting the mask over her face.

Kaelin had to swallow the lump in her throat. "The legends our people have told for years were true. I always doubted them. No one has seen their companion like this in more generations than I can count."

"Since the split of our peoples?" Zendalia asked.

Kaelin nodded shyly. "Yes, I think so."

"Did we take the soul stones?" Zendalia sounded almost sad. "There's so much history that we don't know."

Kaelin wasn't sure how to respond to that, how to pull down the rest of the veil that shadowed them. She jerked her hand back sharply, remembering why they were there, why she had swum and hidden, and why she had thought about sneaking beyond Zendalia while she was distracted. She needed to leave. The added time to her punishment was going to add too much to her soul, and she couldn't live without Neyon. She would die before they took her companion from her.

Kaelin backed away, her shoulders hitting the edge of the cave wall. Zendalia's eyesight was bad enough that if she moved far enough away, she would be rendered invisible. That had to be it. She had to get out, take Neyon with her if they would come, and she had to escape.

"Neyon says you're scared," Zendalia's voice was so clear, so precise. "That you're afraid they'll leave you or be forced to."

The lump in Kaelin's throat lodged, getting stuck and making it impossible for her to swallow. Kaelin backed even more into the wall, her entire tail and body plastering against the sharp rocks. "You can speak to Neyon's soul."

She knew it wasn't going to explain anything, that she had to dig deeper for words to express what she was thinking. Then again, Zendalia had access to all of Neyon now, so she should know it.

"You can speak to Neyon. They're whole now," Kaelin murmured, remembering the tall tales from when she was a child.

Zendalia's head whipped around, their gazes locking. "We're not whole without you."

Kaelin crumbled, her heart thundering in her chest. She wouldn't let herself believe those kind words. She didn't deserve them.

"Kaelin," Zendalia started, coming closer. Neyon glowed

brightly against her skin. "Having this stone was a turning point in negotiations with your tribe. It's what allowed them to trust me, but I never would have known how to speak to them without you. I wouldn't know what to say or even what the threat was. Them not listening to your story is a disgrace to all they hold holy."

Kaelin didn't want to cry. She wouldn't allow herself to break down, not again. She just needed to get out of there. She needed to hide and find herself a new place to hunker down and stay for the duration of her banishment. "They aren't my tribe."

"What?" Zendalia cocked her head. "Of course they are. They're your family, your home."

The light in Kaelin's eyes died, that light she had struggled to hold onto for so very long. She shook her head slowly, feeling coming back to her hands and fins.

"They aren't my tribe anymore. I'm...I'm not going back to them." As soon as the words left her lips, Kaelin knew they were true. She hadn't allowed herself to think or say it before now, but being kicked out again the way she had, she couldn't go back there. They would never welcome her home. They would never be her home again.

Zendalia inched forward, and Kaelin put her hand out to stop her.

"They don't deserve someone as incredible as you," Zendalia whispered. "But you do deserve a home where you are loved, where you are applauded for your abilities, where you are honored for who you are."

"How can you still think anything like that about me?" Kaelin asked, buckling down to the reality of the situation she found herself in. It hurt so much to admit the truth of her reality, but at the same time, the pain floated away into the water around her, and it didn't find her again like it normally did.

"Because I got to know you." Zendalia's voice was almost placating, and it irked Kaelin. "I've seen you face your fears to help a stranger who tried to hurt you. I've seen you ignore the pain of your own body to help another. I've seen the light inside of you, and so has Neyon. They will never leave you, and if you'll allow it, I won't either."

"I don't deserve it."

"Kaelin," Zendalia's voice broke. "I tried to argue for your banishment to be reversed, or at least shortened. I tried to use the knowledge that Neyon had given me to change their minds."

"But they won't let me return, will they?" Kaelin's eyes dropped to the floor of the cave, the full force of the situation hitting her. There was no hope in her tribe. The family that had raised her treated her like she was dead to them—her own parents, all of them, did the same.

"No. Your exile is still in place." That same sadness that was there before edged its way back into Zendalia's tone.

Kaelin nodded slowly, coming back to the realization she'd had moments before. She wouldn't ever be welcomed home. She wasn't the lost child that would change anything about who they were. She was doomed to live exiled from her home, whether it was apart from her people or among them, and the latter would be much worse than the former. Her punishment was never going to end, was it?

"Thanks for trying anyway." Kaelin gave the saddest smile, but that strength she'd found before in truth solidified within her.

"It doesn't mean a thing to me, Kaelin," Zendalia pleaded, coming in even closer as she reached out to touch Kaelin's arm.

Kaelin jerked away. "Of course it does."

"No, it doesn't." Zendalia nearly screamed, her frustration evident. "I wish you had been born in the upper soundings, and then maybe you would understand what's been done to you by your people is barbaric."

"We aren't barbarians!" Kaelin's need to defend her entire life was too strong to resist. She wouldn't let Zendalia disparage her entire people just because of one situation.

"Perhaps not, but this practice of exiling your people, when home is your tribe, is barbaric. It's a deathly tradition that I will eternally thank the king's predecessors for abandoning when our tribes split. I can't..." Zendalia trailed off, her voice softening. "You don't deserve it."

"Why?"

"Because it's cruel and unnecessary, and you did nothing to warrant it. You're not a murderer."

Kaelin froze. Their gazes locked. She'd never seen someone defend her before, not like this, not this many times, not in front of her entire tribe. No one had come to her aid when she'd been presented to the elders. No one had argued for her sake. "I'm not sure I believe you."

"I'll take that over blatant disbelief." Zendalia's lips cracked into a smile. "Will you return with me?"

Kaelin blew out a breath, stretching out her hand. Neyon moved from being wrapped around Zendalia's middle to climbing up Kaelin's arm and perching at the back of her head where they normally resided.

"No." Kaelin smiled, a half chuckle escaping her lips. "My place is here."

Zendalia growled. "Let's rest a bit and discuss it in the morning. Surely, we're safe enough from the kraken here?"

Kaelin glanced toward the entrance to the cave. "For now."

"Good." Zendalia moved in, pressing their lips together firmly. "Let me hold you while we sleep, please?"

Kaelin nearly told her no, nearly told her to leave outright, but they did need rest, and they needed time before Kaelin could bring her back to the convoy and slip away again. Nodding her assent, Kaelin took Zendalia's hand and led her to the back of the cave. She would form a new plan to make everything right while Zendalia slept.

But for now, she would allow herself to enjoy the moment, to believe in the fantasy of them being together in the future.

28

Zendalia's eyes fluttered open, and for a moment, fear wrapped its icy fingers around her heart. Darkness permeated her surroundings and blood thundered through her ears.

Breathe, just breathe.

The words repeated as a mantra through her mind, slowly easing her heart back to a manageable pounding in her chest. Darkness continued to wrap around her so she closed her eyes and focused on what else she could sense. Her body ached, as though stuck in the same position for too long. How long had she slept? No, not her—how long had *they* slept?

A smile spread across her face. The beat of another's heart pulsed against her chest.

Her fingers danced gently down Kaelin's back, the rise and fall of her body indicating she was still sleeping. Zendalia lifted her other hand up and wrapped her fingers around the stone. Instantly light danced on the back of her eyelids. Fluttering her eyes open, she looked at Neyon, and her mind might as well have exploded again. She wasn't entirely sure what it all meant really, but she wasn't sure understanding it really mattered. All she knew for certain was that they had chosen both her and Kaelin and she wouldn't ignore the will of the water gods.

"Oh shit." Kaelin's words burst from her as she pushed up and out of Zendalia's half embrace.

"Good morning to you, too." Zendalia grinned, sure Kaelin could still see her clearly despite the half-formed silhouette Kaelin now became as she put distance between the two of them.

"I fell asleep." A panic radiated from Kaelin's voice, and Zendalia rose, unsure what was happening but positive she wasn't a fan.

"Isn't that the point?" She tried to smile, but the panic she gleaned from Kaelin's face by Neyon's glow dropped any more attempts at lightness.

"Yes, but no." Kaelin swam back and forth in front of Zendalia, but Neyon rested on her shoulder, ensuring she remained at least partially lit, no doubt for Zendalia's benefit. "Oh this is all wrong. Everything is wrong. Since the moment you found me."

"Everything is wrong?" Zendalia asked, feeling the scrunch of her features.

"Oh no." Kaelin stopped pacing and shook her head. "Not you, you're amazing. I'm wrong."

"What?" Zendalia chuckled in her confusion. "You're perfect."

"I…" Kaelin sucked her bottom lip into her mouth and like a weight the truth landed on to Zendalia's shoulders.

"You were going to run again, weren't you?" The gut punch was harder for her to bear than she'd initially thought it would be. The strain in Kaelin's face, the worry and fear, but also the immense guilt that consumed her.

Their eyes locked, and for a moment, Zendalia begged every deity she had ever heard about, whether she believed in them or not, for Kaelin to tell her no. Instead, Kaelin dropped her eyes and lowered her head. The confirmation, though silent, was all she needed. If this was how the future was going to go for them, it would wear her out.

"You were going to run just like you tried to last time. You lied to me about running, didn't you?" Zendalia didn't really need the answer, she had always suspected it. "What do I need to do to show you how amazing you are?"

"It's not your job to show me anything." Kaelin's shoulders were tight, and by that point, Zendalia knew she was trying to be confident when she wasn't.

"You're right." Zendalia now swam to Kaelin's drooping form. She wanted to be calm, but anger and pain raced beneath her skin, filling her veins with a heat the colder water down here could never achieve. "But I don't care. They've broken you, and I won't just sit back and let you believe it. If you don't want to be with me, fine, but I won't—I won't—let you think you're not worth any of this." Zendalia gasped, struggling to pull in enough of the oxygenated water filtered through the mask.

"Zendalia, you need to calm down." Kaelin's voice was suddenly strong.

"I can't." Zendalia gasped more and more. "I need you."

"You don't. The technology replaces my only use to you, but you have to calm down."

"No." Zendalia ripped the mask from her face and with her last breath pushed the words out, "Technology doesn't compare to what you give me, and I would give all of it up in a heartbeat."

"Zendalia." Kaelin's voice rose, panic dancing over her face as she fumbled for the mask Zendalia pulled from her reach. "Please, don't be stupid. I'm not worth it. Please put the mask back on."

Zendalia shook her head back and forth slowly, her lungs screaming for more water, more oxygen. But she didn't put the mask back on. Not even as Neyon floated to her shoulder and slapped her with a thick tentacle. Kaelin had to understand her, and it wasn't about the threat of not being able to breathe, it was about making sure Kaelin saw all of her, saw it in her eyes, her face, and heard it in the words she said.

With a growl Kaelin raced forward, webbed fingers gripped Zendalia's shoulders as she pulled her in for a kiss of life. Oxygen rushed into Zendalia, and she breathed deeply, her lungs inflating and easing the pain she hadn't even recognized she felt.

"What are you doing?" Kaelin pulled back a little, the fire leaving her words just enough for Zendalia to smile in return.

"I need you more than I need breath." Zendalia's heart thundered, knowing this was the moment between them that neither could escape. She was willing to put everything on the line for Kaelin.

"You're only saying that because your brain nearly died," Kaelin said, but a smile played on her lips and her eyes shone with unshed tears that Zendalia knew without a doubt were happy ones.

"No." Zendalia tucked a strand of the dark indigo hair behind Kaelin's ear. "I'm saying it because it's true."

"Please put the mask back on." Kaelin's fingers brushed against Zendalia's arm, the touch tender and soft, awakening even more sensations through her than were there before. She wanted this, and she was pretty sure Kaelin did too, if she could only get out of her own damn way.

"What if I don't?" Zendalia stared into Kaelin's eyes, lifting one side of her lips into a smile.

"But..." Kaelin's furrowed brows smoothed as she understood Zendalia's meaning. "Oh."

"Hmm?" Zendalia asked with a raise of her eyebrows.

Kaelin nodded, the smile spreading farther over her lips before she pulled Zendalia back in for a mix of passion and life breath. Their mouths touched, lips pressing together firmly as water rushed from Kaelin's lungs into hers. Zendalia's eyes fluttered shut as she held onto Kaelin with everything she had.

Zendalia pulled Kaelin in closer, hands on her back with

fingers firmly pressed, nipples brushing nipples as her short nails did their best to dig into Kaelin's skin. They clung to each other, not just for life so Zendalia could breathe, but because they were everything to each other.

"Ahh." Kaelin called out, pulling away from Zendalia's lips. Her chest heaved as she stared wide-eyed at Zendalia.

"I'm sorry, did I hurt you?" Sudden concern filled her, and she wanted to see if she had done any damage to Kaelin's perfect skin.

"No." Kaelin's face flushed, and she shook her head back and forth slowly. "Definitely not."

"You're so sexy." Zendalia buried her face into Kaelin's collar bone, nipping at the skin and feeling heat pool in her core when Kaelin gasped in pleasure at the sensation.

"You need oxygen," Kaelin managed after a few minutes, panting.

"Soon." Zendalia made her way to Kaelin's other side, caring more about her lover's enjoyment. But she couldn't help but feel the pressure building behind her slit as her head became light and floating. Either way, if she pushed the boundaries of how long she could hold her breath in these deep waters, it would make everything that much more pleasurable.

"I want you so much, Kaelin. All of you. Your body, and your mind, and everything that you are." Zendalia panted into Kaelin's ear as their flukes pushed together, slits brushing in a shock wave of pleasure.

"I'm not worthy of you." Kaelin groaned, her fingers digging into Zendalia's arms, holding her close, no doubt because she feared for Zendalia's very life.

Zendalia's eyes watered from the pressure in her chest, her body on fire as it begged for her to breathe, but she wasn't ready yet. Kaelin needed to hear what she had to say. Locking their gazes together, Zendalia whispered, "I'm not perfect, Kae, but I am yours, if you'll have me."

Kaelin's hands were on Zendalia's cheeks in a heartbeat,

slamming her lips against Zendalia's. The sudden rush of oxygen mixed with Kaelin's tongue as it pushed into Zendalia's mouth caused a small explosion of heat to consume her. Moaning, Zendalia's mind wrapped around the sensations swimming through her, the waves of hope and touch that she lived and breathed for.

"I need you." Zendalia moved her lips against Kaelin's, drawing the kiss into her realm of control. Kaelin deserved as much pleasure as she could possibly get from this, from knowing that Zendalia wouldn't leave her, that she was loved. Her heart clenched at that thought, the fullness of realization coming around. She didn't just care for Kaelin—she was absolutely in love with her.

"Yes," Kaelin replied, keeping their lips in contact as her fingers slid between them and found Zendalia's slit.

Zendalia pulled her face back, craving that lack of oxygen she never imagined could heighten any experience, let alone sex. Zendalia groaned, a wild sound that might have scared her if she had heard it in a dark cave alone. But with Kaelin, she knew she would always be protected, she would always be warm and safe.

"You're amazing," Kaelin whispered as she slid her fingers into Zendalia's slit and pulled Zendalia's right nipple into her mouth.

Zendalia gasped as Kaelin rubbed her clit, slow and soft. The pattern was slow, building her orgasm tenuously. It would be like Kaelin to take her sweet time, to weigh all the options of what to do and how to do it before she dove in for the final finish. But Zendalia had never been gifted that kind of patience.

"Harder, oh gods, harder," she cried, arching her back as she tried to move in closer.

She received a chuckle in the darkness, and in the back of her mind, Zendalia noted that Neyon no longer lit up the area. With another brush of pressure against her clit, all other thoughts left her. She was completely wrapped up in Kaelin, in her touch, her breath, her body so strong and tightly bound.

"You are so receptive," Kaelin murmured with a kiss to Zendalia's neck.

The pressure in Zendalia's tail continued to build, piling pleasure on top of pleasure.

Zendalia laughed and pushed her hips harder against Kaelin's too-gentle touch. She wanted everything she could get from Kaelin, but when it was her turn, she was going to give so much more.

"Uh-uh, I'm in charge here."

The confidence dripping from each of Kaelin's words was the sexiest thing Zendalia had ever heard. This mer wasn't someone who had it in spades, but when she did, Zendalia wanted all of it. She deserved it when it came to this. Zendalia moaned but stopped pushing harder against the touch.

Kaelin didn't stop the rubbing, but nor did she speed up or press harder. She wriggled around in a way Zendalia couldn't see but felt in every brush of contact, her nerve endings on high alert as the oxygen continued to deplete.

As though reading her mind, Kaelin's lips were on hers again, passion and oxygen mixing. As quickly as they were there, they disappeared once more but before Zendalia could even consider complaining, Kaelin's second hand slipped through her slit and fingers pressed into her opening.

"Oh!" Zendalia gasped out.

The pressure on her clit mercifully increased, and the speed ratcheted up a notch. Zendalia's hips and fluke undulated, unable to stay still as sensations washed over her.

"More, I need more of you inside of me."

A hesitation in movement and Zendalia found Kaelin's face and cradled it in her palms.

"Is that okay?" Zendalia's voice was raw and rough.

"Yes, of course that's okay, but..." Kaelin took a deep breath "...I can't go in farther without, um, using my entire hand."

A beat of silence hit as Zendalia tried to process while her clit continued to throb, and her body ached for more of Kaelin.

"Umm, it's the webbing." Kaelin interpreted the silence correctly.

"Oh." Zendalia nodded in understanding, hoping Kaelin was looking at her. "I've never done that, but I'm willing to try it with you."

"I don't want to hurt you." There was her beautiful Kaelin, always so worried about what harm she could potentially do. Little did she know she was the gentlest giant in the seas.

"Then trust me. I'll tell you if I need you to stop." Zendalia brought their lips together in nothing other than a kiss, and when Kaelin tried to make it more, she stopped it. This wasn't about breathing—it was about comfort and an exchange of trust.

"Okay," Kaelin whispered.

"Good, because if you don't start moving again, I'm going to scream. And not in a good way." Zendalia bit her lip, holding back the need to move until Kaelin was ready.

Another chuckle from Kaelin, and Zendalia began to join in the laughter but suddenly her mind was preoccupied with far more important things. Kaelin's hands were a whole new form of magic, her fingers rubbing around Zendalia's clit, squeezing the nub or rubbing over it with an irregular pattern, making Zendalia's tail buck in pleasure. Slowly, as though proving how much she didn't want to hurt Zendalia, Kaelin eased her hand into her, finger by finger until Zendalia was filled beyond what she had ever experienced before.

"Are you okay?"

"Oh gods yes." Zendalia gripped Kaelin's shoulders, fingers digging into the flesh for stability as Kaelin fucked her with more strength and completeness than Zendalia had ever experienced in her life. The kraken could have been outside the cave entrance and Zendalia would have remained oblivious as she rode out the orgasm.

She gasped for oxygen, and Kaelin shuffled back up her body, kissing her gently and breathing life into her again.

"Wow."

Kaelin laughed and curled up into Zendalia's shoulder as they floated down to the floor, resting in the same position they had during the night.

"Now, will you please put your mask back on?" Kaelin kissed Zendalia, pushing more oxygen into her lungs.

Her head was dizzy, but it wasn't with lack of oxygen. It was with the aftermath of good sex, but mostly with the realization that this was love, and she would do anything for Kaelin. "Will you come back to the upper soundings with me?"

"I can't, Zendalia. I won't be accepted, and I won't make an outcast of you." Sadness tinged every word, and it shattered Zendalia's heart. She had to remind herself that it would take years to undo what had been done to Kaelin.

"Our people are different, and you're already welcome in my home, in my family cave, and in the halls of the king's castle." Zendalia trailed a finger over Kaelin's cheek, unwilling to give up the intimate touch.

"Because of you."

"For now, but once they get to know you, they will love you for all that you have to offer." Kaelin scooted impossibly closer, using the connection of their bodies to remind each other of what they stood to lose.

"Which is what?" Kaelin asked, the words sounding more like a plea to Zendalia's ears.

"Anything you want. You're an amazing artist, you have an incredible mind, and your physical prowess." Kaelin playfully slapped Zendalia's chest. Zendalia laughed as she continued, "Your fighting prowess is legendary."

"Not sure it would be in the upper soundings."

"With the technology Soulara made you, you just never know."

Kaelin moved in, breathing more life into Zendalia's lungs and lingering long enough for Zendalia to know this wasn't just about life and death.

"All right," Kaelin whispered against her.

"All right?" Zendalia beamed in the darkness.

"Yes, I'll come with you to the upper soundings. But I can't go back to the tribe." Even in the darkness, Zendalia could see the sadness that washed through Kaelin.

"I'll go back and leave with the convoy. You can join us when we reach the edge of the city." It was the best compromise she could think of at the moment.

"I can do that." Kaelin sighed, and the warm bubbles she expelled tickled Zendalia's breasts, piquing her nipples. "Good, now put on your mask."

"Not yet." Zendalia mumbled as she slipped her hand down between their bodies, forcing a small gap between flukes.

"Oh, okay then." Kaelin kissed Zendalia hard as she pushed her fluke hard against Zendalia's.

Zendalia hummed as her fingers found Kaelin's slit open and ready for her. She slid her thumb over Kaelin's clit as she pushed her fingers inside and started a brutal pace, her entire goal to give Kaelin as much pleasure as she had received as quickly as possible. Kaelin cried out as they rocked together, bringing Kaelin to climax.

"Now, the mask." Kaelin gasped out a few moments after she collapsed against Zendalia once more.

"Sure, if we can find it."

Zendalia laughed lightly and then hissed as shining bright lights filled the cave again.

Her mouth dropped open as she focused on Neyon holding the mask with several tentacles.

"Pervert," Zendalia said as she snatched the mask and put it on.

All but one tentacle flopped down, leaving one up making sure Zendalia knew exactly what Neyon thought of her accusation. Kaelin laughed hard, the sound reverberating through the cave, and Zendalia had never been so grateful to have failed at anything in her entire life as she had with trying to kill Kaelin.

29

Kaelin lingered at the edge of the cave. Since she had agreed to go back to the upper soundings, a sense of peace had settled in her heart. She'd sent Zendalia on her way with a kiss, a touch, and a promise to meet up with her, but it would be hours yet until it was time.

She crossed her arms over her chest, leaning back into the wall. The cave felt lonely without Zendalia there, and that truthfully should have been Kaelin's first sign that there was more between them than mere sexual attraction. Kaelin flitted her gaze around, attempting to memorize every last thing about the lower soundings. Having agreed to go back, she didn't want to miss a thing of the here and now. This was her home, and she had no idea if she would ever manage to make it this deep again.

Kaelin shuddered as emotion washed through her. Leaving was scary. She'd never thought it was a possibility before, but Zendalia was right. She had been accepted, at least to an extent, in Reine, and that was more than she could say for her own people right now. She had never been on the in with the tribe, that was for sure, but they had at least tolerated her. Now even that wasn't the case.

The sting from where she'd been hit and slammed backward

echoed in her bones. It hurt, not just physically but emotionally. To be torn from the fabric of what had made her and raised her was the worst pain Kaelin had ever lived through, including the kraken attacks. Neyon floated in front of her, their long tentacles stretching lazily as if they had just had the best fuck of their life.

Kaelin's lips curled up in a smile, and she held her hand out for them. Neyon slunk toward her, wrapping around her arm and sliding up to her shoulder. "So, you've been spending quite a bit of time with both of us."

Neyon squeezed her tightly in response. Kaelin closed her eyes and rested her head against the cave wall. Her breathing evened out as she completely calmed and relaxed, her shoulders dropping and her chest opening.

"Don't think you could have told us that a little sooner, eh?" Kaelin's voice sounded far off, but she knew Neyon would hear every word she said. They had such a tight connection to each other, and she trusted them with everything in her heart. Though she had begun to trust Zendalia more and more with that.

Neyon pulsed vibrations through her, happy little ones that told her they were pleased with how everything was turning out. She remembered stories of the soul stones, but they had been lost for so long that she'd never thought she'd see one again. The fact that Zendalia had one was something special, and she wondered if there were more of them hidden somewhere in the upper soundings. Being able to see into Neyon's mind, to communicate so intimately with someone she had known for so long had been a miracle.

Reaching up, Kaelin stroked Neyon's bulbous head absentmindedly. "Are you about ready?"

Neyon gave her a hard squeeze.

"All right, then. Let's go."

They moved over Kaelin's shoulder and up to the back of her head where they preferred to ride for longer swims. She'd always thought they were lazy, but it was easier for her to sluice through the water than it was for them, and she could swim much faster. Kaelin moved through the water, the cold running over her hips and across her tail as she went.

It wouldn't take her very long to reach the outer edge of the city where she would wait, and she would take her time getting there. She knew she was early. The rocks and boulders that littered the ocean floor had been her companions for so many seasons that she was going to miss them. There were rocks in the upper soundings, but none that looked like these.

The coral that she had used to make her paintings stuck out to her. Neyon had been the one to show her that neat little trick, and she reveled in it. They must have something similar in the upper soundings that she could experiment with. Zendalia would have to show her. Everything was bittersweet as she swam, making her way toward the outer edge of the homestead.

Zendalia swam with the rest of the convoy, steady and waiting for her. Kaelin was surprised to see them and moved faster to catch up. She didn't want them to be waiting for her to leave. Zendalia's eyes widened the instant they locked on Kaelin's form, and her hand raised in a greeting.

"I thought you would be later," Kaelin rushed out as soon as she arrived.

General Honour nodded sharply. "We were supposed to be, but someone made an offense."

Her glare turned on one of her underlings, and it was obvious there would be some kind of formal reprimand. Zendalia shrugged and took Kaelin's hand in hers. "I'm glad to see you."

"I told you I would come."

"Yeah but…" Zendalia shook her head. "Never mind. I'm just happy."

The kiss was unexpected, but the side glance Kaelin and Zendalia got from Honour was full of joy. It was a quick embrace, nothing showy, but that was exactly what Kaelin had needed. Zendalia's people were far more attentive in physical affections than her own, and that was something she could readily get used to. In fact, she was beginning to enjoy it.

"Shall we get going?" Honour interrupted Kaelin's thoughts.

"Yes," Kaelin stated firmly.

As the others began to move away, she risked one last glance over her shoulder. In the recesses of the water, where she was sure none from the upper soundings could see, an elder lurked. Her stomach clenched tightly. She wasn't supposed to be with them, and she didn't deserve to have someone else to take her into their home, but there she was. The elder stayed still instead of rushing toward her like she had when Kaelin had entered the encampment.

Their gazes locked, and a rush of warmth moved through her. Kaelin could have sworn she saw the elder's lips curl up in a smile, but she was too far away to be certain. What she did know was that her hand was raised, webbed fingers spread as far apart as they could go, her hand high above her head in their customary farewell. She always had been the one Kaelin had gravitated toward, the one who had been the softest during her banishment discussions.

Kaelin repeated the same motion, making sure that the others in the convoy didn't see her, aside from Zendalia who stayed right next to her. She blinked three times and the elder was gone. Letting out a rush of breath, Kaelin twisted around and faced the tails of the convoy in front of her.

"What was that?" Zendalia questioned.

Kaelin shook her head slowly. "I don't know."

"What were you doing?"

"Oh, that's our customary farewell. One of the elders was at the edge of the camp and sent me off." Kaelin's lips curled upward into a smile. That was truthfully more than she could have ever hoped for. She'd been sent away so many times without any hope of returning, but perhaps with that, she could one day see her family again.

"An elder?"

"Yes," Kaelin murmured. "She was the most opposed to me being banished in the beginning. However, she never made her opinion openly known to the rest of the tribe."

"Why wouldn't she?"

"It would jeopardize her standing and ability to remain impartial. Her position is to remain neutral. She has to in order for our society to thrive." Kaelin took a meandering pace as they swam. It didn't seem as though they were in a rush to get back to the upper soundings. "How did the last conversation go?"

Zendalia blew out a breath sharply, bubbles exiting her mask in a fury. "They were willing to listen to us about the kraken, but in order for us to work together, they want something."

"What?" Kaelin swam closer to Zendalia as her voice dropped to a lower register. "What could they possibly want from you?"

"Soul stones."

Shivers ran through Kaelin's spine from the top of her head to the tip of her tail. She drew in a deep breath and let it out slowly. "They're very important to our culture."

"I know. I for sure know and understand that now." Zendalia reached up to the stone at her neck and held it. When her cheek dipped to her shoulder, Kaelin could tell that Neyon was with her in that instant. "But I'm not sure how many we have or if we have any more beyond this one. I offered mine—"

"They wouldn't take it."

"No, they wouldn't. Something about Neyon being mine and needing to keep that connection between us." Zendalia's hands shook.

Kaelin reached for her fingers and grasped her hand, folding them together so they were as connected as they could be while still swimming. It was the first true time Kaelin could remember making that connection on purpose, the touch that was centering her more and more. They stayed quiet for some time as they continued to swim through the lower soundings. Honour clearly had memorized the way there because she led them back with no hesitation.

Neyon wormed themself away from Kaelin and started to play with the bubbles that were created by the convoy moving through. They popped one and then the next, gleefully jumping around as they went and keeping up with them at the same time. Kaelin's shoulder bumped into Zendalia's.

"What will we do when we get home?" Kaelin asked.

Zendalia's eyes crinkled, and even though she had a mask blocking her mouth, Kaelin could tell that she was smiling. "I do have to report to King Pregtox immediately about all of this."

"Naturally. Will you mention the soul stones?"

"I don't think I can avoid it. I don't know if he's aware of them either. Soulara only had one that I know of—the one she gave to me." Zendalia shivered, and Kaelin pulled her in a little closer, remembering that she couldn't keep as warm this deep in the ocean.

"Will you ask her?" Kaelin's stomach clenched at the thought. If the upper-sounding mers had all of the soul stones, then they must have taken them when the tribes split all those generations ago. But why? It made no sense for her tribe to keep the physical companions with no way to connect with their spirits or for the others to have a way to connect to nothing. Zendalia had been lucky that Neyon had found her through all the space and without the rituals to bring them together.

"I will as soon as I can find her. Honour said she went surface-side again."

Kaelin jerked with a start. "She went to the surface?"

"She does that sometimes to think, and with the changes to her role in the city now that she's fighting for this treaty, I'm not surprised."

"Can she breathe above the water?" Kaelin's stomach tightened. She had heard of such things with the gods, but never with a flesh and blood mer.

Zendalia shook her head. "I don't think so."

They fell back into a silence, the convoy ahead of them still. Neyon gave up on the bubbles and settled at the small of Zendalia's back, curling up into a ball and taking a nap. Kaelin smiled at them before facing forward again. There was one question lingering in Kaelin's mind, something that she hadn't asked yet but that she desperately wanted to know the answer to.

"What will they give in exchange for the soul stones?"

Zendalia dragged her gaze over to meet Kaelin's. "They'll go to war with us."

Kaelin's world shook. Her people, those who claimed to be holders of life in the waters were going to go to war against the kraken? They were going to willingly murder something? She had never heard of it happening before.

Zendalia squeezed her hand sharply. "They'll not be on the front lines, but they will be supporting our efforts to protect the life in these waters."

"Oh, I guess that makes more sense." Still, the realization that her people would have to walk this line so carefully was beyond what Kaelin had ever thought could happen. They were going to actively help those who were going to kill.

Vibrations echoed loudly in Kaelin's ears. She jerked her hands up and clamped them over the sides of her head as she clenched her eyes tightly. Loud screeching reverberated through the waters, and the convoy in front of them broke formation. Kaelin panicked. She turned on her side and snagged Zendalia's arm to pull her tight against her chest. Their eyes locked, fear lingering in that amber gaze Kaelin had found so much hope in just moments before. They both knew what this was. They both understood exactly what was happening.

The kraken.

30

"Is that the beast?" Honour was at their side as another screech vibrated through the water, her own face mask was already removed, and her lips were pursed tight into a scowl as though the beast were something unappetizing on an offered clam shell.

"The kraken, yes," Zendalia answered, reluctantly releasing Kaelin enough for her to think a little more clearly, enough for her to remember her training as a warrior.

Honour gave a curt nod, a small sharp up-and-down before turning her back on the two of them.

"Troops!" Her voice echoed in the water, usually the cause of instant attention for said troops, it now sluiced over them as a calming wave. "In formation, now!"

A moment of stillness and then bubbles burst around them as they gathered themselves, almost looking as though they weren't terrified for their lives.

And you all haven't even seen it yet, Zendalia thought.

Zendalia squeezed Kaelin's hand and took a deep gulp of oxygen-rich water through her mask. They weren't quite out of the deep soundings yet, but Zendalia could already feel the relative ease of breathing through the device as the water began to thin just a little.

"We are warriors of Reine. We won't allow an incursion to make us scurry away like scared eels, slipping through cracks hoping to be lost in the hiding." Honour sounded clear as she rallied them, boosting them up to the level she needed them at in order to fight.

"Yes, ma'am," the troops all chorused to Honour's call for bravery.

"Then we stand our ground and fight for our home."

"Yes, ma'am."

The troops, nine mers not counting Kaelin, Zendalia, or Honour herself, lined up in a V formation. Zendalia's chest vibrated with the pounding of her heart. The adrenaline of the upcoming battle made her fins itch in anticipation.

"We're waiting for the kraken?" Kaelin whispered.

"Yes," Zendalia answered without turning to face her. If she saw fear on Kaelin's face, she would have grabbed Kaelin's hand and led them both into those very crevasses Honour thought so little of.

"Why can't we just go another way?" Kaelin's voice wavered this time, that fear billowing its way up.

"Because this is the fastest way back to our people. The only other way would be to go back down and rise again on the other side of this shelf." Zendalia watched the convoy stay in formation as they lay in wait.

"But that would be safe." Kaelin had a point, but safety wasn't the concern. Getting back to King Pregtox with the information about the negotiation was. Zendalia didn't have a chance to respond when Honour came over.

"Time is of the essence if we're hoping for the two tribes to combine forces," Honour responded, and until then, Zendalia hadn't noticed that the entire convoy looked at them, mostly with side eyes, but they were all listening. Her stomach dropped. She was acting like anything but the warrior she had trained to be, and she knew it was because Kaelin swam next to her. But Kaelin had proven herself against this beast more times than Zendalia cared to count. They would both survive.

The vibrations increased. The tails of the convoy waved in front of her as they fought to resist the pressure of the water as it came faster and harder. The water turned painful, seeping into Zendalia's skin in a way she had only experienced near the kraken.

"Kaelin, will you hide?" Zendalia whispered. She wanted Kaelin to dip back below into the deep soundings and hide away until this was all over, but she knew at the same time that she wouldn't.

"No." The fierceness in Kaelin's simple answer turned Zendalia's head. Her smile spread across her lips and her chest warmed, with love and pride for the woman who narrowed her eyes and bared her teeth toward something Zendalia could not yet see.

"Can you see it?"

All heads turned toward them. Zendalia hadn't realized she had spoken so loudly, but it didn't matter. If Kaelin could see the kraken, Honour and her warriors would only benefit from the knowledge.

"It's coming directly toward us. It is half buried in the sands, but there are enough metallic tentacles leading the way that it could easily take us out."

"We need your sight, Kaelin." Honour was there again behind her troops, who had all turned back as though having the confirmation of the kraken's presence would somehow improve their own inept sight. "If you are willing to assist."

"Of course." Kaelin nodded and moved to follow Honour to the front of her troops.

"No," Zendalia called, but neither Kaelin nor Honour turned back in response. Had she spoken aloud or had the protest only been in her mind? She hated this. Being separated from Kaelin in a life-or-death situation was only going to cause her stress as she waited for the initial attack.

She shook her head and followed Kaelin. The mer was stubborn—if nothing else she had learned that over the last few weeks. There would be no point trying to stop her or convince her to hide. And Honour was correct, Kaelin could help them with this stand.

Suddenly the vibrations stopped.

"What happened?" Honour asked Kaelin.

Kaelin squinted into the darkness, and what Zendalia wouldn't have given to be able to take what Kaelin saw, the colors and horrors that pressed themselves on to her mind, and know how to help her when the nightmares came in future calm days. Because there would be future calm days. Zendalia had fought too hard to find Kaelin—no technological beast would take that away from her.

"The kraken has stopped."

"Stopped?" Honour and Zendalia asked at the same time.

"Yes. It's stopped and lain down in the sand of the shelf."

"What the hell is it up t—" Honour's words were cut off as a force from behind them slammed into their backs.

Zendalia twisted in the water, maneuvering her form in the space of time it took for another wave of power to push against her, sending her reeling toward the resting kraken.

"There are two of them!" Kaelin screamed as she wrapped her webbed fingers around Zendalia's wrist, stopping her from being forced any closer to the currently dormant kraken that now seemed far less deadly.

"Take the bastards down," Honour roared, and Zendalia watched as Honour and the convoy charged toward the moving technological beast. There were so many tentacles, lit up and flicking through the water, even her people could see them.

Her heart pounded and a smile, wild and savage, made its way across her face. She much preferred the fight to the waiting. Looking to her side, a laugh, crazy and unexpected, floated from her mouth. Kaelin had already raced forward, tail fins spread wide, and her speed quickly overtook that of the convoys. Zendalia pushed her body as fast as she could and joined in.

The tentacles whipped out around her, the lights opening up and siphoning water in through the holes they made. The suction pulled at her scales like it was going to rip them off her tail.

"Fuckers," Zendalia growled low and deep in her throat. She dove forward, fingers pushing into one of the open lights at the end of a tentacle and pulled with all the strength and anger she could muster. This thing was responsible for her father's death. This thing would pay.

But even as the fire and her fury raged, the tentacle slipped from her hands as it was pulled backward with a force she couldn't comprehend. It headed back down toward her, so quickly. She slapped her tail as hard as she could even knowing she wouldn't get out of range fast enough. Closing her eyes, though still moving as fast as she could, she waited for the inevitable pain of impact. It never arrived.

Zendalia opened her eyes just in time to see Kaelin twist around, twirling as though she danced rather than fought with the creature. But after half a turn, she lashed out her tail and slammed it into the tentacle before it could reach Zendalia. Mouth open Zendalia watched in pure admiration as Kaelin attacked the kraken as though she had never known fear in all her life.

"Zendalia." The call, raw and desperate, pulled Zendalia's attention away from Kaelin, who continued to rain damage down on the beast.

"Honour." Zendalia gasped as she saw the general, blood pouring out from her face into the water immediately surrounding her. Zendalia left Kaelin to her battle, knowing she was more than worthy to be a warrior of her own people, even despite the lump of fear that lodged in her chest.

Zendalia pushed as fast as she could, weaving through the

kraken's undulating limbs, though her heart cracked as she watched members of the convoy, mers she had joked with and spoken to only hours earlier, lose their lives to the whipping tentacles, their movements a half beat too late or too early.

"No." Again she couldn't be sure the word actually left her mouth. She swam past a mermaid who looked little older than a child, as she was skewered by a sharp thin tentacle. It didn't look like the other tentacles—there were no lights to warn of its presence. The sword that had moments earlier been clutched in the girl's hand floated out of her grip as strength and life left her body.

Warmth boiled to a burning heat within Zendalia's chest. She plucked the sword from the water before it reached the sandy floor of the shelf. The noise that rumbled in her chest and came out of her mouth was something from a child's nightmare.

Zendalia charged at the thin murderous spear, slicing at it once, twice, three times before the blood-covered tip cracked off and dropped heavy and harmless to the floor. But the fire in Zendalia had only just begun. She ducked beneath swinging tentacles, slicing where she could and easily swimming around those that threatened to take her out. Screams of fellow convoy warriors registered somewhere far back in her mind, but the red rage wouldn't be dulled or ignored.

Every time Zendalia caught a flicker of dark purple from the corner of her eye, the rush raced through her veins once more. Kaelin continued to fight, and Zendalia would be beside her for every battle, the ones she could see and the ones that Kaelin carried deep within herself.

Honour's guttural scream pulled Zendalia back from her thoughts, and she swam around the flailing kraken limbs that blocked her view of her people on the other side of it.

"Honour?" she called and swam quickly to Honour's side, noting the hand the general pressed to her shoulder. Blood seeped through between her fingers.

"We must retreat," Honour hissed as Zendalia brought the

sword up, blocking a tentacle from taking another jab. "Even with your Kaelin, we are simply outnumbered and unprepared."

"Where?"

"Straight up," Honour said, pinning Zendalia with a serious look.

Zendalia's eyes grew wide, but she nodded as she wrapped an arm around Honour's waist. Honour hissed again as she placed her damaged arm over Zendalia's shoulder.

"Troops, fall back!" Zendalia screamed before Honour could give the command. "Straight up, straight for home."

She knew how risky this move was. The steep incline from the lower soundings to the middle soundings could do a number on their lungs and minds, but it truly was the only option. Open waters were dangerous, by any mer standards, one of the universal things both upper and lower sounding tribes remembered and continued to teach. The convoy's original route had followed ledges and cliffs, but now with the threat of the krakens, open waters seemed the lesser of two evils.

"Let's go." Honour tensed beside Zendalia as she screamed the words, only to then let her weight double against Zendalia.

"Zendalia!" Kaelin's voice called out, panic seeping through her name.

"Kaelin!" Zendalia called back as Kaelin came into view. "We are heading straight up."

"Good." Without another word, Kaelin slipped Honour's other arm over her shoulders and swam as rapidly as possible straight into the water above them.

Bubbles surrounded them as three warriors caught up, looked at their wounded general, and reformed a small V in front of Honour, Kaelin, and Zendalia.

Zendalia met Kaelin's eyes over Honour's drooping head.

"So few," Kaelin whispered.

"Yes, but you were brilliant."

"Not brilliant enough." Kaelin pulled her eyes away from Zendalia, head turned toward their new path.

Zendalia wanted to tell Kaelin it wasn't her fault. Wanted to tell her she did all that she could. They were outmatched by a second kraken, and it had taken them all by surprise, but how could she word it when Zendalia felt the death of those left behind stain her hands. She should have done more reconnaissance. She should have known there was more than one kraken. The convoy led the way in silence and with each movement of their tails Zendalia's heart twisted at how many she no longer followed.

31

They had to stop in the middle of the open water. Honour's vibrant green eyes hadn't shown since they moved above the kraken, and Kaelin knew they had to check her. The blood trail they left behind was strong, and if the krakens had any desire to follow them, they wouldn't be hard to spot. But the kraken had never sought out mers to attack. It was always in defense.

"Did you see its face?"

Kaelin turned sharply to the young man they had traveled with. She couldn't for the life of her remember his name, but he had been well trained according to Honour. Kaelin met Zendalia's eyes, and a conversation happened between them without words. With a small nod, she slipped Honour from Zendalia's arms, leaving her to follow up on the man's question.

While still being close enough to hear the conversation, Kaelin cradled Honour's torso in the circle of her tail and checked on the wounds.

"What do you mean, Kett?" Zendalia asked, moving closer to him and looking at his wounds as she talked.

Kaelin ducked her chin and focused on the mer in her arms. Honour's shoulder was probably the worst. The stab wound went all the way through, and she could tell it had some sort of poison in it because the veins against her skin looked like deep webs of black. Kaelin put her hand over it and her flesh was hot to touch.

Scanning down Honour's form, Kaelin found the same poisonous web around the wound to her tail. She cursed under her breath and looked around wildly for anything that she could use to get the poison out. It had to come out, it couldn't be allowed to linger for long, certainly not for the time it would take to get back to Reine where she hoped they had proper healers. She had to find something nearby.

"It had a face," Kett whispered, his voice so angsty that Kaelin glanced from the side of her eyes, needing to look at him and Zendalia, who remained silent while she continued to examine his various cuts and scrapes. Something shiny on the man's belt gave Kaelin the opportunity she needed to ask her own question.

"What do you mean it had a face?" She swam over to him, shuffling Honour in her arms, and snagged the small knife from his belt before repositioning Honour in her tail again. She focused on Honour's shoulder. So close to her heart, the poison would do more damage faster—too fast. Kaelin's heart pounded a little louder in her chest. Silently she willed it to slow, hoping that Zendalia couldn't hear it, but more importantly that it wouldn't drown out the man's reply.

Neyon slipped around her arm and pressed a tentacle to the center of Honour's chest, a light vibration moving through them and into the general. Kaelin drew in a deep breath. Her people had spent years healing others and learning all they could about prolonging a life. But she'd never had to do something like this and never in the open waters. She wasn't a trained healer, and she knew the dangers of doing what had to be done, even for one who had spent years learning this art.

The vibrations from Neyon suddenly stopped, and her companion turned to stare at her. Her eyes stung as unshed tears built up behind them, but she stared unblinking and begging for him to understand.

He didn't. She knew that as surely as she knew that Honour's life would help the fight against the krakens more than her own existence could ever hope for.

"I'm sorry," Kaelin whispered, looked over to see Zendalia still preoccupied with Kett, and took a deep breath, ready to do the only thing she could to help her people.

She brought the shining blade down and pressed the tip into the center of the wound, the nucleus of the growing web. Black liquid, thick and viscous like Neyon's defensive ink, seeped instantly from the new wound. But unlike Neyon's ink, a sheen that warned of danger curled around the edges.

Kaelin closed her eyes and took a deep breath. There were words, so many words she wished she had said to Zendalia, and she hoped she would one day understand the sacrifice Kaelin gave.

She shut out the rest of the waters around her and focused only on her task. She lowered her head toward the wound. That small part of her mind that had kept her alive during the seasons of exile, during the darkest moments of her lonely isolation screamed at her to move back, away from the danger she moved willingly toward.

"Stop." Zendalia's scream came with a bolt of electricity scorching beneath Kaelin's skin.

She gasped, pulled her head back and turned to see Zendalia reach for her, but she was stopped by Neyon's flared tentacles.

For a heartbeat that broke her own heart in two, Kaelin thought Neyon was supporting her, letting her sacrifice herself for Honour. It hurt, it hurt so much to have her own thoughts confirmed as truth. But then she noticed the tentacle that wasn't stretched out. That tentacle was touching Kaelin's temple, carrying the electric shock that stopped her from taking that first suck of the poison to cleanse Honour's blood.

She was just about to bring the knife down and put the tip

into the entry point when Kett rushed forward and grabbed her wrist hard. Kaelin cried out from the sudden jolt.

"What are you doing?" Zendalia asked, her voice carrying a rasp Kaelin had never heard before.

"I have to get it out, otherwise it'll kill her."

"Not this way."

"Zendalia, please." Kaelin's eyes shifted back and forth between the mer who had opened up her whole world and another life dying in her arms. "I can't let her die. You have to understand. Please."

"No, I don't."

"Neyon will explain, but I can't wait any longer." She lowered her head once more, but the zap was strong and more painful through her head once more.

"He already did." Zendalia growled. "You aren't sacrificing yourself."

"It's okay." Kaelin smiled, sad but soft. "Honour needs to live. She'll help win against the kraken."

"Not this way." Zendalia's fingers wrapped around Kaelin's bicep. "I won't let you."

"Why?" Kaelin's tears spilled, warming the water in front of her face. "Why won't you let me respect my people, finally do the right thing?"

"Because I love you, you idiot. And you have more to offer than the backward thinking of a tribe that can't see what a gift you are to this world."

Kaelin stopped crying, mouth dropping open and staring at Zendalia.

"I have to save her."

"Neyon?" Zendalia turned to their companion. The octopus slowly removed the tentacle from Kaelin's temple but narrowed their eyes at Kaelin. She had the distinct impression that if they could, they would have pointed fingers to their eyes and then to Kaelin, letting her know that they were still watching her.

Kaelin swallowed down the lump in her throat and nodded.

As though satisfied with Kaelin's reaction, Neyon flicked several tentacles out toward the open sea beside them. Following this direction, she pushed Honour away from her to float, Neyon floated with her for a few seconds before alighting onto her chest. As soon as she was enough distance away, Neyon charged the water around themselves and Honour and slammed their tentacles down over the wound. Even from this distance, Kaelin heard the snap and crackle of the electrical charge that slammed into Honour's chest. The substance poured from the open wounds and into the water. Kaelin stayed still, fear trembled in every muscle beneath skin and scales. Had she just killed another life? Would Zendalia regret her words? Had she ever meant them?

The crackling charges from Neyon continued until the dark ooze became thin and light, fading from black to red. At the first sight of red, Kaelin moved in and took over from Neyon. The octopus looked ready to pass out, swaying on Honour's chest, eyes all but closed.

"Thank you, friend. I can take it from here." Kaelin helped Neyon back to their favorite spot at the base of her skull and applied pressure to Honour's shoulder, smiling at the lack of dark threads shooting off from the wound.

With Honour in her arms again, she breathed a sigh of relief and swam back to Zendalia.

Kett and his fellow surviving warriors had joined Zendalia as they had watched Honour's life being saved by a familiar and a member of another tribe. They looked to be in various degrees stunned and horrified at what they had just witnessed.

"She'll live, but she needs a better healer to make sure she doesn't linger in the healing."

Zendalia nodded and turned toward Kett. "Have you told them what you saw?"

Kett shook his head and his fellow warriors looked at him, eyebrows raised and eyes demanding.

"He had a face, the kraken."

"He?" Kaelin raised an eyebrow and tried not to react to the sting in her chest at Zendalia not looking at her.

Kett blew out bubbles. "Yeah. He looked kind of like one of us. Face, nose, mouth, but had this weird stuff on his cheeks and chin—it looked like hair."

Kaelin frowned, trying again to catch Zendalia's eyes to see what she thought of it. The only other time Kaelin had gotten that close to a kraken had been when Zen died, and she hadn't had the wherewithal to look into its face.

"It was beyond a hard bubble," Kett continued as though entirely oblivious to Kaelin's heart cracking into tiny pieces.

"Hard bubble?" Zendalia pushed. "What do you mean?"

"I don't know how to explain it." Kett frowned, the shock of the attack no doubt taking over him. "But it didn't look like one of us. He had coverings all over his body, like over his chest and arms and hands."

Zendalia's eyes widened, her lips parting as something hit her. Kaelin could see that from anywhere. Neyon detached from Kaelin's neck and raced to Zendalia, wrapping around her torso and offering what comfort they could. They stayed in silence while Kaelin forced courage to the forefront.

"Zendalia, what is it?"

Zendalia turned and finally met Kaelin's eyes. So many emotions swirled. It took everything Kaelin had to hold back from swimming right into her arms and covering her up, just like she had the first time they had encountered the kraken.

"We should get moving," Zendalia replied instead.

Kaelin nodded.

Zendalia squared her shoulders and took the lead since no one else seemed to be in the right mindset. The others made formation in front of them, and they slowly swam toward home. Kaelin's lips twitched at that as she held Honour close to her. She would switch off with the rest of them when the water became too thin. That was not something she relished experiencing again but it was a necessary evil.

They swam with an urgency, but still slow enough since they were dragging Honour.

"Will we go back for the others?" Kaelin asked, wanting to pray over them.

Zendalia shook her head. "Not anytime soon. We need to make sure the kraken is gone before we retrieve their bodies."

"I volunteer to help."

Zendalia gave a wan smile. "Thank you. I know the others will appreciate that."

Sadness filled Kaelin's heart, but it didn't dig as deep as it had before. She wasn't sure it could. She knew exactly what she had, and that was Zendalia. The more she tried to trust it, the more she found it easier than she expected. She wasn't alone anymore. Zendalia had come to find her several times when she'd thought she was left by herself, when no one would want her.

Zendalia wanted her. And just as importantly, Kaelin wanted Zendalia.

That had been abundantly clear the night before. Emotion choked her throat, making it hard to breathe.

But she could be brave, for Zendalia and just like Zendalia.

"I love you, too," Kaelin said softly, hoping the warriors they followed couldn't hear her words.

"I'm sorry, what did you say?" Zendalia swam a little closer.

Kaelin couldn't make herself look at Zendalia, that age-old fear starting to rear its ugly head again. They swam side by side, and the electricity flicking between their almost-brushing shoulders had nothing to do with Neyon this time.

"I said…" Kaelin took a deep breath "…I love you too."

She would be brave. She finally looked over and met those amber eyes. The ones she knew, without a doubt, she would see every night in her dreams and hoped to see every day she awoke.

She dropped her gaze to Zendalia's lips, her heart ramping up as anxiety washed through her.

Zendalia's face softened. In an instant, her eyes crinkled as a brilliant smile lit up her face, washing through all that worry and pain she still carried in her shoulders.

"I just…I wanted you to know in case…"

"Nothing is going to happen to me, or to us." Zendalia moved in and wrapped an arm around Kaelin's back. She pressed her lips to Kaelin's cheek, lingering longer than would be proper for any non-romantic relationship. "I promise you I won't leave you."

"I trust you," Kaelin whispered, her voice barely loud enough for Zendalia to hear. "And I love you."

"I love you, too." Zendalia put one finger against Kaelin's chin and turned her face so their lips could connect in a tender kiss. "I don't ever want to lose you."

Kaelin smiled, her lips curling up as she relaxed into the moment. The last of the tension that she had been feeling was completely gone.

"Aren't you two just adorable," Honour croaked.

Kaelin's cheeks burned with embarrassment.

Zendalia gasped. "Don't move."

"Wasn't planning on it." Her voice was weak, though there was that hint of humor that Kaelin had come to expect. Tightening her grip as Honour shifted around slightly, she was never so happy to see Honour's brooding gaze. "Want to fill me in?"

Zendalia jumped right to it. "There's four of us left, General. The rest… You were right to give the order to retreat."

"Who's injured?"

"All of us in some way."

Kaelin's head snapped toward Zendalia. "What do you mean you're hurt?"

Zendalia gave her a hard look before lifting her arm to reveal a darkening bruise all down her side. Kaelin's heart clenched hard. She hadn't even noticed. She'd been so concerned with saving Honour that she had completely missed Zendalia's injuries.

"You're hurt, too."

"I'm not."

"Kaelin," Zendalia said firmly. "Look at your tail."

She stopped swimming and flicked her tail around, skimming her gaze down the side of her body. Sure enough, she had a long scratch against her scales, the skin underneath red and angry. "When did that happen?"

"When we were fighting the kraken. When else?" Zendalia touched Kaelin's arm. "When you need a break, let me know. But we don't have time to stop for injuries right now. We need to get home."

Kaelin nodded her understanding. They started to move forward again. The hush that had come over them before seemed to ease up since Honour was awake. She wasn't fully with it, and there was still a great concern about her making it back to the city without dying on them. That same fear that Kaelin had before about another mer dying in her arms didn't quite return. Kaelin was glad for it, because it meant she could focus better on taking care of Honour along with the confession that had just rung between her and Zendalia.

No one had ever told her that before, and even just reminding herself of the words brought a beautiful warmth to her that wasn't there before. She caught Zendalia's gaze and flushed. She was loved. Was it really as simple as that? She knew she could trust it. She wanted to be able to put everything she had into that connection.

It was going to be a long swim home, one that was going to tire out their bones. But that's exactly where Kaelin wanted to go.

Home.

32

Zendalia took a revitalizing gulp of the highly oxygenated water in Reine. They were finally home. Exhaustion pulled at her limbs, and she imagined the weight of it being able to drag her all the way back down to the lower soundings.

"Are you okay?" Kaelin's voice was soft and comforting, a caress to her senses.

"Yes. Maybe." Zendalia shook her head and tried to find words to explain the turmoil of truth that roiled within her. "I think I will be."

"Do you need to go inside?" Kaelin nodded at the castle that loomed up ahead of them. "To report or something?"

"No," Honour answered before Zendalia had a chance to truly work out what Kaelin was asking. "Both of you go home. Rest while you can."

"While we can." Zendalia nodded. She understood well enough. This was only the beginning of the fight. Rest wouldn't be granted so easily again.

"Thank you, both." Honour looked between them, meeting eyes with a slow nod as though the movement still hurt. "We'll talk again soon I've no doubt."

Zendalia returned the nod and turned to see Kaelin. She opened and then closed her mouth.

"I'll explain later. Let's go home." Zendalia entwined her fingers with Kaelin's and led them away from the looming castle.

Like a layer of silt on the surface of the water, the mood pressed down upon them as Zendalia followed the well-traveled water streams back to her home cave. If she had been alone, she would have raced as fast as she could, simply so she could lock herself away in her home and allow all the emotions to wash over her in privacy. But with Kaelin's strong grip in her own, her heart beat just a little easier, and her tail moved with more strength.

Once inside her home, Zendalia took a shuddering inhale of water, but no words followed.

"It's going to be bad, isn't it?" Kaelin's steady voice filled the silence.

"Yes."

"Worse than what we just went through."

It wasn't a question, but Zendalia nodded in response anyway. She tried to meet Kaelin's eyes, but those beautiful violet windows into Kaelin's thoughts avoided her.

"What's wrong?" Zendalia asked.

She shook her head, but Zendalia wasn't having any of it. She had seen these things before, usually from the other side, and while her heart threatened to crack along previously unseen fissures, she had to know for sure.

"Are you regretting..." Zendalia gulped, not knowing what she needed to know more. Coming to the upper soundings? Having sex with her? Saying she loved her? "Everything?"

"What?" Kaelin lifted her eyes then, violet storms meeting the fiery gaze.

"Do you wish that we hadn't met? That you hadn't said..." Zendalia couldn't force the words out.

"Oh, no." Kaelin pushed into Zendalia's arms, her eyes filling with tears. "I love you, Zendalia. I thought perhaps...perhaps now that you were home you didn't need me, want me."

"Oh." Zendalia laughed, relief filling her chest.

Kaelin laughed along and buried her face into Zendalia's chest. Her cheek brushed against Zendalia's nipple, pebbling it into an ache in an instant.

"Oh gods." Zendalia groaned before she could clamp her lips against the noise.

"You'll find I can be quite the benevolent god when I want to be." Kaelin's face darkened, a blush lighting up her cheeks, but Zendalia could still see the fear lurking behind her eyes.

"You're amazing." Zendalia stared into her eyes, daring that fear to show its face.

Kaelin's head lowered at the compliment, and Zendalia kissed the top of her head, taking in the aroma of her hair.

"Are you...are you sure?"

"Yes." Zendalia was delighted. "You are very, very amazing."

"I have no one but you now." Kaelin swallowed, as though needing more time to put the right words together in the right order. "I do love you, Zendalia, but having only one person, it's beyond scary."

"I don't know what the future holds. I'm not good at promises or declaring my feelings."

"You aren't?" Kaelin tilted her head, and Zendalia flushed.

"No." She lifted one of Kaelin's hands and gently kissed the back of it, running her fingers over membrane of webbing,

"Ah." Kaelin breathed the word.

"I have only ever told one person I loved them before."

"Really?" Kaelin squeaked.

"Yup." The familiar voice came from behind Zendalia.

She closed her eyes and groaned.

"Oh." Kaelin pushed herself out of Zendalia's embrace.

Zendalia twirled around to face Soulara as she leaned on the opening to her home, the seaweed curtain pushed aside casually by the back of her hand.

"Soulara," Zendalia spoke, hoping she infused the infuriating mer's name with as much frustration and annoyance as she could manage.

"What?" Soulara shrugged and pushed her way into Zendalia's home proper. Apparently, subtlety didn't work on the princess. Zendalia knew that.

"We're having a private conversation."

"Oh, I know." Soulara picked up a prickly fruit from Zendalia's storage and took a nibble. Speaking around the small piece of fruit in her mouth, she continued, "Talking about love. I mean, it's obvious it's not the first time you've exchanged the words, and many other things."

Zendalia's mouth dropped open.

Soulara laughed and waggled her eyebrows before her face softened, and she looked as though she might begin to blush.

"She's only ever said it to you?" Kaelin's voice was rough, as though she had been deprived of oxygenated water for days.

"Yeah, just the once. We were three and she wanted my last seaweed puff."

"What?" Kaelin's confusion as she looked between Zendalia and Soulara made Zendalia burst out laughing and pulled Kaelin back into her embrace.

Kaelin's stiff shoulders sobered Zendalia up nice and fast.

"I'm sorry." Zendalia smiled. "You're just so adorable. And Soulara is correct, I said it to her when we were three. Her mom makes the best seaweed puffs. You'll understand when you try one."

Kaelin blinked rapidly at Zendalia.

A heat spread through Zendalia's chest, so different from the warmth she had felt earlier.

"I'm sorry. I didn't mean to laugh at you."

"No." Kaelin blinked again, a smile playing a brief visit to her lips. "It's okay. I get that part."

"What part don't you get?" Zendalia replayed Soulara's words through her mind and came up blank.

"You've only said I love you to Soulara when you were three years old?"

"Yes."

"But you meant it? Didn't you?"

"Of course I meant it."

"Whoa, wait." Soulara's eyes widened so far and so fast that Zendalia almost feared her eyes would fall out and go rolling off never to be found again. "You haven't said it before now?"

"Not really, no." Zendalia hoped her voice didn't shake as much as it did in her own ears.

"I'm so sorry." Now Soulara did blush. "I came here to ask some advice because, well, drama in the kingdom. And you all are just about ready to bind yourselves to each other, and now I'm just interrupting that."

"Advice?" Zendalia's own eyes widened.

"Well," Soulara's shoulders shrugged. "I've never seen you so happy, Z. You radiate because of Kaelin. And I thought you two had already. Gods, I'm sorry."

"It's okay," Kaelin said.

Zendalia entwined their fingers.

"I think I've found her, Z."

"The one?"

Soulara nodded.

"Okay, so what's the problem?"

"Many things, but let's just say we are from different tribes, and I figured who better to ask then the lovefish who have the entire city humming."

"The entire city?" Zendalia squeezed Kaelin's hand. The returned squeeze made Zendalia's body lighten as though she were floating along the very top of the water.

"Yeah." Soulara nodded as though deciding on what they had been discussing. "I'm going to leave you two alone. I've got a big order to fill now that father is in discussions with Honour."

"He is?"

"Yup. So, um rest or whatever before the city starts preparing for war I guess." Soulara ran the words together and slipped from Zendalia's home before she or Kaelin had a chance to respond.

As soon as the ripples of water from Soulara's rushed exit stilled, the silence surrounding Zendalia creeped up her back, turning her flesh cold and bumpy. Slowly she turned and found Kaelin staring at her, hands down by her side and her tail resting curved against the floor of her home. She looked so at ease, no obvious tension showed in clenched fists or tightened shoulders. In fact, Kaelin looked perfect and the calmest and at peace with herself Zendalia had ever seen.

"I would have thought it was impossible."

"What?" Zendalia asked, wondering exactly what it was she felt rippling over her skin making sure those bumps remained exactly where they were.

"That I could fall in love with a stranger, let alone one that mere weeks ago had been determined to kill me."

"Bit surprised myself to tell the truth." Zendalia smiled, lifting the left side of her lips just a little higher than the right.

"Well, I can only imagine as you haven't felt safe enough to say 'I love you' to anyone else since you were three." Kaelin nodded, eyebrows twitching together and then back as though she argued with another person Zendalia couldn't hear.

"It's not about safety."

"It's not?" Kaelin's face carried a mix of challenge and fear, but over that she wore a strength Zendalia had always seen, hiding behind the surface.

"Oh no." Zendalia pulled Kaelin tightly to her, tail brushing tail and nipples pressing into nipples. "Safety has nothing to do with it."

"Then what does?"

"I knew you were different, the moment the red haze of revenge lifted. I had no idea that we were so destined though."

"Destined?"

"Of course. Souls don't bond together because they had a soul stone, or because they've been abandoned by their people."

"No?" Kaelin asked, but Zendalia saw the corners of her mouth lift slightly. That was okay. If Kaelin needed the words, Zendalia would say them, scream them at the entire sea every day until she passed into the next life, and she would wait for Kaelin to find her there so she could say it more.

"Neyon knew. For years they knew. Just like they had been split, so had we. But we don't ever need to be split again. We are whole, we are one, and Kaelin…" Zendalia brushed her nose against Kaelin's "…I would be honored if you would agree to being bound to me as I wish to be bound to you."

"Yes." Kaelin didn't hesitate as she followed the word with her lips, pressed them hot and fierce against Zendalia's.

"YES!" A shout of excitement came from outside of the seaweed curtain door of Zendalia's home.

"Soulara!" Zendalia groaned.

"Hey, I had to make sure you didn't screw it up." Soulara peeked her head back through, a smile splitting her face in half. "Congratulations."

To Zendalia's surprise, Kaelin burst out laughing and waved her hand beckoning Soulara to come inside.

"I'm sorry," Zendalia whispered.

"I'm not. She's family, and I can't think of anyone better to celebrate our impending binding with."

"Cheers." Soulara nodded and pushed up her chest.

"I love you." Kaelin turned to say the words to Zendalia.

"I love you, too."

Soulara wrapped her arms around both of them, grinning from ear to ear, "Now, can we get on with the deep sounding chaos and start with the surface pressure?"

"Anything you want, Princess Soulara." Zendalia giggled and gave Soulara a fake bow. "Anything you want."

THANK YOU!

Thank you so much reading Deep Sounding Chaos. We really hope you enjoyed it! We had a blast writing it.

The idea for this book first came to us during an author's zoom catch up where Adrian mentioned a picture she'd seen with the concept of mermaids in space, think of space as the void of water. Neen was so excited it only seemed logical that we should look at writing it together.

After two chats, our single space mermaids book took some incredible turns which has culminated in the beginning of a beautiful friendship and this incredible series *Love, Tails, and Battle Wails*. And no longer looks like what we had originally planned.

But that's what characters do when they take over their own story!

Being from different hemispheres, it's been an interesting and often laughter filled adventure as we find time between our busy lives and opposite time zones to discuss and create this series. There have been 4:30am coffees, late night rum, and tangents in Facebook messenger while the other one is sleeping so they can wake up to a million messages as we get distracted.

We wouldn't have it any other way. We're so proud of this book and can't wait for you to explore and discover the rest of *Love, Tails, and Battle Wails*.

SURFACE PRESSURE
LOVE, TAILS, AND BATTLE WAILS #2

A mermaid. A human. Can they break the surface pressure?

Soulara never wanted to be queen. As the rightful heir, Soulara resists expectations in search of her own path. With a knack for technology and an insatiable curiosity, she explores the deep soundings and the surface. What she finds will kill everything in the ocean.

Autumn Walton is nothing more than a grunt. She joined the military to escape her family and found herself on a planet, mining water, in hopes to save her people. On a day of respite, she meets a strange creature in the water—a creature she'd been told was nothing more than a myth. Now she knows if the mining continues, she'll kill the woman she loves.

From two different worlds, can Autumn and Soulara work together to save the ocean? Or will their forbidden relationship snap under the pressure of duty?

ADRIAN J. SMITH

Adrian J. Smith has been publishing since 2013 but has been writing nearly her entire life. With a focus on women loving women fiction, AJ jumps genres from action-packed police procedurals to the seedier life of vampires and witches to sweet romances with a May-December twist. She loves writing and reading about women in the midst of the ordinariness of life.

AJ currently lives in Cheyenne, WY, although she moves often and has lived all over the United States. She loves to travel to different countries and places. She currently plays the roles of author, wife, and mother to two rambunctious youngsters, occasional handy-woman. Connect with her on Facebook, Instagram, Twitter, or her newsletter.

facebook.com/adrianjsmithbooks

twitter.com/adrianajsmith

instagram.com/adrianjsmithbooks

amazon.com/author/adrianjsmith

tiktok.com/@sapphicbookmaker

NEEN COHEN

Neen Cohen is an Aussie author. She writes sapphic speculative fiction, and while she tries to take things seriously, she thrives being the hyperactive bookworm who rarely stops smiling or laughing. If she had to decide between never reading or never writing again, she simply wouldn't. Rules were never her strong point.

When not writing or working the day job, Neen loves nothing more than dancing, nerf wars with the boys, playing the latest Playstation obsession, and crafting wild and crazy things sometimes for the kiddo, other times because she can.

facebook.com/neen.cohen.82

twitter.com/CohenNeen

instagram.com/neenauthor

tiktok.com/@sapphicspecficauthor

amazon.com/stores/Neen-Cohen/author/B07VSYZF7K